Lost and Found

Lost and Found

Mary Lou Quinn

authorHOUSE®

AuthorHouse™
1663 Liberty Drive
Bloomington, IN 47403
www.authorhouse.com
Phone: 1-800-839-8640

Published by AuthorHouse 02/18/2016

ISBN: 978-1-4969-3880-0 (sc)
ISBN: 978-1-4969-3878-7 (hc)
ISBN: 978-1-4969-3879-4 (e)

Library of Congress Control Number: 2014915998

Print information available on the last page.

Dedication

~In honor and loving memory of my father,
Thomas Martin Quinn~ This one's for you!

Acknowledgements

The author would like to gratefully acknowledge the assistance and support that made this book a reality: Dick Bisbee helped me believe that I could and should write; my sister Terry, who suffered through the first chapters of a rough draft and actually wanted to read more; The Lubec Memorial Library and staff; Jennifer Caven, my editor; My children, Heather and Jamie who will never know how much I appreciate their patience, help and support; and first, last, and always my husband Phil whose confidence has kept me going. Thank you so much.

Chapter One

"—and so, by faith and begorra, me little Maggot, that's the way of the Little People." With his phony Irish brogue, Daddy tries for his real serious look. I scrunch up my face, he lightly taps my head with his forefinger in our very special ritual, and we both dissolve into giggles.

The dream memory slips through the crevices of my unconscious to be replaced with a feeling of loss. The sound of banging joined with a profane verbal tirade from outside assaults my consciousness, and the name "Wayne" mingles with a brand of swearing in a guttural voice that has a familiarity to it that I'd rather not acknowledge.

I struggle to the surface of consciousness and roll into a wall. What the hell!! Where did that wall come from? Where am I? I hate rolling out of bed only to hit a wall. It's a dead giveaway that I'm not where I think I am. I think I'm in a closet. I force my eyes open to scan the place and locate something familiar—my backpack dumped at the foot of an end table next to my bed—and there's my black duffel slouched on a chair in the corner. Now it comes back to me. I'm in a little utility room in the middle of the Barrens Motel. My impeccable timing again. It was all that was available, but it was really set up as a crash pad for someone else. I'm guessing that someone else is named Wayne. The ranting on the other side drifts back into my brain and my teacher mode can't help but admire the variations and uses of the f-word that filter through the screeching, yowling, and banging. Quite creative, really.

Okay, I think I'm awake, and it sounds like an obnoxious female drunk out there. I can relate. Been there, done that. It's time to move. I get off on the right side of the bed this time, pull down my T-shirt, (stupid thing always rides up), pad over to the door and check the slide bolt. It should hold. I can yell too.

"Go away! There's nobody here!" That was dumb, of course, since I'm here.

Silence.

More swearing, now laced with threats, comes slurred and crashing through the air; then, as quickly as they began, they vanish. Now what? Here I am wide awake in the middle of the night standing in an oversized closet in a town I'd never heard of until a few months ago. It's going to be hell getting back to sleep.

A noisy crash and sounds of tearing are suddenly behind me. I swing around to the noise, and there's my tormentor, hanging through the window over the bedside table. The screen's ripped, and there's a head of dirty blonde hair—not just the color, it's pretty grungy too— one shoulder, one arm and one boob inside. The propped up window has fallen down and trapped her, and she looks like a bizarre hunting trophy. Her hand slaps the wall. "Aw shit, shit, shit!" Her wailing bounces in waves inside my head. It's a whine now, and I think it's laced with some pain, if it's possible that she feels anything at all.

I reach out by the door and flip the light switch. That wasn't such a cool idea, because now I'm temporarily blinded, but I manage to find my clothes. Wriggling into my jeans and sliding into my sneakers give me time to adjust my sight and assess the stark reality of the situation, not sure if I'm really awake, caught in a macabre dream or on autopilot. I can't leave her there, and I can't just stand here. Looking at the mess hanging in the window, I vaguely recall an incident that must have left me looking similarly absurd.

It was one of the many times my dad came and bailed me out and one of the many times I let him down. A wave of remorse crashes over me again but I need to get back to the present.

"Hey! Can you hear me? Am I getting through?"

"Yeess."

"Hang in there, I'll go around and help you out."

There are tears mingled with barely decipherable obscenities. I slide the bolt back and tug on the door. Damn, she almost broke it but a good yank and it's open. As I step out, I spot Winnie, the owner, halfway down the line, hair done up in big curlers, gauzy kerchief with flopping ends, a chenille bathrobe over sweats, and mules slapping on the cement walkway. It was an image out of a fifties comedy.

"What's going on?"

"We've got a blonde drunk looking for Wayne. Right now she's stuck in the window and needs help."

"Damn, it's Sheila. That's her car. Jesus H., she can be a handful. I'd better call the sheriff. They know how to handle her. Go ahead and do what you can, but don't put yourself out. I'll be right back, okay?"

I'm trying to wrap my mind around what's going on here and manage to mumble "right".

This place had been my last hope. After slogging through what should have been a four hour trip, I decided that instead of heading down to Bar Harbor with more bumper to bumper traffic I'd make a left hand turn out of Ellsworth and away from the world of traffic lights. I would have appreciated the sense of calm that comes from leaving an urban area, but I was drained by frustration. Every 'No Vacancy' sign I passed sapped more of my energy, and the 'poor me's' set in. Of course, I could have saved myself some grief by planning ahead, but that's kind of hard when you're running. Everything was booked solid for the coming Fourth of July holiday, which in this neck of the woods appeared to be a bigger deal than Christmas. Winnie had been behind the counter engaged in banter with a middle aged couple about a family called the O'Dells. I couldn't help but overhear enough of the conversation to tell me about the coming celebration's events in town as well as the name of the proprietress, Winnie McCarthy. I hadn't wanted to seem impatient because I knew it was my own fault that I was running out of options, but I was getting rather tired. I sat down on the 60's avocado green cushioned chair and leafed through some old magazines lying on the table next to me, while the couple and Winnie continued their reunion.

Finally the couple left, and Winnie had come around the corner in a shuffle, her short sleeved flowered blouse hanging off her shoulders as if it were still on a hanger and her legs looking like broomsticks in her pink polyester pants. She looked spunky for her age, and I guessed she didn't miss a trick. "Dear, how can I help you?" she asked; not, "Do you have a reservation?" or, "What's your name?"

4

"I was wondering if there was any chance you had a room left. I know it's a busy time, but I've tried everywhere up the coast and I'm worn out." A little display of how pitiful I was couldn't hurt.

"Oh dear, I really have nothing but a small corner room that I keep for my grandson. Sometimes he needs a place for himself when things get a bit…well, you know…at home."

As I went around the end of the motel now, I wondered if things were a "bit…well, you know…" at home for Wayne tonight. My conjecturing about Wayne came to an end as I took in the picture of Sheila. There's plenty of light from the security pole lamp, and I can see the problem right away. She had leaned a pallet up against the building and used it as a stepladder. Apparently it fell back as she'd tried to get in the window. Now her feet are thrashing, and she is truly hung up. She's as much of a scene from behind as from the front and definitely has no fashion sense, not that I'm one to talk about fashion. She's packed into hip-hugger pants that don't quite make it to her hips, and her flip-flops are dangling from her grimy feet.

I lean the pallet back up against the wall and try to guide her feet to the top of the pallet so she can get a foothold and take the weight off her top, but she can't or won't budge. I pick up the window prop stick—no high tech here—that had landed in the dirt and climb up beside her. She starts to struggle, but I whack her across the fanny with the stick. It's my way of getting even for her waking me out of a sound sleep.

"Hold still, dammit. I've got to open the window and widen the tear in the screen. You hear me?"

A mewling whimper is her only response. I guess that to be an answer. I get the stick wedged in and widen the rip, then wrap an arm around her waist and slide a hand under her chest to get her uncaught.

5

"Okay, take it slow and we'll ease you out."

More whines and whimpers, but she does pretty well. Her head comes out and… oh-oh. The weight of both of us is too much for the pallet, and it cracks and gives way. We both start falling backwards, and in my mind everything goes into slow motion. My last thought is, "Oh shit, this is gonna hurt!" It did.

As we tumble back, her butt lands on my belly, and my head whacks against the ground. Her shoulder or head slams me along side the face. A 1-2 punch and I'm out!

Pulsing blue lights through my eyelids. *Just ten more minutes, Mom, then I'll get up.* I'm clawing my way up from an abyss. What's going on?

It's work, but I crack open my eyes and try to focus. *The pain. A handsome guy with deep brown eyes is staring down at me. Am I dreaming? Have I gone to heaven or is this the devil in disguise?* The nerves in my body start popping like firecrackers.

"Dammit Hal, turn off those gad blessed lights. I'm having enough trouble getting my people settled."

"All right, Winnie. I hear you. Come here a minute and watch this one. I think she's coming around."

The vision moves away with the sound of creaking leather. Yeah, that fits, cop. Winnie's face, full of concern, takes his place.

"How you doin', dear? Can you hear me?"

My jaw feels bolted together, but I manage a grunt. "That's it, dear. Take it slow and easy. Check for hurts."

You have got to be kidding. It would probably take less time to check what doesn't hurt. While I'm doing the checking, the blue flashes stop, and I can hear static radio chatter. Oops, another motor and more lights. Yuck, more cops. Cop A, the devil with deep brown eyes, grumbles "cut it," and Cop B blessedly shuts down his light show.

I've got my wind back and can even articulate a few words, but moving is another matter. While Winnie mother-hens me into a sitting position, I can hear the cops chit-chatting.

Cop B: "Sheila?"

Cop A: "Yeah. I think she's okay and pretty much done for the night. Check her out and put her in your car. I'll see to the other one."

Cop B: "Right."

Ol' creaking leather comes back to the other one. "How's she doing, Winnie?"

I got in first, "Just fine, other than a knot on my head and six broken bones. Just fine."

He grins. "Feisty! Let's do a quick concussion check." Don't we sound official!

He checks my pupil responses with his flashlight and my ears for bleeding. My pride hurts more with every passing moment.

Cop B comes back, reporting that Sheila is loaded up and passed out in his cruiser. My eyes focus on name badges so I don't have to look anyone in the eyes, which is a stretch with Deputy Harold Grimes. The devil with the deep brown eyes is at least 6'4". His

7

sidekick is a short squat guy by the name of Howard Jones. Deputy Grimes directs him to give him her car keys. He'll park her car out of the way. Somebody will pick it up tomorrow. Okay with Winnie? Yeah. Take Sheila home and get back on the road. He'll do the paper work. This guy certainly knows how to take charge and give orders.

Winnie and Deputy Grimes escort me back to my room, Winnie apologizing and spilling over with concern. By the room light, she checks my head for blood and informs me that I'm not bleeding but my face is starting to swell. Great! The deputy tells me he'll get a statement from me in the morning, 10:00 am at Josie's Diner.

After settling that, and after reassuring Winnie that I'll be fine, the deputy struts off, and she scuffs off in her slippers. I'm finally alone in my room, which looks as pitiful as I feel.

The lights off, I'm back in bed but too wired and too sore to drop off to sleep. I think back to the dream I was so rudely awakened from and try to remember what I'm doing here in this little storage closet of a room.

My first visit to the area had come at the end of a camping trip up in Baxter State Park, a short getaway before the black fly season hit at the end of our last spring break. I had taken a different route back to Old Orchard Beach, exploring the coast of Maine. Mundy was one of the places I'd discovered, and the sight of bald eagles had left an indelible memory. Dad had thought I needed to leave and almost threw me out of the apartment. I'd made arrangements for a nurse to come in and stay with him, but it didn't stop me from worrying. The doctors had made it clear that, though they couldn't say for sure, they did know he didn't have long to go. It had been Dad's idea to try Maine when I'd dragged my sorry ass back to my home in upstate New York.

I had managed to graduate from college and go into teaching, but home had gotten a little uncomfortable due to my ever escalating drunken escapades. When the teaching position in Alaska had come up, it was like an answer to a prayer. It was the other end of the earth and away from all those people, places, and things that were causing all the problems in my life. It would be a grand adventure. It had been an adventure all right, but not of the grand kind. Dad was ever the understanding one and welcomed me back, but trying to land a job had been difficult. The place wasn't the same, and I didn't know which had changed, me or home. My old friends, such as they were, had gotten on with their lives, were married and had kids. I hadn't done anything on a positive note, and time was slipping away. Dad could see how frustrated I was getting, and he knew I wasn't going to stick around. I wonder if he already knew he was sick and wanted to get me away before I noticed. He suggested I try another direction and head east instead of west this time, so I did. I'd gotten as far as Old Orchard Beach just before Christmas and even managed to get a job at a prestigious private school starting in January. It seemed that everything was going my way, and the move had been just what I needed. But something was still wrong.

Going home after Alaska had been a real jolt, and though things were looking better, I still had that feeling of being out of sinc with my surroundings. I was on the outside looking in and I couldn't break through that glass wall. For some reason, suicide was looking like an easy way out of this world. One of the other teachers at the school guessed that I was struggling and took me under his wing, and that's when I had to take a look at my life style and, more specifically, my drinking and drugging. I wasn't going to be able to hold onto a job for long if something didn't change, and I was ready to give up the misery that was my constant companion.

Getting and staying sober had been a lot of work, but I had help and it was just in the nick of time. When I visited Dad again—sober—I found out that he had lung cancer and that it was terminal. He wasn't about to let that interfere with my life, but the haze had cleared enough that I could think of him for a change rather than myself; and besides, I was still looking for his approval.

Friends in Maine helped me move him up to my apartment in Old Orchard Beach, and the school wasn't too far away. Dad had spent the last three years with me, but he was gone now. We had been everything to each other since Mom had died. I guess you could say it had been just the two of us against the world. During the last year of his life, Dad had been bedridden, and it was tough watching him sink deeper day by day. I wanted to put some distance between that life and me, so here I was, still moving east.

True to form, I chose the worst possible time to pull up stakes, the beginning of the summer season in Maine. That's why the storage closet. It was all that was available and at a price I couldn't refuse.

I still wondered what Dad had been hinting at but couldn't quite grasp the clues as I thought about our last conversation concerning family and roots. I'm here now. I'll worry about why later. Sleep has always been a good escape. I finally escaped.

Chapter Two

Ow! I'm all tangled up in the sheets, it's a pain to move, and my mouth feels like it's full of Elmer's glue. Suddenly it dawns on me like a sledge hammer that I've got that meeting at Josie's with the tall cop. I fumble for my watch on the bedside table. Barely enough time, but I'll make it.

A hot shower has got to help. Thank goodness the mirror in the bathroom is only nine by twelve. I'm pretty scary to look at. Here I am almost thirty years old, and I bruise like a little kid having a tumble on the playground. It's pretty pathetic. Squeezing into my jeans is painful. I'll bet my backside is beautiful too. The trailer with all my worldly possessions is still attached to the truck, so I decide to hoof it down the hill into town and the diner. How far could it be? I grabbed my backpack. Whatever I need is in there somewhere; it just may take a while to find it. In my rush, I nearly knock over the chambermaid as I shoot out of my closet of a room.

Winnie had given me the tip that Josie's Diner was the best place in town for that morning eye opener at reasonable prices. I don't exactly look like I'm swimming in dough, so I appreciated Winnie's suggestion. I'd tried it out earlier and it felt comfortable. I was guessing it was one of the town's local gathering spots.

The owners of the place, Dwight and Josie Wayland, weren't locals but from New York. As a New Yorker myself, I had always made a distinction between the city and the Adirondacks where I was from. Dwight and Josie were from the city, and you'd think they'd stand out like a handful of sore thumbs, but they didn't. Perhaps it was Dwight's laid back 'I live to fish' attitude, or maybe it was Josie's outgoing, fun-loving character. There was none of the snobbery I had come to expect from city folks living in Maine.

I felt immediately comfortable around Josie. She had no trouble coming up to me and making me feel like we were long lost buds. A wallflower she was not. With bushy hair that was a true carrot red and freckles that no amount of makeup could cover up, she was the spitting image of Little Orphan Annie in her fifties. I'm sure she must have been teased unmercifully most of her life. In comparison, my red hair didn't seem such a liability. I admired her presence and style. She wore bright colors and huge earrings that were startling yet not out of place on her. All right, I admit I was jealous of her confidence and comfort in her own skin. She definitely held her own with both locals and people from away.

The two of them had done a great job turning an old building into a top-notch dining place specializing in breakfast and lunch. It still had the original tin ceiling and wood floors that groaned and slanted a bit. The diner had a fifties feel to it with plenty of tables and some naugahyde booths around the walls. They did a brisk business even early in the morning.

Ten o'clock must be a slack time between breakfast and lunch, as the place is almost empty when I arrive. I am astonished when

Josie greets me by name and is all-sympathetic as she ushers me to the same booth I had the first day. It's not just my face that is a dead giveaway; she also knows all about how it got messed up out at the motel. Small town, of course; by now everybody has probably heard something of what went on. I'm grateful that there aren't many people here to stare at my face. I'm not exactly Miss Congeniality without my morning caffeine fix, which is woefully late today.

Josie has my water and coffee on the table before I'm barely settled. I'd noticed yesterday that water was a mainstay for customers. It was a nice touch that was missing in most places I'd been. Josie's water was not a glass full of ice but good cool water with enough minerals to make a meal.

This morning it's nectar from heaven as I gulp it down and sip my coffee—something to cut through the glue.

"Josie, this is like a transfusion, life-giving and desperately needed."

"Whatcha gonna have to eat? You need more than coffee to keep your strength up."

"I couldn't do your cooking justice just now. I've got a meeting with the local law about last night."

Speak of the devil. Deputy Harold Grimes appears at the door. Josie gazes at the deputy and sighs as if drinking in Michelangelo's David. My guts suddenly clench as I watch him bow his head to get his tall muscular frame through the diner's door. Dominance comes through with every razor-sharp crease of his uniform, a perfect fit. He knows how good he looks, not a speck of sweat on his ball cap, spit shined low-cut boots, and that heavy leather belt with all his tools of the trade. I watch the easy riding belt and I'd like to take its place. I look up from the belt to catch his quick cop-scope of the interior. He moves like a panther tracking its prey through the jungle. I want to say "come and get me" and slide my hands under that uniform. I feel the heat flash over my body and the dampness well up between my legs.

I hate being at the mercy of my body, and I hate being at a disadvantage because I'm so easy to read. You should always have the upper hand. It's the best protection, and right now I need protection.

Without taking his eyes off me, he asks Josie for a coffee and moves closer to my booth. He tilts his head from one side to the other in a quasi-serious examination. "You're a mess."

Tell me something I don't know, Mr. Perfect. What a bastard. I'm no stranger to this tactic of intimidation and control. "Anything you say …. Cowboy."

Now that was dumb, but this guy was really rattling me, and I was not at my best, an understatement of the first magnitude. He didn't like my comeback. I caught the instant fiery flash from those eyes but he recovered quickly. He backed off with his hands up in mock surrender. Oh, puleeease! Give it a rest!

"My mistake, sorry. How are you feeling?"

"Just about the way I look."

He seats himself in one smooth motion, breaking eye contact and emanating an all-business attitude with clipboard at the ready and cap pushed back.

Josie puts his coffee and water down to one side in a deferential manner. "Thanks, Josie. You might as well pull up a chair and listen in. It'll save her having to tell it twice."

Oh, aren't we cute. If he's trying to show how at ease he is compared to me, he's doing a hell of a good job.

Josie clasps her hands to her breast and flutters her eyelashes, "Why thanks, Cowboy," and deftly pulls up a chair, elbows on the table, chin cupped in hands, all innocence. He didn't like the comment any better coming from Josie. I was beginning to think I was trapped in a grade B movie.

"Okay, we're ready for the statement. I suggest you leave the questions to me, Josie." Now it's down to business. He explains that they're sort of informal around here; he'll make notes from my statement, I'll check it over, and if I'm in agreement, I sign it. Sounds painless enough. Oh, let's not bring up pain!

We do the identification bit, full name and address. Margaret Mary Murphy is easy enough, but an address gets a bit tricky. Both Grimes and Josie do a groan at my name, but Grimes closes Josie's mouth with a look. What is it with my name? When I was signing the register card at The Barrens Motel with my first initial, last name, and truck license plate number, I had caught Winnie staring as intently as a crow eyeing its next meal. "You related to the Mundy Murphys by any chance?"

"Not that I'm aware of, but I suspect I share ancestors from the old country with a lot of Murphys." That response usually ended any further prying.

"Where you from originally, if you don't mind my asking? I like to see how many different places people come from."

I'm brought back to the sequence of events by Deputy Grimes. I'm a little fuzzy on the times, and Grimes refers to his log to line it up. He had it all down and was probing into my background, when

I noticed that he'd quit taking notes. I figured this was above and beyond and none of his business. I don't like being pumped for information and I shut down quickly. The hackles went up.

"Do you need anything else for the report?" I ask as I point to his notepad. Do I spot a flash of rage? He shrugs it off and asks me if I want to press charges. I couldn't see where it would do any good. I just wanted to put the whole thing behind me. They both nodded agreement. Grimes said he would check with Winnie next, folded up his clipboard, rose, squared his cap, fished a dollar out of his pocket, and laid it next to his coffee cup.

Josie got as far as "Why thank…" but he was turned and half way out the door.

Josie sighed, then got up and wiggled into the booth. "Your name. Now tell me about it."

You can't resist Josie, and my resistance level was way down anyway, so I filled her in on the short history of my Mom and Dad and my quest for roots. Josie told me there just happen to be an older woman in town with the same name.

Then she switched from gossip to interview mode. What was I gonna do? Where was I gonna stay? Very good questions. I told her I was at loose ends and looking for a place to land for the time being. My stay at the Barrens was looking mighty short-lived.

"Done any waiting?"

"Oh yeah, and a little cooking as well, mostly baking."

"Ha! I knew it. Here's the situation: I've got a girl in the back room who's a top-notch waitress, local to boot, but she's about five minutes away from going into serious labor. Actually, she's not due for a few weeks, but it's her first, and it's really taking a lot out of her, but she's hanging in there because she knows I'm in a bind with the Fourth coming up. Bless her. Are you interested?"

"Sure. It sounds great." And as I was beginning to realize, you can't say no to Josie. Things were moving fast, but I liked not having time to think.

She laid out the details: hours, basic wage, etc. I liked it even more. This wasn't a thirty-nine hour a week setup. You were part of the staff and treated as such. Then she threw in the clincher. She and her husband had used the small apartment upstairs when they started out. Now they had an older fixer-upper house a couple blocks away. The apartment was being used for dry goods storage, but all the necessities were there and plenty of room for one person. We could work out an arrangement.

I was overwhelmed and getting dizzy, but I held up my hand, "Josie I gotta be up front with you. I've been through the whole nine yards of drugs and booze. I'm a risk."

She reached across and squeezed my hand, "Honey, I know people. You'll be wanting to hit the meetings. Winfield, one of our regulars, pure gold, comes in every morning, he knows the circuit. Half of this town goes and the other half oughta." Another squeeze, "You'll do, you'll do."

My eyes filled up, and I was having trouble breathing. Josie was having none of that. She jumped up. "Come on, I've got about two minutes before the nooners start." And she was off. I took a deep breath, swiped my eyes, and hurried after the fireball, caught up in her energy.

Chapter Three

Walking into the kitchen of Josie's was an experience. There was a century's difference between it and the dining room. The kitchen was completely stainless steel and well organized from top to bottom. I had been in many restaurant kitchens, and they were usually not places you wanted customers to see. It might put them off their feed. With short bursts, Josie gave me the lay of the land. It was like a dream world. By now, I really admired Josie's low-key presence with the public, but the kitchen made me believe that the name 'diner' was a misnomer.

Though he had appeared laid back, Dwight was all efficiency and definitely in his element at the grill. I met Wanda, the pregnant waitress, and she looked like a huge popover. Did Josie say she was having twins? I stood mute as Josie told her about my coming on board. I was watching for any signs of resentment about me taking her place, but her exhausted expression beamed with what I took to be relief.

Standing at a triple sink and gawking in our direction was a young man. Josie bustled over to him, "Robby, we have a new person working with us." Robby didn't seem to be aware of Josie but hadn't taken his eyes off me.

"Gee, were you in a fight? Your face looks all beat up."

Thank you for that announcement. I suddenly felt self-conscious and uncomfortable. The kid's direct comments were unnerving. With my usual saber tongue I shot back, "You should see the other guy."

"You fought with a guy?" Robby's awe was startling. My mind was doing a fast analysis of this young man in his teens. What's wrong with this picture? I glanced over at Josie who had been trying to get my attention.

"Rob's number one in the kitchen, aren't you Rob? We're like family." I looked back at Rob, and he was beaming with a childlike innocence.

I understood. "Well Rob, my name is Margaret, but you can call me Maggie. I wasn't really in a fight. It was an accident with another girl. We sort of collided."

"Oh," Rob slowly processed what I had said. "Is Maggie a nickname? Robby is a nickname. My real name is Robert Williams. You know, you're tall."

Robby was about five feet six inches, a skinny kid with pimples and just a tiny bit of dark stubble on his chin and upper lip. This bit of facial hair gave the impression of more maturity than he actually had, which is what had caught me off guard. "Nice to meet you, Robert," I said as I reached out and took his hand. I needed to lighten up. He was my students' age, for crying out loud.

As an underpaid teacher I had taken many a summer job. Waiting, which was one of several, is like riding a bike; you just climb on and adjust to the new bike, but you don't forget how to ride. Josie brought me an apron, an order book and pen. "We'll go over the particulars later. Shirley will be in to take over in a while. It's show time!" On our way out, Dwight shot me a one liner, "Hope you got A's in penmanship, I have no intention of going blind just yet."

The place had filled up just in the few minutes we had been in the kitchen. Josie pointed to one end of the room, and I grabbed some menus and was off. Everything else left my mind as I concentrated on the job. My customers were tourists who took the generic menu very seriously. I'd always threatened to write a book entitled *Stupid Questions*. You have to have a sense of humor and patience waiting. Come to think of it, that holds true for teaching as well. I would tell my students that the only stupid questions are the ones you never ask, but that doesn't hold with customers. I got my first memorable questions right out of the gate.

"Now, this clam chowder, is it Manhattan or New England clam chowder?" I bit my tongue. This came from a woman dressed in a sequin studded French terry running suit with matching sun visor. It was all I could do to keep from giving her a history lesson on shellfish and tomatoes in New England. I assured her it was fresh, rich New England clam chowder. In fact, I'd had it for lunch the day before, and it had been out of this world. I was ready for the next question as she tried to delicately inquire about the type and parts of the clams used in the chowder. This woman had some serious hangups.

I hoped Dwight could decipher my waiting shorthand. It wasn't so much a matter of penmanship as the code you used. Every place was a little different, but if Dwight was as experienced as I thought he was, I was covered. For having been dropped in cold, everything went smoothly. Thank goodness for specials boards. My mind was not up to memorizing the specials and spieling them off.

The time flew by, and then a flushed, bleached blonde rushed in at quarter to one. She put on the brakes as I looked up. The expression on her face said 'Who the hell do you think you are?' I nodded to her as she made a beeline for the kitchen.

Suddenly I was ravenous and felt like a wind-up toy that had run down. Shirley had arrived, and I needed to eat something. I had gotten the impression from Josie that Shirley was going to be coming in at noon. Something told me that punctuality wasn't a word in her vocabulary.

Josie and Shirley were swapping rushed words as Shirley tied on an apron and headed out of the kitchen and out onto the floor. The main lunch rush had dwindled to a trickle, so I nodded to Josie, and she waved me into the kitchen.

"Dwight, throw on a couple of burgers for Maggie and me. We'll park here near the kitchen so I can have a smoke and talk. "Move in," she said, so I schooched into the little corner booth to listen to Josie. I'd be working the early morning shift, leaving me the afternoons and evenings, so getting to meetings and taking care of business wouldn't be a problem. Being able to get things done while businesses were still open was a plus. They roll up the sidewalks at five around here.

When would all this start? My head was spinning trying to take it all in. Josie hollered out to Dwight, "Let me have your keys. Maggie's going to take a look upstairs." Dwight ambled over with a wad of keys that must have weighed two pounds. "I see you've been shanghaied." Josie flipped through the keys until she located the one she was looking for and held out the wad to me by that key.

"If this is being shanghaied, I've had worse."

"You say that now…" and he cocked a mischievous grin in Josie's direction.

"Dwight, stop harassing the girl. You go on up and check the place out. See what you think. You look like you travel light. If you like what you see and are willing to depart your current plush abode, you can move in today. Dwight will help out after we close up, won't you, dear?"

"See what I mean? I'll be glad to help you move in." I enjoyed the playfulness of these two. For the second time today tears were welling up, but Josie would have none of it. "Now, get outa here and take your time."

My philosophy of people and life in general had always been you have to take what you can get because you deserve nothing and everyone has an angle. I might have to take another look at my philosophy.

Chapter Four

Josie's was at an elbow on Water Street. The street took a turn west and inland, and the coastline did just the opposite. As I climbed the back steps to the apartment, my anticipation grew. At the top of the stairs, a deck extended the length of the building, and the view was spectacular. From this vantage point, I could look south and take in the entire harbor to the mouth of the Mundy River. When I turned to the north, there was a great expanse of rugged coastline with very little sign of human development, just a few dirt roads and a small pebble beach at what was now low tide. It looked like a fascinating place to explore.

Trying to dampen my enthusiasm so I wouldn't be disappointed, I filled my head with foreboding about what the apartment would look like. I wasn't feeling very deserving of anything at the moment.

The key turned easily, and the door swung open. Wow, it was great! Visions of my little closet room at the Barrens made this place look like a palace.

There were boxes everywhere. I wandered around them as I took in the general floor plan, every doorway a new discovery. The only furniture in the place was a chrome legged kitchen table and three plastic covered kitchen chairs. These were smack dab in the middle of a dining area piled high with paper products for the diner. The kitchen was small but loaded with cupboards and more counter space than my last apartment.

The bathroom was a treat compared to the closet at the Barrens. In that little cubby-hole, I could sit on the john, wash my hands in the sink, and stick my legs in the shower stall, which was the only way to shave them. This bathroom would only need a new shower curtain to replace the stiff crackly plastic one that was there. The window looked out on the deck, but I wasn't too concerned about modesty when I was two stories up overlooking the harbor.

The most interesting discovery was in one of the two bedrooms. There on the floor were stacks and stacks of old newspapers, very yellowed from time. There must have been decades of newspapers crammed into this room. The banner on each stack said *The Tidewater Times*. I was intrigued and made a note to ask Josie about them. Being a history teacher was a choice I had made based on my curiosity about the past and my need to know. Of course, like everything else about me, I tended to extremes. Curiosity is supposed to kill the cat, but the saving grace is that cats have nine lives. There were stairs at the opposite end of the apartment that led down to the diner, with a street door and a side door right into the landing below. I checked the street door and it was securely locked. The door to the diner was locked from the diner side, but it had a slide bolt on this side. I could have my security from anyone walking in from the diner besides Josie and Dwight, and at night I could bolt it on my side just for good measure.

I'd seen enough. It was beyond my wildest dreams. It had only been a short time ago when I had picked up stakes and joined the ranks of tourists going up the coast to enjoy a Maine summer. I thought I was leaving the hive of human activity in the land of 'no' and 'rude' that I called Southern Maine, only to get trapped on the turnpike with thousands of others as we were siphoned into fewer and fewer lanes due to road construction. The fact that I had overestimated the speed at which my truck would travel hauling a trailer and the amount of traffic there would be had severely hampered my forward momentum. Now it seemed that forces were moving me along at a good clip, so I might as well sit back and enjoy the ride.

I bounced down the steps to the diner, keys jangling and my backpack flapping against my side. "I'll take it! I'll settle up with Winnie, do some errands, and be back at five." It only took an instant for those words to leave my lips. Doubt crept in, and thinking this was all too good to be true, I asked Josie, "Are you sure you want to do this? It's not too late if you want to change your mind."

"Girl, I know my mind, and I don't go around changing it all that frequently. Besides, you can do the job, and Wanda needs to be off her feet."

"Josie, I don't know how to thank you. I'll see if I can help Winnie get the screen fixed at the hardware store and then head over here."

"While you're there, get a key made." After a tussle she got the key off Dwight's wad and handed it to me. I was so excited I'd forgotten about all my aches and pains, but I wasn't crazy enough to jog back to the motel. I took it at slow saunter.

Winnie was bustling around in the back of the office wearing a polyester pant and blouse ensemble that looked like the same vintage and design that she had been wearing when we first met, only the color had changed from pink to blue. As I opened the squeaky screen door and stepped inside, Winnie stopped what she was doing and came up to the desk.

"How you doin'? I see you have some souvenirs from last night. I'm really sorry about all the trouble. Sheila's not so bad once you get to know her. She just adores my grandson Wayne and their two kids. They're really just kids themselves." If last night was any indication of adoration, I wanted no part of it. "I hope everything got straightened out. Harold stopped by this morning. He said you might have some friends in common from Old Orchard Beach."

"Winnie, I'm sure last night was just a gigantic misunderstanding and it's over with. I met with Deputy Grimes, Harold, and that's the end of it." My mind was starting to whir again. The deputy and I had had our little sit-down session, but he'd never said anything to me about mutual friends. "Did Deputy Grimes say who these friends were that he knew?"

"No, he didn't go into any of that. He just went over the records and then left." I wasn't going to delve in any deeper about the towering deputy with Winnie.

"Winnie, Josie is renting me the apartment over the diner so I'll get my stuff together. Do you want me to take the screen to get fixed at the hardware store?"

"Oh, is it because of last night?"

"No, no, Josie offered me a job, and the apartment is part of the bargain."

"So you'll be staying in Mundy then?"

"Well, for now. I try not to get too far ahead of myself. What about the screen?"

"The motel has an account at the store. I'll give Greg a call and let him know you're coming; could you bring back the receipt?"

"Right."

It wasn't going to take me long to pack up because I'd never really unpacked in the first place. I wouldn't be sorry to be gone from here. The chambermaid or Winnie had cleaned up the remnants of Sheila from the wall and the window. What was left of the screen popped right out. Next stop, the hardware store.

It was no Home Depot, just an old nineteenth century white clapboard two story building. The door had a bell attached that tinkled as I walked in and onto well-worn wood floors that creaked in places. The nuts and bolts of the business were in this front room. Going up a few steps to a back landing, I found the cashier's counter and a section with everything for painting inside and out as well as crafts. For a small town and a small store, the place had at least one of everything you could want, just not a great variety, which is fine for those of us who hate to make decisions.

A girl looking like she was just out of high school came out from the back. She had lanky brown hair tucked behind her ears, with tendrils escaping to dangle in her eyes and getting caught up in her wire frame glasses. She was wearing frayed jeans shorts that rode low on her hips and a tank top that didn't quite cover her bra straps or her midriff. It exposed a Celtic Knot tattoo. With no makeup and hiking boots, she looked like a tomboy with a sexy twist. I got the impression that she was ready and willing to take on the world.

I had seen her the day before up against an unused side door with her nose in a book. That person didn't quite fit the image that she was putting out right now. I hadn't been able to see what she was reading and I didn't want to be nosey. At this moment I felt like I was looking at my younger self as I surveyed her manner, a distant look and care less attitude. I could relate to the complete picture—tomboy, reader—and I could have gotten a tattoo on one of my drunken holidays. I just hadn't.

She walked up to me and said, "Is this Winnie's screen?"

"Yes. I don't suppose you could get it fixed by closing time?"

"No problem; Greg can have it done in an hour." She nodded toward the back of the building.

"Could I also get a key made?"

"Sure." She eyed me up and down as she took the key.

We walked over to the grinder and she picked out an appropriate blank and started to grind away. Over the noise I introduced myself. She didn't miss a beat but there was that look again. She said she was Terry, "with a y" Murphy. How about that, another Murphy. I quickly added I was originally from New York State, which was probably dumb. In Southern Maine I'd gotten used to the reaction to New Yorkers; like black flies, they were annoying and just as unwelcome.

"One Murphy to another, I gotta ask, is there something I should know about my name? I keep getting these looks."

"It's no big deal, just a lot of us around this town. Ya might say we're all one big family." This was said with disdain.

"I guess I'm a little over sensitive." She looked at my face and we both broke up laughing.

How Dwight had any energy left after working all day was beyond me. He was all muscle with only a slight paunch starting to appear at his waist. Most of my things I could move myself—heaven forbid I should have to ask for help. I liked to think of it as my way of being independent. However, my things had been supplemented with some of Dad's possessions that I either couldn't unload or didn't want to let go of. A filing cabinet that weighed a ton and Dad's stuffed chair were the most unwieldy, even for both Dwight and me to wrestle up the outside stairs and into the apartment.

"What have you got in this thing, gold bricks?"

"It was my dad's. I haven't had a chance to open it so I couldn't tell you, but I'm not that lucky. For all I know it could be crammed with coupons that my dad was fanatical about clipping for years."

Chapter Five

After Dwight left, I moved the boxes for the diner into the room with the papers. I had no energy left to unpack anything. My duffel had the essentials for a day including my alarm clock, which I would definitely need to get me out of bed tomorrow for work.

I plugged in my old box fan, set it in the window, pulled a sheet and my pillow out of a plastic trash bag, and settled down for the night. My body had come to a screeching halt but my mind was still racing. Past, present, and future tumbled around, bouncing into one another as the fan droned in the window, and then there was blessed oblivion.

The alarm went off way too early. I didn't hit a wall this time, but I did roll off the futon as I reached to silence the alarm. I padded over to my trash bag linen closet for a towel and hopped into the shower. That brought me around.

Drat! I'm down to my last change of clothes. I'd better do some brain-picking of my own with Josie this morning. At least this isn't the first day at school. One time the apartment I was living in ran out of hot water on the first day back to school, and it put me off my game all day. Not to mention that I think I'd made a pretty scary impression on a bunch of new faces.

Speaking of faces, a good night's sleep had done wonders for mine; it almost looked human again. The bathroom was equipped with a full length mirror, so I took stock of my appearance. Even though I had always been self-conscious about my height, I'd finally accepted the fact that 5'8" wasn't all that bad. Having that couple of extra inches had come in handy a few times. With my height had come thinness. The greatest impact on my self image had come from a comment when I was in my early teens, about the same time I found a solution to my troubles in a bottle. My childhood girlfriend came from Swedish stock, and when she hit puberty she blossomed into a full fledged garden while I was struggling just to bud. We were walking home from school, aware of the boys looking at us. It was Liz that they were looking at, and that's when I heard that derisive phrase "Get a load of the carpenter's dream hanging out with Liz." My instinct was to knock them all cold. That was always my answer until I discovered booze. Liz got invited to all the keg parties, and for a while she would have me tag along, but we were going our separate ways.

As I stared in the mirror, I took pride in the shape I had cultivated. I had put on muscle and kept it toned. I wasn't top heavy, but there was enough of me to be enticing. I would soon be turning that corner into thirty, and I dreaded getting old. Right now the shape that I was so proud of was dotted with multicolored bruises to go with my freckles. My nice firm buttocks had a fist sized black bruise that would take some time to heal. Thank goodness clothing would cover up most of the signs of the other night's event.

I had nothing in the place to eat and a coffee maker somewhere with no coffee. It was looking like this was going to be one of those really full days again.

Downstairs at the diner, Josie and Dwight were already in full swing. I smelled the java brewing as I walked through the door.

"How'd you sleep last night?"

"Like a baby, but I could use another twenty-four."

Josie ran through the schedule of duties, promising that there would be more once I got used to where everything was. She was going to break me in easy. Sure. Six o'clock rolled around and the place was packed, all regulars expecting to get what they always get. I had the cold water and hot coffee down as fast as possible. The other 'usual' orders slowed me down a bit, but I joked with the guys and they were good natured. I was all set to pat myself on the back for a flawless performance when this old guy came in, sat down at a small back table and said, "I have tea."

He was missing most of his teeth, and his hands looked like gnarled tree roots, but there was something about him that was calm and patient and showed through his rheumy blue eyes.

"You're new here, so I didn't want you to be put out about the coffee. Never did get a taste for the stuff. By the way, my name's Winfield."

I took a step back. Winfield's straightforwardness had thrown me off. "I'm Margaret....I'm...I'm a friend of Bill W."

"Well, nice to meet you Margaret. You going to be working here now?"

"I'm filling in for Wanda for the summer."

"That's good. Wanda needs to be able to enjoy this first baby. Will I be seeing you at the meetings?"

"I plan to start getting to some soon." Boy did that sound lame. Winfield looked right at me. "Don't plan, just do. I look forward to seeing you." He handed me a meeting list for the area that I stuck in my apron pocket. Then he gave me his 'usual' order and I put it in and then went on to other customers.

Josie was in and out of the kitchen carrying big tins of hot steamy fresh muffins. At nine o'clock Robby arrived with a big smile on his face. We swapped good mornings, and he dutifully set about doing up the coffee mugs and breakfast dishes. We were working like a well-oiled machine.

I was bringing out breakfast for a table of four tourists when he came through the door. Deja vu. Totally distracted, I nearly served up one of the gentlemen's breakfast on his lap. That would have gone over well. The clatter caught Deputy Grimes' attention. He did a double-take when he saw me working. It made me feel good just to see a tiny ripple in his impeccably unperturbed manner, and it was also telling. Maybe Mr. Perfect can be rattled after all. I excelled at rattling people. Dad said it was a bit of the leprechaun in me.

"Deputy Grimes, it's nice to see you. Are you having just coffee or would you like something to eat?" This as I dutifully set down coffee and water.

His look was intense, and I could feel the wave of red heat crawling up my neck and face as he scrutinized me. Once again I was at the mercy of my body, and it made me mad.

"You look like you've recovered from your ordeal."

I guess that was suppose to be an off-handed compliment, but I wasn't buying. "I'm pretty resilient. It's time to move on."

"I can see that. New job? You planning on staying in Mundy, are you?"

"Well, for a while. I plan to play it by ear. Oh, by the way, just for the record, my current residence is upstairs….for your report." I couldn't believe what I was saying! I sounded like I was trying to pick him up. My insides were starting to turn to mush as his deep brown eyes bored into me. We were in a staring contest, and I was going to lose.

After what seemed an eternity, he said he'd have one of Josie's morning glory muffins, and I beat a hasty retreat. Get a grip, girl, he's just a customer. What is it about this guy that gets me so hot and bothered?

I was racking up a long list of things I wanted to ask Josie about. She seemed to be in the know about everything going on around here. I wanted to know a little more about Deputy Grimes. Knowledge is power, and it was time for me to turn the tables on this guy.

It had been a while since I had waited tables, and by noon I was wearing out. Shirley was nowhere in sight, so I just kept plugging out of sheer force of will.

She managed to make it to work, only a half-hour late, but better late than never. Josie was ready for a break and so was I. I needed to eat something and chat. We sat down together in the spot by the kitchen and I jumped in. "We need to talk."

"You're not going to quit? You did great this morning."

"No, no. I need to pick your brain about some things, that's all. First, what's with Deputy Grimes?"

"Oh, if I were only twenty years younger, I'd crawl into his pants in a heartbeat. He's a hunk. I think he likes you, if that's what you mean. He seemed real interested in you yesterday."

I had to admit there was something about him, but I wasn't about to let on that I was just as inclined as Josie to find out what was under that uniform. "That's not exactly what I'm looking for. I thought you might be able to tell me a little bit about him. You know, the circumstances under which we met were a little strange."

Josie eyed me like she was reading a book and got this Cheshire cat grin on her face. "Sure. Over the years you pick up a lot of stuff if you listen. Hal grew up in Mundy. In school he was the star of the basketball team, they're called the Storm Petrels. Anyway, he and Howie were like Mutt and Jeff, always together. Hal had bigger aspirations than Mundy could take care of, so he went off to join the service. I think he went into the Navy Seals."

"Ok, wait a minute, who's Howie?"

"Howard Jones, Sheila's brother."

"Howard Jones. Why does that name sound familiar?"

"He's a deputy just like Hal. They're sort of a team again. When Hal came back to Mundy, Howie was already a sheriff's deputy, and he got Hal to join up."

The memories of that night started swimming around in my head, complete with the name badges that I had been staring at. Howie was the one that Hal had been giving orders to, and Sheila was Howie's sister. How bizarre!

I wanted to hear more but knew I had other things to take care of, so I found out where the nearest Laundromat was and where I could turn in my rented trailer. The Laundromat was practically across the street, but for all the other things I needed to take care of, I would have to travel thirty miles or more. I might actually have to plan out an itinerary to get things done.

Up in the apartment, I threw my dirty clothes in a trash bag. I wouldn't know what to do without these all-purpose containers. Looking around, it was easy to be overwhelmed by so much needing to be done. Where to start? Better yet, what did I really, really need to do? The trailer was costing money every day, so that had to be taken care of as soon as possible. Besides, with it hooked to my truck, I felt tied down, and I wanted my freedom back.

The Laundromat was called the Wash Tub, and it was hidden behind the hardware store disguised as a one-story ranch affair. The small sign hanging from chains by the door was the only clue to what was inside.

After years of frequenting these places, I knew what to look for in a good one. There were lots of washers in a variety of sizes and an equal number of dryers, a couple of seating areas, and a bathroom. This last is especially important when you're sitting there listening to rushing and sloshing water.

I was in luck, the place was almost deserted. It had a bill-changing machine, which was great because I didn't usually carry around enough quarters to do laundry. I fumbled for my wallet and pulled out a five. That should cover it. The machine sucked up the bill then spit it out at me. Oh, great! Well, I knew some tricks to make the bill more likeable. I straightened out the corners, folded it lengthwise and opened it up, then fed it back into the machine. Success. The quarters crashed into the metal cup at the bottom. I was going to need laundry detergent. I don't usually buy it in the Laundromat, but it's nice to know when you're in a pinch or a hurry that it's here, even if there isn't a great selection.

With my bag, handful of quarters, and soap, I shuffled over to the machines and started stuffing, sorting as I stuffed. I wash everything in cold water; that way I don't have to worry about special care items. Not that I had anything special for summer duds.

Once the wash was going, I made a pit stop in the bathroom, and then sauntered over to one of the molded plastic seats, the kind you get as lawn chairs. I thought I'd use the time making a list of things I wanted to get.

The only other people in the Laundromat were a large older woman, sixty-ish, and a small tow-headed five-year old. I hadn't been paying too much attention to anything but getting the clothes going; now, however, they were hard to ignore. The little girl—the woman called her Jenny—was tearing around the place with a clothes cart like it was a racer. The woman kept up a barrage of insistent chatter telling her she shouldn't be running around. Jenny countered this verbal assault by ignoring the woman and setting up a barrage of her own, asking over and over if she could go to the store. I felt like I had walked into a war zone. Listening to this bombardment would be hard to take for an hour.

The machines all had digital time readouts on them, and I had a watch. I decided to jog back to the apartment and do some chores rather than stay in this annoying verbal combat zone.

It's a good thing I'm in good shape, or the jog back and forth would have done me in. The afternoon was fading away, and I still wanted to get rid of the trailer, which meant getting into Tylerville, the county seat of Tyler County. The drive alone would be forty-five minutes one way. All that just to take ten minutes to drop off and pay for the rental. I was in a whole new realm here. To capitalize on the drive, I could do some shopping and have dinner someplace. Tylerville wasn't all that big, but it was bigger than Mundy.

I took the drive over at gawk speed, checking out the little villages along the way. It gave me time to think about my drive up here. The last person who had moved up to this neck of the woods had been teased unmercifully about being relegated to the back of beyond, and now here I was in the same place. The thought crossed my mind that I might have had an ulterior motive for coming this way. Jeff Chandler, his wife Beth, and their two boys had been my surrogate family.

When Jeff got stationed at the State Police Barracks in Tylerville, I remember looking the place up just to find out where the hell it was. Jeff was happy about the change which had come with a promotion from sergeant to lieutenant. His feelings about Southern Maine mirrored my own. There were way too many people and problems all zooming around at warp speed.

Beth saw it as a move to a better environment to raise their two kids in. The natural beauty of the county was awe-inspiring. I wondered if Jeff still thought it was paradise. He would be a good person to give me the lowdown on the area. Thinking about Jeff set off pangs of missing my friends down south and wondering what in the world I was doing here. It was comforting to think that there were at least a couple of people I knew. You would think with all the moving I had done, I'd be able to handle change with a little more finesse, but that wasn't the case. All of a sudden I really wanted to touch base with Jeff.

The rental people were very friendly and helpful. They didn't even take as much of my money as I had calculated, but then, I always round up so there aren't as many embarrassing moments. I asked about the State Police Barracks and if they could recommend a good restaurant. They came through on both counts. I was given a complimentary map of the town, and the guy pointed out where I was, where the barracks was, and where the restaurant was. I could take it from there. I gushed my thanks and went out to my truck to decide where I wanted to go first. I was getting quite hungry, even though it was still a bit early for dinner.

With the trailer gone, my faithful old Jeep Comanche and I both felt lighter. I'd had the truck for years and been all over Maine in it. I'd never had any pets, but the truck had been my companion and security blanket for those times when I felt needy. I admit I even talk to it, but it doesn't talk back, at least not in so many words.

I opted to go to the restaurant to eat during the senior citizen hour when I'd be less likely to encounter noisy children and obnoxious tourists. Captain Black's was not one of your run of the mill seafood restaurant chains. The dining area had a picture book view of the Mundy River, which ran the length of the county. I was pleased to be seated near the window so I could take in the scenery and be less self-conscious about eating alone. The place was quiet and genteel without being expensive and snobbish.

I ordered lobster stew that was to die for if the cholesterol in the cream didn't get you first. It was served with a side salad and a fresh baked mini loaf of whole wheat bread. To top this you had a choice of whipped butter or homemade strawberry preserves.

As I ate, I was intrigued by the many ospreys that were fishing in the river, stunning when the sun shone on their wet feathers as they rose from the water carrying their catch. I could have sat there for hours, but I did want to try and see Jeff.

I used the map to find the barracks but then drove right past it. You had to take this country road that twisted, turned, and dipped, with care. Let's face it; all the roads in this county were country roads. That was half its appeal, no traffic.

The barracks building was down off the road, and I was so intent on watching what was ahead that I didn't realize I had passed it until I came upon another landmark. I didn't have to worry about ticking other drivers off as I drove slowly back, because there were no other vehicles on the road. It was actually pretty nice.

There it was. How could I have missed the bold State Police shield on the sign out front? Granted, the place looked like an ordinary house, but it had no windows, not even a door in the front facing the road. The parking lot was to the side, and the door was to the rear.

It was strange that my coming here could cause such mixed feelings. Visiting the State Police Barracks was not my idea of a good time but visiting with Jeff was different.

I peered in the door window, and there was Jeff bent over doing paperwork at a desk that was surrounded by electronic equipment. I knocked, and his head shot up with a puzzled look that turned into a broad smile as he waved me in and got up.

"Maggie, you're a sight for sore eyes. What the hell are you doing here?" he exclaimed, as he wrapped me in a bear hug.

"I had to see if you were keeping paradise to yourself."

"How's your Dad? He making you take a vacation?"

"Dad died this spring. I couldn't stay in the apartment with all the memories."

"Oh, Maggie, I'm sorry. You know he's in a better place now, and he'd want you to be happy."

"I was glad I could be there with him at the end. You know, in an off-handed way he let me know that he came from around here someplace. He never shared anything about his family. Maybe that's why I'm here. I don't know. I just packed up my stuff and headed east."

"You look like you've had a bit of a tumble. You still sober?"

Coming from anyone else, I might have taken offense, but Jeff had been there when I needed help getting Dad moved in and sometimes when I just needed to vent. "I'm still sober, but it was rough at the very end. To be honest, I thought about just doing all Dad's pills and ending it. There's nobody left. But I'm here."

"You'll have to come out to the house for dinner. I can give Beth a call. She'll be crazy to see you and so will the boys."

"I'll have to take a rain check. I just finished eating over at Captain Black's. I'd like to see Beth and get her take on the school systems around here. I've just started a summer job, but if I'm going to stick around I'll need to find something for the fall." I filled Jeff in on my situation and promised I'd get in touch to set up dinner arrangements.

As I was pulling out of the Police Barracks parking lot, there was one lone truck that I had to wait for. I could get used to this slower pace. The driver of the truck and I locked eyes for a moment, and I could swear it was Deputy Grimes in civvies…but figure the odds. Maybe with a small population you got to see people you knew even out of town. It had been a long time since I'd lived in a small community. I was used to getting lost in a crowd.

I basked in the warm glow of my visit with Jeff all the way back to Mundy. Another day had come and gone, but I was settling in.

Back at the apartment sitting in Dad's old stuffed chair, the smell of Dad and his Old Spice wafted into my senses, sending me back to his bedside. I closed my eyes.

"The search continues in Tyler County for two missing fishermen out of Mundy. County officials say the crew of the *Double Nickel* was last seen off Sail Rock…"

"Maggot, have I ever told you about growing up there?"

"Where, Dad? You never said much of anything about when you were little."

There was that black hole, that empty space, a missing piece of me that was always just out of reach.

I must have dosed off. When I roused myself, the apartment was dark except for the light streaming in from the street light through the curtain-less windows. The only thing left to do was move from the chair to the futon. My bed wasn't set up yet. Tomorrow would come too soon again.

Chapter Six

Josie wasted no time in gearing up my role at the diner. Bright and early she got me started on muffins and preparing the home fries. These were the real deal, baked potatoes, skinned and cut up, then fried on the grill with lavish amounts of butter, seasoned with salt, pepper, and paprika. I got right into the baking, but I still had plenty of time to go work in the trenches. By mid-morning slack time arrived and I wasn't even tired.

I was just about to take a break when a towering figure filled the doorway of the diner. I stood stock still examining every aspect of his demeanor. He wore the same impeccable uniform. There was no jovial familiarity with the other customers, so I didn't have the feel that he was a regular. My skepticism kicked in, and I wanted to know why he was here. I didn't cause a scene, just acted nonchalant while taking his order. Of course I was far from it. I wished they had a shot that would inoculate me against the idiocy my mind seemed to go through whenever I got near him. Let's face it, I got horny. It isn't fair.

"How are you settling in to the new job and all?"

Like he cared. "Oh, I'm doing great. Josie has me baking, but I haven't managed to do much unpacking yet." *Now don't start babbling, girl.* "Am I going to see your smiling face around here every morning, Cowboy?" Why was I trying to be so antagonistic? His response was an intense silence with a cold stare as a chaser. Well that got me a big fat F in Waitressing 101.

"I'll have coffee and a muffin."

Josie must have noticed my foot sticking out of my mouth, because she came over with coffee and muffins and plopped down at Deputy Grimes' table. "So what's the local scuttlebutt, Hal? You going to be working on the Fourth this year?"

"I've pulled the graveyard. We're all on one way or the other for the holiday, but I don't mind. You and Dwight going to the fireworks?" I placed his water, coffee and muffin in front of him and moved on to take care of other customers.

I didn't stick around when Shirley arrived; there were too many things I wanted to get done. I went up to the apartment. Standing in the middle of the floor, I looked around. Where to begin? I decided to organize all the boxes of things for the diner and the stacks of papers, which reminded me that I hadn't asked Josie what was up with them. All the things that weren't mine went in the bedroom closest to the stairs leading down to the front of the diner. Josie or Dwight could come up and grab what they needed, whenever.

I really had little to show for my life. I set up my bed, a twin, and threw my linen closet bag on top of it. I'd make it later. A small chest of drawers and a bedside table and lamp rounded out my childhood bedroom set. Pitiful.

The living room was easy enough, although I'd have to live here awhile playing musical furniture to get things where I wanted them. My ever-ready futon, Dad's overstuffed chair, an armchair, and my comfy rocker were the extent of my major furniture. I'd spent some long hours in that rocker correcting school work. A blanket chest doubled as a coffee table and storage. The filing cabinet that Dwight and I had hauled up here could be an end table. I had every intention of going through it some day, but I hadn't had the desire or time after Dad died. I had a Tiffany lamp that I'd gotten at a Portland import shop, a splurge to add a little color to my life. It would go great on the filing cabinet if I could find some outlets.

My one concession to modern times was my computer and one of those nondescript computer table setups. It was going in a corner where I had discovered a hidden outlet; I could work at creating a presentable office space later. I usually was able to jerry-rig whatever bookshelves or setups I needed with things at hand.

Thank goodness a kitchen table came with the place, not that I'd necessarily actually eat at a table, but it made a good work surface. I did have a TV. It had kept Dad company while I was at work, his window on the world. In the evenings we would watch the news together. This was almost a contact sport. Dad would rant and rave in very politically incorrect epithets about various subjects and people that came up.

I wondered what the cable situation was here. Phone service, electric in my name, what else was I going to need to take care of? Oh yeah, food! It's amazing how my stomach can growl at the most appropriate time. I'd check out the local market for the basics and pick up a pizza at the Quik Stop, Mundy's version of a Big Apple.

I was doing all right for cash, what with the money I brought with me plus the tips I was making, but there were two more big things to do: post office and banking. The list was getting longer. I was used to having all kinds of businesses to pick from, but that wasn't the case here. There was no shopping center with a dollar store, no shopping mall with big name chain stores or specialty shops. Instead there were just the bare essentials for survival: hardware store, grocery stop, and gas pump. What more did you need? Moving here was more of a challenge than I had anticipated. I couldn't just hop in my truck and start swearing at the congestion as I whipped through traffic to get to Wal-Mart or Home Depot. Even so, I felt like quite the little domestic today with all I was getting accomplished.

The market was within walking distance as was most everything in town, but I wouldn't be able to haul groceries and pizza. Swinging my backpack over my shoulder, I bounded down the stairs to the truck.

Well, it was no supermarket, but it was bigger than a corner grocery store or convenience store. It was fun checking labels and expiration dates and an eye opener as well. I could see I would have to be very careful, because I was finding way too many gone by sell by dates. Not good.

I was almost finished but lost in my own little world when my cart got shoved. It took a minute to pull myself back to the present. Must be a scuffer. That's what I call the little old ladies that scuff around a store using their carts like walkers.

"Yo, bitch!" As I looked up and focused, it wasn't any little old lady but the broadest, hairiest hulking ogre I had ever seen leering at me. I couldn't imagine why he had fixated on me until he opened his slobbering mouth again.

"Well, looky here. If it ain't the fucking bitch that beat up Sheila. Right proud of yourself ain't ya? You got no binnis here. Why dun ya take your sorry ass and get the fuck outta town?" He gave a nasty shove of his cart right into my ankle. Pain and adrenaline immediately took over, and I was swinging my backpack before I knew it. He was so plastered that the contact felled him like a tree.

Now what had I done? Between his booming voice and the thud he made when he hit the floor, he'd attracted quite a crowd. Now my flight instincts took charge and I was looking for an exit. Was this Wayne? Hard to believe this was Winnie's grandson.

Mumbling something about this person being ill I started to back up with my cart, as a couple of guys bent over the lout and tried to bring him around. "Bear! Bear, can you hear me? Bear, you sorry son of a bitch, you're shit faced."

The name was perfect for the guy. I put as much distance between me and Bear as I could and moved toward the frozen foods department to hide out. Maybe the chill air would calm me down. While I was doing what I thought was a pretty good job of being oblivious to the commotion, Winfield walked up to me.

Those rheumy blue eyes were reading me like a book. "Pretty impressive put-down of a drunk twice your size. I missed you at last night's meeting. There's one at the Old Grange tonight at 7:00."

I really was in no mood to hear this right now, and I was looking for an exit. "I've been really busy with the job and trying to get moved in." I didn't even know if I still had the meeting list he had given me the day before.

"Tsk, tsk, tsk." Winfield sighed as his head sagged from side to side. "First I was too busy, then I was too tired, then I was too drunk."

Oh, Jeez… I hate getting thumped with slogans like that, and they sting when they hit a nerve. It was obvious that I wasn't going to get out of this gracefully. I knew I was getting overly sensitive, and a meeting would do me good, but there was so much I wanted to get done.

"Where's the Grange?" Winfield gave me directions, adding it was the only building on the outskirts of town that said 'Grange' on it. Well, duh. I must need a meeting, because even that last comment irritated me.

It didn't dawn on me that Winfield had kept me occupied while Bear and his entourage left the place. He had probably saved my sorry ass from more explaining and uncomfortable circumstances. I'd have to remember to thank him. Maybe I'd make the meeting.

I had plenty of time to put away groceries and have my pizza with an hour to kill. I had no problem finding the Grange. It was on a rise on the outskirts of town. 'Grange' was or had been written on the front of the building, but years of weathering had left very little that was recognizable. It was a two story white clapboard structure in an advanced state of peeling. The sides of the building had those tall four-pane windows, and their black trim was in a race with the white to see which could disintegrate first. Birch and poplar trees framed the building on three sides, surrounding a dirt and gravel yard that acted as a parking lot.

I was way too early, so it wasn't surprising that no one was here. New place, new meeting, and here I was twiddling my thumbs. I might as well explore the woods around the building. The shade would be a welcome relief from the glaring sun and baking heat. Summer is not my favorite time of year.

My exploration was cut short when I heard the arrival of another pickup. The truck was probably as old as mine, but with the rattle of a leaking exhaust system and scattered dents that proclaimed it as a working truck. What stepped out of the truck could only be described as a wizened old leprechaun. The jeans he was wearing were clean and still stiff enough not to have seen many washings. He was in a Kelly green sweatshirt, white socks and sneakers at one end and a Notre Dame ball cap on the other. It made me sweat just to look at him in this summer heat, but there wasn't so much as a bead of sweat on his gaunt body. His skin was more weathered than his clothes, and he walked with such a stoop that I half expected him to topple over at any minute. My back ached for him.

I must have been quite the sight stepping out from the treeline. He had taken in my truck and now his gaze rested on me. Suddenly I felt like I was at my first meeting, awkward, confused, and wondering, as I so often did, what I was doing here.

He waited for me as I came across the dirt lot to a set of rutted steps leading to the hall. "Well, hello. I'm Kenny. Are you new in town?" He offered his hand, and I hesitated only a second before grabbing on to it. He had a firm grip that belied his frail appearance.

"As a matter of fact, I just got into town this past weekend, and I'm in the process of moving in. Oh, my name is Margaret."

"Well, welcome Margaret. It's good to see another female face around these halls. I'm afraid we old codgers outnumber you gals. If you don't mind me asking, are you new to the program?"

"No. I've been around a few twenty-four. Do people give their sobriety date up here to qualify?"

"Lord, no! We aren't that highfalutin here. Do they do that where you're from? I haven't been out of the county."

Kenny was cute in a cunning sort of way. I imagined he didn't miss a trick, but I could believe he hadn't been far, a true local.

"Some of the places I've been the people introduce themselves with their sobriety date, but it has always seemed a sort of pride thing and I can't afford the ego trip."

"Well, Margaret, it sounds like you've been around. I mean that in a good way. We could really use some ladies with some time in the program. There are a lot of newbies coming from the courts, and they don't want to listen to us old men."

I was home. My sponsor had always pounded into me, "can't keep it if you don't give it away." When I'm feeling down, working with another drunk always picks me up. Could fate have sent me here? I'd just go with the flow.

Kenny and I set up chairs, put out literature, and got the coffee going. The hall was surprisingly cool. The walls had the twelve steps and the twelve traditions on pull- down shades, and those slogans that I had been beaten over the head with so many times that I had a love-hate relationship with them were all there too. Helping to set up was a great way to break the ice.

Winfield came in just as we were finishing up. "Margaret, glad to see you found the place. I see you've taken over my job." For a split second I got defensive, but it passed, and all three of us laughed. I really needed a meeting!

When the coffee was done, we took our Styrofoam cups out on the wooden steps and I got to be the rose between two thorns.

"Kenny, do you know who this is? This is the gal who took on Sheila and Teddy single-handed."

"You don't say."

"I didn't take anybody on, and who is Teddy?"

"Teddy is Theodore Cox, also known as Bear. He's a friend of Sheila's and rather protective of her in his own way."

A thousand crude comebacks were swirling through my brain but I didn't know these gentlemen well enough to share them. "Well, they could both use the program." Wasn't I just little Miss Priss?

"Sheila did come once or twice. The courts may have sent her. It's hard to tell, but she didn't stay. Remember I said we don't get too many girls around here. Maybe next time she tries you can help her out."

Kenny was sweet. He was already setting me up to make a twelfth step call. The question was, could I survive one?

The parking lot began to fill up, and a variety of guys trickled in to get coffee and come back out for a smoke. I sat and listened to the conversations, thinking how much they were like those at the meetings I used to go to.

Just as we all started to filter into the hall, two girls about my age drove up in a maroon van. They seemed to be nervous, furtively looking around as they came to the steps. I held out my hand and greeted them. The surprised look on their faces said that maybe greeting wasn't done here. We went around the room and introduced ourselves and I tried to remember the girls' names for after the meeting.

It was a good meeting that drifted out into the parking lot. The two girls, Tina and Joanne, were new and skittish, but we agreed to keep in touch and maybe get together for another meeting. I wished I had a phone number to give them, but all I could do was write down my address and where I worked just in case they needed to talk, and I got their numbers in case I needed to talk to someone. As I was doing this in what was by now an almost empty parking lot, a rumbling old K-car in faded ice blue rolled by at just below normal speed. I thought Tina and Joanne were going to bolt as they looked over at the cruising car.

Lo and behold, if it wasn't Sheila behind the wheel. There was someone in the car with her, but I didn't recognize him. All I could tell for sure was that it wasn't Bear. I hope this didn't mean I was going to get my chance at twelfth stepping right now. Sheila and I took each other in, and then she gunned it and was over the rise before you could say Jack-be-nimble.

That was it for Tina and Joanne. They couldn't wait to be long gone. I said my goodbyes as doors slammed, and Joanne drove away with Tina in the passenger seat.

I had felt connected once again and yet here I was all alone in a dirt parking lot. It was only eight-thirty.

Chapter Seven

The Fourth was getting closer, and you could feel the excitement building in the town. Josie was letting me play around with my favorite coffeecake. I'd picked up some things I needed, so if it didn't go over, Josie wouldn't be out anything. The cake was a dense sour cream raspberry swirl concoction that could pass for dessert.

More people from away were coming in just after the regulars were finishing up. I'd only made two coffeecakes as an addition to the muffins that Josie's was known for. I figured the regulars weren't ready for any changes, but people from away might be game.

Robby was my guinea pig. I cut him the first slice out in the kitchen. He looked to Josie.

"Go ahead, Robby, make sure it's good enough for Josie's." She winked at me as I placed the slice on a plate with a fork and offered it to him. Rob took his taste testing very seriously, and all of a sudden I was worried the coffeecake wouldn't pass muster. I waited.

"Wow!" he said, as he consumed the final mouthful. "Josie, can we have this every morning? It's real good."

"Too much of a good thing isn't good, but it sounds like it stands up to our standard."

"Thank you, Robby. Josie's right, it might not be good every day. We'll keep it as a special treat, uh … if that's alright with Josie."

"Robby, how about if you come up with a special name for this cake that Maggie made, and we'll put it on the special board."

"I don't know if I can, Josie. You really think I can?"

"Of course you can. You're my number one man."

"Can we name it Wow! Raspberry Wakeup Cake?"

"I don't know if it will live up to the wow part but I definitely like the wakeup part. What do you say Josie? Will all that fit on the board?"

"We'll make it fit."

I was chalking the last letters on the board when Deputy Grimes came in. I made a quick promise to myself to keep my mouth shut so I wouldn't insert my foot again. It was hard watching that swagger. Whenever I was drawn to a boy when I was a kid, I would lash out and pound the shit out of him. All the while I thought he was trying to tame me, when he could always have claimed self-defense. Maybe that was why I ended up with so many bruises when I got into relationships, but that was one of my problems. I didn't know how to have relationships. I could get away with that kind of behavior when I was little, but it wasn't flying now.

"What'll you have, Deputy Grimes?"

"I'll have a piece of that raspberry stuff you were putting up on the board. Josie usually comes up with some good tasting specials. Oh, by the way, I hear you've been getting around. It might be a good idea to try and keep your nose clean."

Instant boil. I was *not* going to explode. *Count to ten. Don't let him push your buttons. Don't give him the power.*

"Oh?" I walked away to get the coffeecake and cool off. I was praying I wasn't turning red, but I couldn't be that lucky.

"Maggie, what's the matter?" Josie's concerned expression was like a mirror. This was not how I'd planned to start my day. "Just oil and water. They don't mix well, you know."

"Are you still having trouble with Hal? Haven't you two young people gotten beyond that? Do you want me to take care of him?" Boy, was that a loaded question!

"No. I'm fine, thanks."

When I returned with the coffeecake, I had a better handle on myself, but Josie decided that I needed a little help anyway.

"Hi, Hal. Maggie was just about to go on break." She was looking at Hal as I put the cake in front of him. I couldn't tell if there was some signaling going on between the two of them, but I was surprised when Deputy Grimes turned to me. "Why don't you join me; I wouldn't mind the company."

He wouldn't mind. How about me minding? "I'd say I'd been outnumbered here."

"I'll bring you over some coffee. Sit. Get acquainted." I felt like a little kid whose mother is trying to set her up on a blind date. But I supposed if he was going to act like a regular, I couldn't go on with a daily grudge. I sat down. Now what? This was really awkward.

"So, are you meeting new people?"

"Practically everyone I meet is new to me."

"You aren't making this very easy. I'm concerned. You need to be more careful about who you get involved with. There are some pretty unsavory people here."

"Look, I can take care of myself. I didn't come here to take the top dog spot. I've seen some of Sheila's stable and I'm not impressed."

"What's with the Wild West lingo?"

"You said it. I get around."

"That's intriguing. If you are trying to pique my curiosity, you have."

"I'm not trying to do anything but settle into a new place."

"Can you tell me why you decided to come to Mundy?"

"No."

"Is that no you can't or no you won't?"

"Is that a personal question or a professional one?" This whole situation was going over like a lead balloon. It wasn't like me to be so sensitive. I wasn't ready to bare my soul to this guy, and besides

I really couldn't tell him why I had chosen Mundy because I didn't know.

"How about we bury the hatchet, if you don't mind me using a western phrase?"

"OK, but if I remember correctly, in the battle between Cowboys and Indians the Indians lost, and I hate to lose."

"What are you doing the Fourth?"

"I hadn't thought that far ahead. I get the impression it's a really big deal in Mundy."

"Josie's is closed on Sundays, and since the Fourth is on a Sunday, you won't have to work. If you'd like we could hit the town and take in the fireworks before I go on duty. It may not seem like much from a big city point of view but everyone gets involved.

Was this a date? I didn't want to get my hopes up because I couldn't pin down how I felt about this guy. Mind and body were at war and which would win was anyone's guess. I had to say something.

"Will you be coming in tomorrow?"

"I'm not working then, but I could stop by."

"Your offer sounds like fun and I'd like to take you up on it, but I have a few things I need to get straightened out. Could we make plans tomorrow for Sunday?"

"Sure, but I'll probably be in early." He was so at ease and I was ready to jump out of my skin. *Good one, Margaret. Was that a 'yes' or 'no' you just gave him?*

"I've got to get going. Tell Josie her wakeup cake was terrific, as usual." He got up, put money on the table, waved to Josie who had been watching us at a discreet distance, and was out the door. I just sat there.

Josie wasted no time in hustling over to find out what went on. "Well, did he like the cake? Have you two decided to be friends?"

"Let's see. He told me to tell you your cake was terrific as usual."

"Didn't you tell him you made it?"

"I didn't get the chance."

"What were you talking about, then?"

"Cowboys and Indians." That got a queer look from her.

"We decided to bury the hatchet. He wants to show me around on the Fourth and take in the fireworks."

"So, did you say yes?"

"I think so. I'm not sure, but he's stopping by tomorrow morning." Josie was shaking her head and her earrings flashed like her own private fireworks going off. "Why are you fighting this so hard? You two should be hitting it off real well."

"The operative word in that is hitting. I've got so much to do and there's so much that I don't get that I just don't want to rush into anything. Besides, hooking up with someone isn't even on my 'to do' list." Josie got that look again as if she was reading me like a book. She smiled and got up. "Josie, when Shirley comes in, do you think we could talk?"

"Sure, but right now the next wave has arrived."

When the time came, we sat at the back table next to the kitchen. I asked if there was a phone line up to the apartment and she said yes. I didn't know how to get down to what I wanted to ask, so I continued talking about taking care of the utilities. I could tell she was getting restless. She knew I was dancing around the real questions. "Maggie, what do you want to know, really?"

"Give me the low down on Sheila, Bear, and Wayne. What's up with these guys?"

"It's a nasty situation. Sheila's got two kids by Wayne, I think. The state is always threatening to take them away, but when things get hot she doles them out to Winnie, Wayne's grandmother. How Winnie survives them I'll never know. They're hellions. But what do you expect with their home life? Since her brother is a deputy, that's probably helped her get out of a lot of scrapes. They all grew up together, Hal, Wayne, Howie, Sheila and Bear. Sheila and Bear are the same age and the youngsters of the bunch, so they got pretty tight. They all liked to party and I hear some of them are still into that and the drug scene, but I'm not really privy to what goes on in that world."

"Sounds like just one big happy family."

"Pretty close, although I wouldn't use the term 'happy' in that context. It must be hard on Howie. He's no angel, but he's on the drug task force that all those agencies are involved in. You know…DEA, state, and county sheriff. I always thought it was kinda strange that Hal didn't get on it instead of Howie. You know, sort of like a career move. But Howie's been the one that's lived here all his life and been with the Sheriff's Department longer. So give. What happened with you and Bear?"

I could look back and laugh at it now though it wasn't funny at the time. "Don't even make it sound like some social engagement. The lout shoved a cart into my ankle, bellowing obscenities for the world to hear. He was so trashed. It was a case of slobbering drunk meets Murphy backpack, and that's all she wrote. Maybe I should have this thing registered as a lethal weapon."

"You *are* a scrapper. I know as long as I'm in my right mind there's no way I'd take him on. I give him a real wide berth."

"You could say I wasn't in my right mind."

"On another subject all together, could you make another couple of those cakes tomorrow? They went over big today, and Saturdays we get a different crowd of people. We've got an account at the market if you want to pick up what you'll need."

I said I'd be happy to. I needed to get back on that horse even if it tried to take a bite out of me. In a small town with one grocery store, you couldn't avoid going in there or running into people, for that matter. I was finding that out the hard way.

I figured I had better get started before things started to close up for the holiday weekend, so I used the public phone down at the Quik Stop. It was on the outside corner of the building with no privacy and a lot of noise, but if I plugged one ear I could just make out what was being said through the receiver. Wonderful automation and menus tied me up. "Press one for a problem with your phone, press two, etc." Once I got a live person he set me up with an installation on Monday by five. That was quick; I figured I would have to wait at least a week. The electric company just had to do paper work and verify everything with the Waylands because the apartment had electricity already hooked up. The post office and bank were practically next door to each other. I gave the post office my new address and got the ball rolling to forward my mail which had been on hold down the coast. I could use my paycheck from school about now.

With all those errands out of the way, I set out for the market. This time I was making sure I didn't get ambushed, but then, nothing is fool proof. Everyone in town seemed to know who I was, but I didn't have a clue about them. It tended to be a bit of a handicap.

There was no need to lollygag; I knew what I wanted and where it was. I was honing in on some seedless raspberry jam when I heard my name.

"Hello, Margaret, good to see you."

"Hi Kenny, it's good to see you too. There aren't too many people I can say that about yet. Uh-oh, is that Sheila down by the register?"

"Yup, that's Sheila and her two kids, Ross and Kayla."

I definitely didn't want any more confrontations. I don't think Kenny understood why I was hanging back. Gone was my rush to get in and out of here, and you couldn't just melt into the crowd, there wasn't one. Kenny was talking to me and I was nodding but not listening as we inched forward toward the checkout and Sheila.

The little girl had straight dark hair with pale skin and freckles that stood out in relief. Her enormous dark eyes were ringed with circles and resembled a doe's caught in the headlights. She was so thin that her joints looked swollen compared to the rest of her. I was looking at a malnourished child with absolutely no vitality. Ross seemed to take after his mother in the looks department. He had a thick head of unruly dirty blonde hair and his skin was sallow, too, but he was fidgety. His sharp, cruel-looking eyes gave me the creeps. I could picture him torturing animals, and it made me shiver. From his behavior, Ross must be the elder. Kayla was hanging off Sheila, and Ross was running verbal rough-shod over her. He wanted what he wanted and he wanted it now!

The most nutritious thing in the cart was a half gallon of milk. Among the sugary convenience foods was a half-gallon of coffee brandy, someone's drink of choice. No wonder these kids looked like concentration camp survivors.

"Hi, Sheila, how's it going?" Immediately she looked down at the brandy, then up at Kenny and over at me.

"Hey, Murf, getting them a little young aren't you?" Kenny turned red and my mouth fell open.

"Now Sheila, that's no way to talk. Not in front of the children. This is Margaret."

I waited for an obscene outburst but instead her response was "I saw you out at the drunk school. Kenny's always trying to recruit people." I was astonished that she didn't remember the motel, and then it dawned on me that she had been blotto and probably in a blackout. Why the reaction by Bear if Sheila didn't care what happened that night? I wouldn't say she was entirely straight at this moment, but she was more lucid than before. Kenny gave me a little nudge. I guess I was supposed to say something, but all I could think of was 'attraction not promotion,' a snippet I had picked up at meetings. It was a tradition or something. I just knew I wasn't going to push AA at her, and I don't think she was attracted to me or AA for that matter. It was all I could do to croak out "Nice to meet you." "Yeah, whatever," she replied, and we were dismissed. She finished up and left, and now I was eager to do the same. Questions were stacking up like a compost pile, and little thoughts were pricking my subconscious. She'd called Kenny 'Murf,' and what was this 'drunk school' stuff?

After that wonderful encounter, I decided to give Tina and Joanne a call, so it was back to the pay phone. Now I had a number I could give them for when the phone did get connected. It wasn't like I needed an excuse to call but my old behaviors kicked in, and I had to rationalize every move I made.

Between the heat and my emotions, I was restless most of the night, so it was great to get back to work the next morning.

"Maggie, would you consider working tomorrow instead of Monday? I've got a feeling it will be dead on Monday, and I want to take advantage of the foot traffic and the goings-on that will be right here on the street tomorrow. I know you have a date with Hal, but with Wanda gone and Shirley with other commitments…."

"Woo, back up. First I do not have a *date* with Hal. Second, I don't really know what's going on tomorrow. Third, I'm not sure how long Hal and I can be in each other's company without coming to blows."

"I didn't mean to get pushy. Each year, craft and food vendors line the streets around the village square, and there are all kinds of activities and entertainment before the fireworks. Usually we're open, and it's a nice steady crowd. With the Fourth falling on a Sunday and the condition Wanda was in, I had written the day off, but you're working out so well, we could handle it. It's only for a short day. Dwight, Me and Robby will be here but we need another body. What do you say?"

Dwight stuck his head out of the kitchen at this moment and gave me an evil wink and nod in Josie's direction. "I told you, you might be in for more than you bargained for."

"Josie, if you promise to take a breath and slow down, it just so happens that this might work out for me. I'd be happy to work tomorrow and have Monday off; that way, if the phone guy comes early, I'll be available." Even without Dwight's prodding, I was reminded that it was hard to say no to Josie. There was also that nagging trepidation on my part about hanging around with Hal all day. I was really up for a good lay, but my mind was working hard to override my emotions. It was time to talk to Cat. I was ready for her kick in the ass.

Before my thoughts could travel any further down that path, Josie was handing me a sign. "Great. Here, hang this up in the window of the door." It was a neatly printed sign with Fourth of July decorations and the hours we would be open for business. It had been a done deal. I couldn't help laughing, and Dwight and Josie joined in.

We were in the kitchen planning for the next day's specials while preparing today's. The traditional entrée was salmon. Josie wasn't sure if she wanted to do salmon wiggle, salmon with dill sauce or a shrimp-salmon plate. This was all new to me, so I just kept nodding in agreement as if I knew what she was talking about. I'd make whatever she wanted; just give me directions and ingredients.

Business was off to a brisk start. I was knee deep in customers when Hal came in. He was even more of a hunk in civvies and could easily pass for a downeast fisherman. There was that maddeningly alluring swagger with a muscle shirt showing off his tawny firm biceps. I wanted to jump his bones!

Chapter Eight

Even though I didn't have to rise and shine before dawn, my inner alarm clock had me up and ready to go. My memories surrounding the Fourth of July got mixed reviews. Holidays had always been uncomfortable for me and just being in a new place didn't change that.

At work we had a steady stream of customers having everything from just coffee to full breakfasts. Some were obviously killing time waiting for the events of the day.

Robby came in just as the vendors began setting up their booths along Water Street. There were some crafts and several food stalls. These set Josie off like an M-80 firecracker.

"Every year when we're planning the celebration I ask them to puhleease…put the food vendors down at the other end of the street, and every year it's the same old thing. 'We've always done it this way.' Without us businesses there wouldn't be any Fourth of July celebrations!"

I noticed a cute little shack on wheels directly across from the diner that advertised 'fish-on-a-stick.' It was this particular individual that Josie seemed to have a running feud with. Personally, I didn't see what the hubbub was about. The vendors would bring walk-in customers who would order something just to lay claim to a seat.

Robby filled me in on all the activities that were planned for the day. I didn't really understand what he meant when he talked about running across crates in the harbor or the fireman's large fish relay, but both sounded intriguing to watch.

"Do you like fireworks, Maggie? Did you have them where you grew up?"

"Oh yes, my mom and dad brought me to them before I was born." A quizzical look took over Robby's face, so I had fun regaling him with my family fireworks stories. It was enjoyable retelling those days; our little family had had quite the time.

Our fireworks had been over a lake surrounded by the Adirondack Mountains of New York. The booming would echo around the lake as the sulfuric smell of black powder drifted over the surface of the lake. Our favorite place to watch the display was on a grassy hill in a park where there had been an old pre-Revolutionary fort. I would imagine that I was in the midst of a raging canon battle. Before the fireworks, we would visit the old fort area where skeletons of soldiers and Indians had been unearthed, and lifelike displays of dungeons and surgeries with bloodstained mannequins captivated my imagination. Robby's mouth had fallen open when I told him my parents took me to the fireworks before I was born. I had better be careful about how I phrased things. He liked it when I told him about the sparklers that set off a grass fire one year as we waited for the action to begin.

It was comforting to remember those family moments. There had been a lot of other not so happy memories as I grew older, but I wasn't going to let them rain on my Fourth this year.

It was a nice full day and tips were good. I had plenty of time to run upstairs and shower the smell of grease and fish out of my hair, dump my stinky clothes in one of my all purpose trash bags that was now acting as a laundry hamper, and figure out what to wear. I was actually worried about wearing the right thing to a Fourth of July celebration. How crazy was that? In the back of my mind I was thinking about running into Hal. I wanted to make a good impression on him. I was craving company, but at the same time, there was something annoying about that guy.

I had decided on a crisp white tee with the sleeves rolled up. I could play the game of showing off my tan with the best of them. The capped sleeve came down just enough to cover those maddening shoulder freckles that redheads are cursed with. My khaki shorts weren't short-short but just short enough. I had let my hair down and kept it tucked behind my ears, hoping the rinse I had used would both keep it from bushing out and finish off any lingering greasy fish odor from the diner.

I was starving. At the bottom of the stairs I saw Robby with some friends looking happy as always. I waved and he came jogging over. "Is there any place left to get something to eat?"

"Most of the booths have closed up but the Icebox is still open. It's that little place down by the pier. We're headed over there for some ice cream, but they have other stuff you can eat."

"It sounds good. I'll give it a try." I had noticed the place in passing but hadn't ever stopped there. Robby bounded off with his young acne-faced friends, shouting that he would see me there. I headed out toward the Icebox at a much slower pace, perusing some of the diehard vendors who weren't yet ready to close up shop for the night but wanted to squeak out that last couple of sales. Some of them had cute handcrafted items, and others looked like their wares were straight out of a carnival prize catalog. There was one booth that caught my interest and overrode my growling stomach. It was selling pictures, postcards, prints, and magnets with pictures of Mundy's olden and not so olden days. You could be transported down this very street as it was a hundred years ago. There had been more hustle and bustle with many more businesses and people.

While I was being transported back in time, the vendor was trying to strike up a conversation with me about yearbooks and team photos. They were his big sellers this year. The man had quite a collection of old school photos. This grabbed my attention when I thought I might be able to see what Hal and the others were like in their high school days. The vendor was very obliging and pulled out a couple of decades of the Mundy Petrels, Mundy's basketball team. I made a guess at Hal's age and found what I was looking for. There were younger faces of Hal, Howie, and Teddy Cox, although it was hard to believe I was looking at the same hulk that I'd met up with in the grocery store. The vendor had continued to carry on a one sided conversation and was reeling off names that didn't mean anything to me. I did grow more attentive at any Murphys, and I got my first glimpse of a young teenager named Wayne McCarthy. Yes, that was Winnie's grandson. I'd never actually seen him, but there was a family resemblance that Sheila's kids shared. It was getting late so I thanked the guy, but I wasn't about to start an album on Hal. He looked put out about not making a sale, so I gave him my best smile and took one of his cards for the future.

The Icebox had a crowd of people, most getting ice cream, some waiting for food orders. The building itself was a whimsical A-frame with gray driftwood stain. The outside was festooned with old wooden lobster traps and colorful buoys that had never felt the touch of salt water. The lawn area that went down to the water's edge was covered with people in lawn chairs, on blankets, and at picnic tables with red and white striped umbrellas. To the left of the Icebox was a dilapidated fish processing plant that appeared long defunct and was now a gathering place for seagulls that weren't ready to call it a day yet. They were perched in row upon row on the roof as they eyed the food possibilities of the crowd. I'm not sure which outnumbered which, seagulls or people.

I finished up a fried seafood dinner and started on dessert. Kids and dogs were running everywhere, the kids with ice cream smeared across their faces and down their chins. I was enjoying a great big chocolate cone, trying not to drip down the front of my shirt while looking over the throng that had come for the fireworks. I wasn't quite sure what to do next or where to light so I could enjoy the evening.

The pier and parking lot were alive with activity, everyone waiting for the great light show to begin. As the dusky light was fading to dark the noise level was rising. I thought I heard a familiar voice. I scanned the crowd and there she was. Sheila's obnoxious obscenity-laden mouth and pale skin that seemed to luminesce in the dim light made her stand out in the crowd. She was getting rowdy among a group of characters, one being Bear. Just watching her catapulted me back to Old Orchard and the old party ways that had caused so much trouble. I realized exactly what she was doing and was totally flabbergasted at her blatancy; she was dealing right in front of everyone including her kids. I started to feel the rage building in me. There's nothing like a reformed whore, and that's just what I was. I'd been there and I recognized the moves. She was obviously well lubricated.

I felt myself being drawn toward Sheila as if her screaming obscenities were a siren song. I started toward her with no idea of what I would do or say and no thought of making a scene. I had tunnel vision and I was on a mission. She saw me coming and must have read the look on my face. She had a leash in her hand and suddenly it became a weapon. I was on auto pilot headed for disaster when, from the corner of my eye, I noticed movement behind me and the flash of a uniform. Just then someone grabbed hold of my arm, and I was swung around like a tether ball, smack into Hal's chest.

"I wondered if you were ever going to show up." I looked up at him but I couldn't get my mind to focus. He was wrapping his arms around me, but I was craning my neck to turn and see what was happening with Sheila. I could just make out Howie in uniform saying something to Sheila, and she was staring and gesturing over at me.

"Hey, Earth to Margaret." I tore my eyes from Sheila and tried to come back down to earth. "Let it go. What were you going to do, get into another fight with Sheila?"

"I haven't ever gotten into a fight with her. She's dealing right out here in front of you and everyone and with all these kids around."

"Calm down. It's being handled. By the way, I'm off duty right now, in case you haven't noticed. Tell me, do you enjoy making a spectacle of yourself?" He let go of me so I could turn toward Sheila and the crowd that had converged on her. Many of them were staring at me including Robby. That got my attention, and I could feel my face flush.

"I didn't mean to cause problems, Hal, it's just… I don't know."

"It's okay, Maggie. Come on, lighten up." He slipped his arm around me with a lighter touch and pulled me into his chest. I wanted to nestle in under his arm and breathe in his scent and hide from the prying eyes of others. He walked me up to a grassy knoll with big boulders that acted as guardrails by the side of the road. They made great seats for the fireworks. I was experiencing wonderful trilling vibrations up my spine and I'd have been happy to give up watching fireworks in exchange for making some of our own back at my place. I was melting like a piece of cheese in a grilled cheese sandwich.

The fireworks thundered over the bay and echoed out to sea. I wasn't thinking of historic canon battles but was letting the sights and sounds wash over me in what was a very sensual experience. I was dreaming about the remaining night and the thought that I didn't have to go to work in the morning. The fly in the ointment was the fact that Hal *did* have to go to work, and shortly.

When the fireworks were over, the chaos began as everyone tried to drive out at once. Hal and I just strolled past cars waiting in line. We were actually holding hands. Hal walked me up the backstairs and then it got awkward.

"Well, I had a nice time. I hope you enjoyed our fireworks."

"Thanks Hal, I really did have a good time and thanks for rescuing me from myself. You want to come in for awhile?"

"I'd love to, but I'm on duty shortly so I'd better be going. I'll see you around." With that he left me standing on the doorstep, and he was gone down the stairs. This evening didn't exactly end picture-perfect. Not even a good night peck on the cheek. At least he didn't shake my hand.

I went into the stifling apartment, turned on the fan, and decided that I needed a cold shower to match the mental bath I had just received.

Chapter Nine

My night was spent tossing and turning. Even the fan in the window and the open back door weren't giving me much relief from the heat, and my mind finished off any chance I had at sleep. I kept rehashing the evening with Hal and the totally unsatisfactory end to the night. Sheila had stolen another night from me. Why was this happening? How could I put an end to her insinuating herself into my life? I wanted to quit renting space to her in my head. Just being around users made me a little crazy. To be honest, which was hard for me, Sheila's behaviors were uncomfortably familiar, and there was still a part of me that wanted to slip back into that world of oblivion where nothing bothered me. Mixed in with Sheila and Hal were memories of family provoked by the conversation I'd had with Hal. Pesky unanswered questions sat at the edge of my consciousness but not quite within reach.

I finally gave up. My automatic inner alarm clock had been preset for diner time with no snooze button, so I might as well stop fighting it and start my day. I was going to have to walk it off, occupy my mind with new experiences rather than playing in old garbage. I decided to start exploring Smuggler's Neck, the name of the intriguing coastline that had beckoned me from the minute I stepped up on the deck of my new apartment. It sat north of the bay that Mundy was on and had been an unofficial commercial spot in Mundy's early history, hence the name Smuggler's Neck. I had gleaned its name and history during my brief excursion to the library. There had been quite a ruckus coming from places on the cliffs with flickering light, perhaps from a campfire. Maybe it was a camping area now. I thought of the bugs and didn't feel like clumping into a campground at the crack of dawn. Taking the coastal route around the Neck would cut down on the bugs and be easier traveling. I could be alone. The higher elevations could wait until some other time.

The tide was just starting to go out, so there was barely any exposed beach yet. I had lived on the coast long enough to know that you should always be aware of what the tide was doing. I could get so wrapped up in exploring that I'd almost gotten trapped a couple of times by incoming tides. Here the tides were averaging twenty-five feet, which means the water comes and goes pretty fast.

Donning long sleeves, pants, and some old sneakers, and armed with a flashlight, I started my trek. I wasn't going to heft anything else down the beach. Without sleep I didn't have the energy; empty hands and empty head were my goals.

Predawn to sunrise on the Maine coast has got to be one of the most serene and beautiful sights there is and one of my favorite things to experience. The hues of color change so gradually that they are like a musical picture gently washing over your senses. Amethyst and purples blending into pink and magenta set the backdrop for yellows and turquoises to peek through at the horizon line. When it's calm, as it was this morning, the water is a perfect reflection of the sky. I found these predawn excursions to be rejuvenating and almost better than sleep.

The tide had left piles of kelp among rocks which were encrusted with barnacles, periwinkles, and mussels. I slipped and slid over them, my sneakers struggling to gain purchase. Every so often, bits of exposed beach offered my legs a rest. Climbing over rocks on a beach was sometimes as strenuous as mountain climbing and required considerable agility. The kelp and seaweed were giving off a heady aroma in addition to providing an obstacle course to navigate. All in all, a very exhilarating morning jaunt.

The sun wasn't quite up, but the sky was brighter when I noticed something colorful on a piece of beach hollowed out of the cliffs by the tides. It was too far away to make out so, of course, I had to get closer.

As I scrambled up to the spot, I recognized the source of the color, a striped tube top. Holy shit! My legs let go first, then my bladder as I landed hard on the slimy green rocks, my hands shooting out for balance and making contact with razor sharp barnacles. There, like a large rubber baby doll, lay Sheila, gently lolling back and forth with the outgoing tide. No longer with a glowering expression of hate, Sheila's face held a startled glazed stare.

Like history repeating itself, my past came crashing to mind. I hadn't thought about the episode in Alaska for years. I had tried to forget the past, compartmentalize it, and, yes, run away from it. It now was obvious that none of that had worked. In an instant, the names and faces of the people who had driven me close to suicide and given me a double dose of distaste for law enforcement all came spinning into my mind. This was not the first time I had run across a dead body in a watery setting.

The other body had been in Navy dungarees, floating face down in the Bering Sea. Bobbing in and out near a deserted inlet, the young Navy enlisted man had been stabbed to death for being a drug informant for NCIS.

"Shit! *Why me?*" I cried. Not now, not here, not when I was starting a new life. I don't know how long I just sat where I had fallen. Poor Sheila. Her tube top had split open and allowed one ample breast to escape, making her look for all the world like the Pillsbury Doughboy in drag. I didn't think she had been dead for very long, but that was an amateur's guess.

Gradually the acrid odor of my own urine seeped into my consciousness, along with the memory of Mrs. Slaven, a towering gray-haired battle axe, looking down on me. "You're a disgrace, a girl your age a bed-wetter. Your mother should have told me. I'm not paid enough to deal with this in the middle of the night. Stop that blubbering! I've got a good mind to make you sleep in your mess. This wouldn't have happened if you'd done as I said and gone to the lavatory." What had I done to make my parents leave me with this terrible woman? Whatever it was I wasn't going to do it again.

I was drawn back to the present. I forced myself to stand and take stock of where I was. The wet salty taste of tears added to my confusion as I looked over at Sheila. She had stopped lolling back and forth. The tide had left her stranded there on that little piece of beach, exposed. Something made me look up at the cliff top. Did I hear rustling in the bushes up there? Was I being watched?

I had no idea how much time had passed. My legs were too rubbery for climbing over rocks, so I began to slog through the wet sand and sea foam, tripping and sliding along the beach, my wet pants chafing the insides of my thighs, adding physical discomfort to the black terror in my mind.

I stumbled up the back stairs and into the apartment. I felt dirty all over. Just get out of these clothes. I stripped in the bathroom, threw my wet stinking things in a trash bag, and climbed into the shower. The sight of Sheila nagged at me. I had left her exposed and alone. I had to do something. I couldn't pretend I hadn't been there and seen what I saw.

It was all I could do to drag myself from the shower. I didn't know if I would ever feel clean again. With no phone and the diner closed I was cut off, all alone, scared. *Don't think about that. Get to a phone and call the police.* I was talking myself through this. Throwing on clean clothes and grabbing my backpack, I headed for the truck and the Quik Stop. The outside phone would be available even if they weren't open yet.

I pawed through my backpack for change. Come on, there must be something in here. It was unbelievable that this place didn't even have 911 yet, so I had to find a number in the phone book for the state police. However this was not the time to focus on when Mundy would make it into the 21st century. I felt like I was wearing mittens as I struggled to do this simple task. Once I got someone on the line, all sorts of things came tumbling out. I wasn't making much sense. I don't know what I said, and I wasn't very clear about where Sheila was. I think I got it through to the officer that I really needed help, because he told me to stay right where I was and someone would be out.

When I hung up I was shaking all over. I hadn't even thought to ask for Jeff. Standing outside the Quik Stop waiting for the police, I must have looked like a druggie in need of a fix. As early morning customers started to wander in, I tried to ignore the sideways glances I was getting.

It seemed like forever before a state trooper pulled up in his blue Chevy Caprice cruiser. I rushed to his door before he even had time to get out of the car. "I'm Margaret Murphy. I called. If you follow me in my truck I'll show you where she is. We can't drive all the way, she's on the beach." I was babbling again, and the trooper was giving me a very reserved look. Just as I was getting in my truck, I noticed a sheriff's car drive up next to the state trooper. Great, let's have a gabfest. Oh hell, it's Hal. He must be at the end of his shift. I didn't care. I was leaving and they could follow or not, their choice.

I waved and started off. I was refusing to think about anything. I didn't dare. The adrenaline rush was still giving me the shakes. At the diner, I pulled my truck around back, and Hal and the state trooper parked on the street which was still surprisingly quiet. The town hadn't been up as long as I had.

Be cool. No emotion. "Hal, Officer, we'll have to go up the beach." I couldn't bear to look at Hal in his crisp uniform. Looking straight ahead, I headed out in a power stride. The sun was rising steadily in a clear blue sky, and the tide had gone out even further. This time I wasn't climbing over slippery rocks but slogging through wet sand, my sneakers sinking in. The trooper came up to one side of me and Hal was on the other. None of us said a word. I looked down at their polished boots and wanted to apologize for them getting dirty. I was starting to lose it again, wondering if Sheila would still be there. Had I been dreaming this nightmare? This train of thought vanished as we approached her body.

The flies had found her, and the ocean water had left a crust of salt on her skin. She looked even paler in the bright sunlight. The trooper instructed me to stay back while he and Hal went and squatted next to the body. I felt embarrassed for her, having guys peer at her in such a vulnerable state. The trooper used his radio and then they came to where I was perched on a boulder.

"Margaret, what happened here?" —this from Hal, as if I was responsible. I didn't like the accusatory tone I was hearing and, I was relieved when the trooper pulled rank with his body language. "Ma'am, do you know who that person is?"

"Yes, her name is Sheila Jones."

"How do you know her?"

Now I looked over at Hal. How was I supposed to answer that? What had I gotten myself into? Hal was not going to be any help. "I met her last week when she broke into my motel room. She was drunk. I've seen her a couple of times in town since then." The trooper just nodded.

"Is your residence near by?"

"I rent the apartment over the diner where we parked."

"As soon as we get some backup at the scene, I'll need to get a statement." I just nodded. Hal and the trooper looked up and I looked over my shoulder; there were people coming up the beach. It was too soon for police backup, so it had to be curious locals. My guess was that half the town had scanners. Howie was in the lead with that short bulldog figure of his. Hal recognized him at the same time as I did and went to head him off.

I couldn't hear what was being said, but there was a heart-wrenching scream from Howie as Hal struggled to hold him back. I heard something about a 'she' but I didn't have a clue who the 'she' was. Howie just kept staring at me with that uncanny family resemblance.

The beach became a zoo of people with crime scene tape making a cage around Sheila. I had to get out of this place. The trooper who had first shown up escorted me back to the apartment through the throng of people. I could feel my face turning red. It was all I could do to keep from running.

We had just gotten to the apartment and were sitting at the dining table when Josie came flying up the stairs and burst in. "Are you all right? Is it true that Sheila is dead?"

"You need to leave ma'am, I'm taking Miss Murphy's statement."

"The hell I'll leave! I own this building and Margaret works for me." Go Josie! Now she looked like some fireworks you didn't want to mess with, and I could use a friend right about now. She sat down, and I guess the trooper decided he wasn't ready to do battle with this redheaded fury.

We went back to the questions. "When was the last time you saw Ms. Jones alive?"

"I saw her at the fireworks last night."

"Did anyone else see her there?"

"Of course, there were hundreds of people and her brother and Hal, Deputy Grimes."

"You didn't have any other contact with her?"

"No, I did not." I was getting defensive. "Could we just finish this? I don't know anything else."

"Did you see anything out of the ordinary out there or hear anything?"

"You mean besides a dead body washed up on the beach?"

His lack of response indicated he didn't appreciate my acerbic remarks. Lack of sleep was taking its toll. "I don't know if it means anything but there was a lot of noise like shouting and lights like a campfire."

"When was this?"

"It seemed like it was all night. I was having trouble sleeping, and sound travels over water. Oh, I think I dropped my flashlight in the rocks when I fell. And it might be nothing, but I thought I heard a rustling coming from up on the cliff."

"Thank you for your cooperation. I'll be in touch." That must be a standard cop line. I couldn't wait. Josie was holding my hand as the officer left.

"You look like shit, girl. I was going to see how you made out last night, but I guess this isn't a good time."

As the officer was leaving, another wide-eyed guy was peering in my back door. "I'm here to hook up a telephone line for a Margaret Murphy?"

"I'm Margaret. I see you found the place alright."

"Yeah. Hey, what's all the excitement about down there?"

"There's been a death. I don't mean to be rude, but could you just do what you need to do, and then you can go down and find out more from whoever is down there."

"Okay, okay."

"This is turning out to be one miserable day off. I didn't sleep all night and now with this mayhem it doesn't look like any kind of nap is in the cards. Josie, do me a favor and don't give me any more time off; I don't think I can survive it."

Josie was more than happy to commiserate with me and still try to pump me for information about last night. I made iced tea for the two of us and just sat back to relax.

"Oh Josie, I screwed up last night with Hal, and Sheila was the catalyst."

"Tell me all."

"She was bold as brass dealing drugs down on the pier before the fireworks. Her kids were there. I just lost it. I guess I put Hal in an awkward position, but he at least kept us from coming to blows. Howie was on duty and he got involved. The whole thing put a wet blanket on the evening. Now with this happening, Hal thinks I had something to do with it."

"Well, she won't be ruining anymore relationships."

"That's the problem. All I thought about last night was how to get her out of my life, and now this."

"It was only a matter of time before Sheila's lifestyle caught up with her. I've seen it over and over again: car accidents, overdoses, freezing to death in a snow bank, or just getting sick and dying. It's a shame but there it is."

"Thanks, Josie, I needed to be reminded of that. My sponsor told me when I first got sober that it wasn't normal for someone my age to have so many dead acquaintances."

"You're too young to be worrying about reading the obituaries. That's the pastime of the old like Winfield."

There was another knock on the screen door. Now what? "I'm here to hook up your cable." This place was becoming Grand Central Station. The cable people had told me it would be about two weeks before they got to me. "I wasn't expecting you for another week."

"I had the time and was in the area so I figured I could get you done early."

"You *are* from Coastal Cable, aren't you?" Josie stared in disbelief. "Yeah, of course, we're the only cable company in the area. I hear there's been quite a lot going on here."

Bingo! Here was another scanner owner. Well there's a plus. Sheila got my cable installed a week early. Now I can watch what's going on downstairs on the television. "Okay, I just need a hookup over there in the corner. I think that's the cable line there. Is there anything else you need to know?"

"Naw, this is real easy, most everything's done out at the pole." Good, I was glad to hear it.

Josie finally left. I had cable and a phone; now I needed some sleep. A change in weather had brought a heavenly cool breeze off the water. The sky had gotten cloudy and it looked like it was going to rain.

I sat on the deck eating a sandwich and looking down the beach toward Smuggler's Neck. There were still people milling around in small groups conjecturing about what had happened. They had probably taken away Sheila's body by now. There was a big RV with Maine State Criminal Investigation written on it and people in blue jumpsuits going back and forth like members of an ant colony. I went back inside, flopped down on my futon to enjoy the breeze and was out like a light.

Chapter Ten

I was disoriented when I woke. I had been in blessed oblivion. *What time is it?* I had slept through the afternoon. The events of the morning came crashing back, so I peeked out the back door. Had it been a dream? Traffic had let up on the beach, probably because the tide was coming back in, but the signs of some happening were still evident. It hadn't been a dream.

I needed to talk with someone I could trust so I could get a handle on what was going on with me. I'd call Catsy, give her my new phone number and hash things out with her. I already had a pretty good idea what she would say, but hearing it from her mouth would calm me down.

I suppose technically Catherine Collins was my sponsor, at least that's how it started out, but we had become fast friends. She was a surrogate big sister and knew me better than I knew myself. At first I only knew her by her nickname, Catsy, short for Cathy C. The name fit like a glove because she always had at least three demanding cats in her home. She took in strays and I qualified.

When I first met her, she was celebrating her tenth anniversary of sobriety and I was inching my way through my first week. It had been like crawling on my belly through broken glass. I was sure I was different and didn't belong in with these convicts, drunk drivers, homeless bums, and hookers. But I had never seemed to belong anywhere. My life was a mess, but I wasn't quite willing to concede that it was because of drugs and alcohol. It was the drugs and alcohol that helped me survive and blot out all the problems. I felt like people were out to get me, and life was totally unfair. I went to meetings grudgingly. They were someplace to go since I had pretty much worn out my welcome everywhere else.

No job, no prospects, and no insurance left me few options. If I could pull my act together, I might be able to get a job, but what was I to do in the meantime? Meetings killed time. I'll never forget that first meeting. I sat on my hands because I still had the shakes. My feet never stopped tapping and jiggling. Catsy got up to get her medallion and tell her story. There were a million reasons why I wasn't an alcoholic and I would haul them out as my armor against any criticism or suggestion that I might be right where I belonged. But that night as Catsy told her story it was as if she were reading my diaries as she dispatched each reason or loophole I had held onto with her own experiences.

I broke into tears, and for the life of me I couldn't explain why I was crying right there in the meeting. My outburst got Cat's attention, and she cornered me as I was about to bolt from the hall. She gave me her number and we made a date to have coffee and a hot fudge sundae, her treat.

That memorable night had started me on the road to recovery. I knew it wasn't good to put all my faith in Catsy and she wouldn't allow it, but she was always there for support, even if that support was a good swift kick in the butt.

I punched in her number. Two rings, "I'm here." I could hardly speak. I felt better just hearing those two words. Trying to be nonchalant, I asked her how she was doing, but there was a hitch in my voice. "Don't try to bullshit me. You sound terrible. What took you so long to call?"

"I just got my phone in today."

"They don't have other phones where you are?"

"Alright, I thought I was doing okay, and the corner pay phone gives absolutely no privacy."

"Doing okay, my ass! So you're calling from your own place? That was fast. Where did you finally end up?" I told her about Mundy, my job and the apartment. So far I had conveniently left out the rough spots.

"How did you decide on Mundy? I knew you were going up the coast, but Mundy? I've never heard of it."

'Why Mundy?' was the question I hadn't been able to answer to anyone's satisfaction, including my own. I had come across it on my way back from camping in Baxter State Park where there were still patches of ice and snow. It had been one of those toss-of-the-coin decisions I'd made on what direction to take while on spring break from school. For some reason, decisions had never come easy to me, and flipping a coin had become an easy way to make them. I headed east through vast expanses with little or no human habitation. Then just when I thought I was lost, I came up on Route 1 and traveled south to the coast, exploring spits of land that fingered out into the ocean. Mundy had been on one of those fingers.

When I got back from my excursion, I shared my adventures with Dad. He'd been the one to insist I take some time off. "Maggot, stop moping and go have some fun." That April night burst into my mind as clearly as if Dad were right here beside me. We were watching the evening news together, one of our rituals. It was Dad as usual – verbally attacking the TV, cursing the state of the world, and all in a roar. I sat there and nodded in agreement or grunted some response. Just then, a news story came on about a missing fishing boat and her crew out of Mundy. There was a big yellow dot in the middle of what was suppose to be Tyler County. It grabbed my attention, because I'd just come back from there. What was odd was the sudden silence; neither of us spoke for a moment as if in suspended animation.

The news story only lasted a few seconds and then Dad got a faraway look in his eyes. "Maggot, did I ever tell you about my growing up on the coast?" A hint of his teasing brogue was peeking through.

"Are you kidding Dad? You've never said a word about growing up. I thought you were hatched from a blarney stone." It made him laugh which made me happy until the coughing started. I socked the oxygen to him, and when he calmed down the moment was gone, and we went back to watching the news the way we always did.

"I discovered the place coming back from camping before Dad died," I told Catsy. "It's a curious little village, and besides, it's as far as I got before calling it quits for the day." I began to fill in the gaps with all those rough spots I'd left out.

"You've been indulging in a mighty fine self-pity party, Maggie. You know you can't run away from drugs and booze. It's everywhere, and you sure as hell can't run away from yourself."

I started to sob. "I hope you've made some meetings and didn't pick up. You know I can't help after the first drink. Did you call me because you want me to tell you it's all right? Go ahead. Get drunk, you're fully capable, but don't give me a load of shit to justify it."

"I don't want to drink," I whined, "but my life is getting so complicated, you don't understand."

"Whoa, back up. This is Cat you're talking to. Let's take the drama out of this scenario and get off that tangent you're on, and then we'll talk."

How quickly that old way of thinking had slipped right back into gear. Even to my ears I sounded like a newcomer to sobriety. I started spilling my guts to Cat and listening to myself. Maybe I could figure out what I was doing here. We must have talked for hours. Even her cats got in on the conversation as they purred and walked all over her. One of them– I think it was the extremely overweight money cat - sounded asthmatic.

"Maggie, keep in mind H.A.L.T. - Hungry, Angry, Lonely, Tired. What does the word tell you to do?"

"Stop what I'm doing and take care of the hunger, anger, loneliness or lack of rest."

"Young lady, you sound like you have all four of those conditions." As she said this, my stomach growled, and even with the nap I'd had, I still felt bone tired.

"Talking to you has relieved the loneliness Cat, but I think you're right."

"This is just a suggestion. Get a cat. Remember your track record for picking men? You're spending entirely too much time in your own company."

"I'm not ready to make a commitment like having a pet. It's hard enough taking care of me."

"We'll see. Stay in today. Don't drink, go to meetings, and call me. You know what to do. Now eat something delicious and go to bed."

By the time I got off the phone with Cat, all the muscles in my body were loosening up. I hadn't realized how wound up they had been. I hadn't had time to make any goodies, and it dawned on me that the only thing I'd eaten all day was the sandwich at lunchtime. I filled a big bowl with cereal and milk, poured a glass of juice, and sat down in Dad's chair to find some mindless TV viewing while I crunched my dinner.

We were busy at the diner right from the start. Everyone was talking about the death of Sheila Jones, and conjectures and rumors were flying. The old and the young, tourists and fishermen, housewives and businessmen all decided to flock to Josie's, ground zero. Here they tussled for salacious tidbits of news and created such a racket that I felt like I was at the Icebox with seagulls swarming over scraps of food.

Maybe I was just self-conscious, but I felt like everyone was staring at me or giving me sidelong looks and then turning to their tablemates and conferring in hushed tones. I had to get a grip. I used the business routine to stay aloof. I took orders, put together the specials, and worked on desserts. Even Robby didn't have a chance to ask me questions as I bussed in dishes to keep him busy. Josie looked at me with concern, but she was respecting my wish to stay out of conversations.

Then Hal arrived. The sight of a uniformed deputy sent a hush through the diner. What was everyone expecting, a pronouncement from the law to settle the rumors, or did they think he was going to spill some juicy details for their morbid curiosity? I was still stinging from Hal's comment out on the beach yesterday and really wished Josie could wait on him, but she was up to her elbows in customers and trying to keep the coffee flowing.

I went to his table with a mug of coffee and a glass of water. Thinking to keep the atmosphere light, I asked what on the menu would satisfy his craving, but he was having no part of that. Oh no, not him.

"Margaret, we need to talk." No Maggie, no niceties or small talk, just a command in a forceful undertone. At least he hadn't shouted it out in the diner. I wanted to tell him to go to hell, but I held my tongue.

"Besides conversation, which I am not at liberty to give out at this time, is there anything you would like to order, Deputy Grimes?" For a split second, his face went ashen and he looked perplexed, but he recovered with icy coolness.

"I'll have a blueberry muffin, heated with extra butter, thank you. When can we talk?" He was really being persistent.

"What is it you want to talk about?" I could be just as icy.

"I'm off duty at 4:00; I'll come by your place then."

I could only stare at him as my mind churned through what he had said and what he was obviously leaving out. Whatever he wanted to talk about wouldn't be official if he was going to do the talking on his own time, that much was clear. I was reserving judgment on whether that was a good thing or a bad thing. I didn't have any particular plans but committing to a 4 o'clock meeting quashed the opportunity to go shopping anywhere. Not that I had a deadline for fixing up the apartment, far from it. I just didn't like being corralled.

"I'll probably be home by then." This set off another expression of disbelief that I might not be at his beck and call. What the hell, it was kind of fun rattling his cage. A packed house gave me the perfect excuse for moving on to other customers. Hal wolfed his muffin down, dropped his money on the table, and left. What a prick he was being about it. We finally had a lull just before the lunch crowd was due to arrive, and I was in need of a break. I poured myself a cup of coffee, snagged a muffin, and sat down at the corner table by the kitchen. Josie was handling the sprinkling of customers that were left, but she grabbed a coffee and scooted in beside me. "Maggie, there's someone I'd like you to meet."

I rolled my eyes. "I'm in no mood for match-making or blind dates."

Josie laughed a deep belly laugh, tears streaming out of her eyes as she tried to get control back. "Lord, no! It's nothing like that and besides he's married." As if that had relevance. "His name is John Driscoll. He's from New York, too, and retired up here about the same time Dwight and I did. No doubt you discovered the bundles of newspapers up in your apartment."

"I was meaning to ask you about those, but it's been so hectic that it slipped my mind."

"This whole place used to be the office and printing space for the local newspaper, the *Tidewater Times*. It was crammed full of old printing machinery, desks, and old papers. The building had great potential, but we couldn't even begin to start on it until we got rid of the stuff. I hate to throw anything out, but Dwight was for calling the disposal company and just gutting the place. Then we met up with John, and he was enchanted with all the paraphernalia. I guess he couldn't quit the newspaper business cold turkey. He'd been an editor for one of the more prestigious newspapers, and reporting and publishing ran in his blood. Those were his words, not mine. He decided to get the local paper up and running again single-handed. Instead of us having to trash the lot, he bought the whole kit and kaboodle and set up across the mall."

I didn't think I liked where this was going. The last person I wanted to meet was a reporter. Josie was going on about a local happening right here in Mundy and something about publicity for the diner. I had tuned her out. I couldn't see how someone's death would be good for the diner or the town, for that matter. I tuned back in when I caught something about an in-depth piece on substance abuse in the county, and I started to cringe. People just don't get it. You could have all the programs and all the news articles you wanted, but it wouldn't change a damn thing. Alcoholics and drug addicts die. That's the inevitable finality of the disease. There might be a delay due to incarceration or hospitalization but you'll still end up at the same miserable destination. All this other crap just made the do-gooders feel better, as if they had some power over another person's life. There was an expression that I used to live by that I shared with fellow abusers: "I'm here for a good time not a long time, life sucks and then you die." That wasn't my mantra today, but then the difference was that today I was sober.

"What does he want with me?"

"Well, I told him a little bit about you, like you found her body, you work for me, and you live upstairs. You know stuff like that."

"Josie what else did you tell him about me for crying out loud?" I could see my anonymity going up in smoke.

"Don't get in an uproar. I just said you were from away, and boy what an introduction to the town with Sheila breaking in on you and all."

I let out a groan. Everyone would be connecting the dots now. "I'm not all that whacked out about being featured in the local press. Isn't there some way I could just remain anonymous?"

"Girl, there is no way you can stay out of the spotlight in this town with your name and the run-ins you've had. Remember this is a small town; news travels like wildfire."

"So when am I suppose to meet this guy?"

"He's coming in around twelve-thirty. Shirley will be here by then."

"What makes you think she'll be on time today?"

"We're the center for the news of Sheila's death. She'll be here."

The unwelcome prospect of meeting Josie's friend, Driscoll, now consumed my mind, with no room to give Hal and his problems a thought.

Then there was another distraction. As part of the early lunch crowd, Winfield came in with a stunning older woman. I couldn't imagine the connection these two could possibly have. She was graceful in her movements and immaculate in her appearance, something that seemed uncommon in these parts. A deep tan said she was an outdoors person. I could imagine her gardening with prize-winning roses and hearty vegetables that she would put up for the winter—not because she needed to save money, but because she enjoyed the work and the independence. Her blouse was a sleeveless cotton oxford in a pale mint green, and she wore a white skort—those two in one things, skirt and shorts—and white leather Keds that were cushioned around the ankles. She kept herself in shape. She wore simple round button earrings that I was betting were clip-ons and the only other pieces of jewelry were a small gold cross on a short chain, a simple but elegant watch, and a wedding ring/engagement set that looked impressive.

There was something about her. Now I was the one staring. Her hair must have been a deep auburn at one time, because there were strands of that color interspersed with a head of thick white hair. No dye job for her. It was sad to see older women with thin hair that you knew had turned white years ago sporting bright dyed hair in a straw matted look. I hoped I looked that good and had that air of confidence when I was her age. I hadn't seen her with Winfield before, even though he was a regular.

I went up to their booth. "Ah, Margaret, I've brought someone I'd like you to meet. I apologize to you both for waiting this long." Winfield had me jumping with curiosity. "Margaret Mary Murphy, may I present Margaret Mary Murphy Doyle." My mouth fell open. I glanced over at Josie, and there she was with a wicked grin plastered across her face. "I'm very pleased to meet you, Mrs. Doyle." I stammered out. "I heard there was someone in town I shared a name with."

"I understand you've met my brother, Kenny. He speaks very highly of you."

"Kenny is your brother? He never said anything about a sister or us having the same last name. Come to think of it, I don't know whether or not I ever mentioned my last name but he doesn't miss much, especially in this place."

"People around here naturally assume that you know everyone. It's been a pleasure meeting you, Margaret. Perhaps we can get together for tea. You're more than welcome at my home."

There was warmth to her words and a sincerity that caused me to melt inside. I longed for a friendship with this woman. "Thank you Mrs. Doyle. I'd love to get together with you sometime. You could give me a different perspective on Kenny. I've even done a little reading at the library about the Irish that settled here. How are you on history?"

"Oh, Margaret, you don't have to call me Mrs. Doyle, just call me Margaret. I can give you some interesting insights into the history of Mundy. I'm a member of our local historical society."

"That's great, and you can call me Maggie." It was nice to have a genuine conversation with a person rather than an interrogation. Granted, she was old enough to be my mother, but I wasn't about to get overly picky about my friends. I wasn't exactly rolling in them. The earlier mention of newspapers had activated my craving for historical exploration. There's nothing better for deflecting scrutiny of your own background than to delve into the ancient history of others. I was an expert at that.

The day was more than half over for me, but it was a roller coaster ride that promised still more twists and turns and gut wrenching situations. Shirley was indeed here even before her scheduled time, which gave her an opportunity to have Josie bring her up to speed on the local gossip. Shirley came on like I was an interloper in her bailiwick. We had not really hit it off from the first time we had met. I don't think she takes well to change, a typical local. I didn't think of myself as a threat, but I got the impression that Shirley did.

I'd just gotten my apron off when a slightly paunchy gentleman with close-cropped steel gray hair came into the diner. He waved at Josie and strode up to the counter that held our baked goods of the day, what was left of the items I had assiduously been making in every spare minute I had. "Josie, when are you going to have some real food like prune Danish here? Bring some class to this neck of the woods?"

"John, you just don't quit, do you? How many times do I have to tell you that to stay in business you cater to the majority of your clientele, not the oddballs?"

"Oh, Josie, that cuts me to the quick."

"Your hide's too tough. I'd need a jackhammer to penetrate your thick skin, which is why I suspect we have this same conversation every time you come in. Why don't you try the cream cheese cherry braid or the carrot cake that Maggie made fresh today?"

"I haven't had my vegetables yet, so give me a slice of the carrot cake, and I'll wash it down with a mug of your always excellent coffee. Speaking of the maker of these delectable edibles, where is this Margaret Murphy who is so newsworthy?" He craned his neck to take in the diner.

I wanted to seep into the cracks of the floorboards. Driscoll sounded like a typical overbearing, obnoxious New Yorker who always knew best and was always right. I was trapped next to the kitchen with no way to slink out of the diner. When his head swiveled in my direction, we locked eyes, and I was nailed to the spot. I happened to notice that Shirley had a great big smirk on her face as she handled the remainder of the lunch crowd. She was getting a thrill out of watching me squirm.

Driscoll came and sat down at the table near the kitchen, the one I'd begun to get possessive over. It was for our breaks and our conversations, not this brazen outsider. Look who was calling the kettle black. I was the real outsider, the newcomer, and Driscoll's presence made me acutely aware of that.

Josie brought the coffee, water, and carrot cake to the table. My eyes pleaded with her not to leave me alone with this guy. When the three of us were seated, Josie made the introductions.

John Driscoll got right down to business. "There are four reasons why anyone moves to this isolated corner of the world. Retirement is one. That's what brought me and Josie here. You don't look old enough for that. So your job brings you here, you're returning to your roots, or you're running away from something. Which reason fits you?" With that first question asked, he forked up a piece of cake and washed it down with a gulp of coffee. No delicacy there. I doubted he even tasted what he was eating.

Strike one for me. I couldn't even answer the first question. "I've never quite compartmentalized my decisions that way."

"Where did you come from when you decided to come up this way?"

What did it matter where I came from? In my mind I was feeling guilty, and I hadn't done anything wrong. Could Josie possibly begin to realize just how miserable I was feeling right now? "I came up from the southern part of the state. I like to travel."

I watched as he devoured the slice of cake and slurped the rest of his coffee. I was waiting for a big belch to signify the conclusion of his feeding. Instead he caught Shirley's eye, held his mug up, and nodded for a refill.

"Since you are being evasive about your past, let's press on to more recent events: to wit, your confrontations with the deceased and why you were where you were when Sheila floated onto the beach. Oh, for your information, they're calling it a suspicious death with something more definitive expected after the autopsy."

"This interrogation is over the top. Even the police didn't ask all these questions."

With one stubby-fingered hand on the table and the other with middle finger extended aimed at my chest he punctuated his words. "Apparently you don't fully grasp the position you're in. Let me see; you fought with the victim, flattened one of her friends, stuck the cops on her, and 'found' her dead body. I don't know about you, lady, but in the cops' handbook, that makes you suspect numero uno. Do you see why I'm interested in your side of the story?"

"Mr. Driscoll, I think you might be a wee overly dramatic about the situation. This may seem a cliché, but I'm just an innocent bystander in this."

"Well, lady, you may be an innocent bystander, but it appears to me that there is something about you that draws this action like a lightening rod. I'd like to find out what that is. I'm a bloodhound when it comes to a story. Once I get the scent, I follow it wherever it takes me."

I had to turn the tables on this guy, or he would never leave me alone. Play the innocent. Ask him for his view and knowledge of the area. Get him to talk. You can never tell what you can pick up that way, and although I really didn't enjoy the thought of massaging this guy's ego, I'd do it just to get him off my back.

With the ego massaging of Driscoll I was there another hour. I gave little innocuous snippets about teaching, camping, and Dad dying. Finally, three mugs of coffee, the carrot cake, and the last of the cream cheese cherry braid later, the inquisition came to a halt.

"Margaret, I make a better friend than an enemy. You are either incredibly naïve or you're holding on to some powerful secrets. Josie, you know me. See if you can talk some sense into this young lady. Oh, by the way, the edibles rate right up there with a New York deli. With talent like that you should stay out of trouble." He settled up with Josie, and I just put my head down on the table. Was this day over yet?

I was determined not to be at the apartment when Hal showed up. I needed to get out for a while. With just my backpack and with no particular destination in mind, I backed the truck out and headed up river. Driving set me free. I felt back in control just being behind the wheel of my truck. I pulled into a little turn-off to a nature preserve. A nice long walk in the afternoon heat would be the perfect workout. I'd be able to face Hal even if I would be all sweaty. That brought a grin to my face.

There was a placid little pond back in the woods with mossy banks and spruce trees that had laid down a rusty carpet of fir sprills. I sat cross-legged in the shade and pulled out binoculars to check the treetops for interesting bird life. Bird watching was a pastime I had picked up in sobriety. It emptied my head, and hours flew by in artistic grandeur. I never ceased to be amazed at the variety of God's creations. They had always been there, but I had been so out of it that I couldn't see past my nose. I pulled out a bag of gorp to munch on and thought how easy it would be to snooze the afternoon away in this peaceful place.

The screech of a blue jay and the sound of crackling twigs made me aware that I wasn't alone anymore. This was public land to be enjoyed by everyone, but I really liked it when I could have places like this in complete solitude. I looked at my watch; I had just enough time to make it back as Hal showed up. Perfect.

I circled back to my truck. There on the edge of the turnoff was another one. I'd left enough room where I had parked so that they could have parked right next to me. Oh well, maybe they knew a better trail into the woods. I threw my backpack into the truck and hopped in. Ouch! I suddenly realized why someone might choose a different parking spot. The other truck was in the shade, but mine had been sitting in the sun. Talk about a hot seat! I hadn't been thinking. I could barely touch the steering wheel. I hopped out as fast as I had gotten in, rummaged around for my old sweatshirt, and spread it on the seat. It was times like this that I wished I had air conditioning that I could crank up and cool down with.

As I put the truck in gear and was looking to pull out, I noticed someone coming out of the woods near the other truck. He didn't look much like a nature freak, but I suppose neither did I. Jeez, there was something familiar about the guy. I must be hallucinating. Everyone seemed to look like someone. I guess I was just homesick, and besides, this guy reminded me of a lizard, skinny and slimy. A glance at my watch again told me I had better get a move on. I wanted to make a point with Hal, not blow him off.

Hal had the sheriff's cruiser which he had parked conspicuously outside the diner. He was sitting in it waiting for me. Oops, I guess I was a little later than I had planned. He saw me pull around to the back and met me at the foot of the stairs. Any other time and I'd have had romantic expectations of an evening to come. But Hal wasn't putting out any romantic vibes, and I just wanted to figure out what was so urgent, clean up, have something to eat, and go to a meeting.

The silence was awkward as I opened the back door, tossed my backpack and keys on the table, and waved toward the living room. "Come on in and have a seat. Were you waiting long?" He walked over and sat in Dad's overstuffed chair. He was much taller than Dad had been and looked like he was sticking out of a kid's chair. I flopped down on the futon that I'd made up before work.

"Margaret, I had to tell the state police everything about you and Sheila. They think she might have been murdered. If there is anything that you are holding back or didn't mention to the police, now's the time to let me know so I can help you."

"I don't understand. What are you saying, that I know something about this woman? How could I? I had just got into town, and she just happened to be a drunk and a local dealer. It's not my problem."

"What makes you think she was some kind of a drug lord?"

"For crying out loud, I didn't say she was some kind of drug lord. She was using and selling, probably to support her habit, and from what I can tell that was pretty common knowledge. You should know that. You're the deputy." From the look he gave me, I knew I had crossed the line. It must have sounded like I was belittling him for not knowing his job. I was being defensive, and everything I said was coming out wrong.

He got ramrod straight. "I guess you don't want to cooperate and you don't need any help."

"I can't do something when I don't know what it is you want. I thought I *had* cooperated. I told the police everything I could. What is it you think I'm not saying?" My voice was rising. Soon I'd be screaming and I didn't want that. I felt I'd lost control. I had to calm down. *Take a deep breath. Remember what Cat said, take the drama out of it.*

"Maggie, if you didn't have anything to do with Sheila's death but whoever did thinks you know anything that could implicate them, you could be in danger."

"*If* I didn't have anything to do with her death, what is that supposed to mean?" Now I *was* hurt. How could he possibly believe that I had a part in this? Driscoll's words came back to me, and I wondered why this was happening to me.

"Maggie, you have been rather close-mouthed about yourself and what you're doing here. That can be taken in a lot of different ways, not all good."

I get it now. Something happens, we blame the outsider, the newcomer. It can't possibly be a local who's responsible. Welcome to a small town. I sat back, astonished. "Hal, I don't know what to say. I appreciate your concern, but I don't think there is anything that can or needs to be done. I'm sure everything will work out for the best. I have to believe that."

He looked as if he had a battle going on inside of him. I suddenly realized just how self-absorbed I'd been. As Cat would say, 'It's not always about you.'

"Hal, I'm sorry. Your partner and friend just lost his sister, and this whole mess has put you in a difficult situation. How is Howard doing? I know you're trying to help him." The memories of Dad's death and the arrangements that had to be made came whirling back. You operated on autopilot until it was over, and then it hit you when you were left alone.

"Howie's out on bereavement leave."

"Please tell him I'm thinking about him. Nobody deserves to die like that. I can't imagine what it must be like for her kids."

"Yeah, well, Howie has lots of family."

I wanted Hal to go. There was nothing more to say. He seemed to be deciding something and then got up and walked to the door. I was relieved that he was leaving.

"Maggie, if you need anything just let me know."

"Thanks Hal, I will." He left with his hat in hand as I followed him out onto the deck and watched him go down the steps. I was confused.

I certainly couldn't read some people well, especially men. Funny, it seemed that all of a sudden people were coming out of the woodwork to get to know and help me. I wasn't ready to believe I needed help, and my suspicious nature told me that everyone wanted something from me. A meeting was what I needed for a good getaway from all this. I had time to get to the meeting at the Grange and maybe corner Kenny and tease him about Margaret.

I was early for the meeting. Kenny showed up overdressed for the weather just like before, and we went in to make coffee and set up. As I followed him up the stairs I tried to visualize him and Margaret as children. Kenny looked like somebody, but I wasn't sure it was Margaret. There was definitely no similarity in the way they moved.

"Kenny, I met your sister today. She seems like a wonderful lady. Why didn't you say something?"

"It's more fun to be pleasantly surprised, don't you think?"

"Pleasant surprises I can take. It's the other kind I'm not fond of. So, who else are you related to? How about Terry down at the hardware store?"

"Terry's my youngest daughter. You two met each other, did you?"

"We had a nice conversation, but she never said anything about her aunt having the same name as me. Just like her old man."

"We Murphys tend to keep to ourselves." I thought that must go with the name, because Dad fit into that category.

The meeting was on gratitude, and just sitting there and listening, I realized I had a lot to be grateful for. Cat had been right again. Gratitude got me out of my self-pity mode. I missed Joanne and Tina. It wasn't until 7:10 that I gave up expecting them to walk through the door. There were some new faces—new to me, that is. One older woman had fifteen years, and there was a guy around my age named Del who seemed well grounded in sobriety. He looked like a fisherman and good looking to boot. I didn't ask if Del stood for something or if it was a nickname. I was trying to keep my ears open and my mouth shut. After the meeting I stuck around to help clean up and so did Del. It was a beautiful evening.

Back behind the wheel, I wasn't ready to go back to the apartment. The dusky sky was beginning to glitter with stars and there was a cool breeze. At the edge of the parking lot I got out my medallion and flipped it. Heads, back to town, Tails, up river. Tails. I put it in gear and headed out of town.

I was floating, taking it easy, watching the sky go through color and light changes as stars began to twinkle on. With no streetlights or neon signs to diminish the starlight, it was like being in another time. I had never seen so many stars.

I was thrust from my reverie by glaring high beams in my rearview mirror. I hated it when people were so inconsiderate. I adjusted my mirror down so I wouldn't be so blinded. I didn't want to let a little irritation spoil the evening. I was putzing along so whoever was behind me could pass and I'd have the night back to myself.

Ugh! Crunch! *What the hell? What's happening?* I'd been hit. The steering wheel was slipping out of my hand. My chest ached from the seat belt. I needed to get my bearings. I readjusted my mirror so I could see behind me. It was difficult to tell who or what was there with those damn high beams. Whoever it was had dropped back. It was probably just a drunk who hadn't realized how close he was and how slowly I was going. It probably served me right for gawking along. *No need to panic, Margaret.*

I guessed it was time to pick up the pace and concentrate on my driving. No need to putter along like a stereotypical woman driver. Now what? The lights were picking up speed and coming right for me. This was crazy. Suddenly the tranquil starlit night was becoming a desperate and lonely war zone. I stomped on the accelerator. *Come on, baby, let's show them what we're made of.* Maybe I could just outrun this nut.

I kept glancing in the mirror as much as I dared as I sailed through the woods racing as fast as my little truck would go. Up and down hills. I looked back again. Had I lost him? I hit a straightaway. Oh no! There were the high beams again and now they were gaining on me. The truck was maxed out. I started desperately praying for some sign of life, some place to get off the road, but there was nothing as far as I could see.

I hung on to the steering wheel, knuckles white and nails biting into my palms as I braced for another hit. My heart was pounding so hard it became a drumming in my ears. What was with this game of cat and mouse?

Another crack and my head flew forward against the steering wheel as it was ripped out of my hands for just a second and that's all it took. The truck was out of control. I grabbed the wheel and slammed on the brakes. That was definitely not the brightest thing to do. My headlights showed boulders and brush swirling by as I went into a spin and came to rest up against some alders in a cloud of dust. The truck sputtered, then stalled out.

My head ached and I was disoriented. Then fear revived me and I clawed at my seatbelt, shut the engine and lights off, and reached for the tire iron I carried under the seat. I didn't know where I was, what direction I was pointed in, or what direction I had been headed. But the big question was, where was the vehicle that had hit me?

I got out of the truck and crouched next to the door. I looked in both directions and could just make out tail lights in the distance. That gave me a direction. I stared at those lights until my eyes stung and they disappeared. I was immobilized. I don't know how long I stayed crouched next to the truck afraid to move. The buzzing whine of mosquitoes finally pried me from the spot.

I had to take stock of my situation. I got in and started the truck. So far so good, the headlights worked. Could I get out of here? A little maneuvering and I was ready to get back on the road. It was definitely time to head home. No more side trips. I was afraid to look at the damage that had been done to my truck, but I was still in one piece.

All the way back I anxiously watched for other vehicles. I didn't know if I was afraid of seeing another car or if I wanted the assurance of others on the road. I kept mulling over what had happened. Had it just been a drunk driver, kids out having a good time—or something more sinister? Should I call Hal and ask for the help I'd turned down this afternoon? These were the kinds of decisions I still had a hard time with.

The adrenaline had worn off and left me with a crushing headache. The stairs to the apartment felt like Mount Everest as I slowly pulled myself up by the handrail. I didn't have any energy left to call anyone, and besides, the only way to get a hold of Hal was to call the Sheriff's Department. He and I hadn't gotten around to swapping phone numbers. It would have to wait until tomorrow when he came into the diner. That would give me a chance to run it by Josie. Maybe she'd have a cooler head than mine.

Chapter Eleven

When I showed up downstairs, Josie's first comment was, "You look like something the cat dragged in." That's exactly how I felt, but today I was ready to do some talking. Once I got baking, what Hal had said and the escapade on the way home from the meeting just poured out of me. Josie took in everything and didn't interrupt once. She probably figured she had me talking, better not jinx it.

"Have you checked the damage to your truck?"

"No. I was too tired last night and it was dark. I was just glad to get home."

"When we have a break this morning, you should run out and check on it. Then you'll have something concrete to report."

"I was hoping I wouldn't need to do any reporting. I'm sure it was just some kids joyriding out in the boonies."

"Your insurance company is going to want to have a report if there is a lot of damage."

I looked a little sheepish. "I've only got the minimum liability insurance. If anything needs to be fixed, it will have to come out of my pocket."

"Talk to Hal. It never hurts to let guys know you need their help. You know you could win a lot more boyfriends with a little less independence."

"Josie, don't start. I'm not looking for any boyfriends."

"Oh, really?" Well, maybe I was but I wasn't about to let her know that.

For the first time I was sort of looking forward to seeing Hal. On a break I checked out the truck. The plastic grill was broken on one side, but that was cosmetic. The turn signal on the left-hand side was gone and would need to be replaced. That was the front. The sides didn't look the worse for wear, but then I got to the back. The tailgate and bumper had been creamed. Evenly spaced vertical dents had smashed in the tailgate, making it almost impossible to pull down and even harder to push up and latch again. My two bumper stickers in black and iridescent silver were mangled. One used to say 'K.I.S.S. Keep It Simple Stupid.' Now it read 'K.I.S. Keep It Stupid.' The other had said 'Turn It Over' but now just said 'Turn O r.'

I came back into the diner down in the dumps. That truck was very special to me. It had been with me during the last of my drinking and drugging days, my last possession. I had lost just about everything else. It had gotten me to many meetings. I considered it my lifeline and maybe even my running shoes. They didn't make Comanches any more.

"Do you know any good auto body mechanics, Josie? The truck is going to need some work."

"That's too bad. The closest place I know of is Charlie Haggarty's Garage over in Sutton. He does just about everything with any kind of vehicle you've got."

"Where is Sutton?"

"You've been through it. It's between Wilcox and Tylerville. It's more of a crossroads than a town. There's the garage, the Sutton Methodist Church, Crossroads Gas and Eat which is like a convenience store, and this tiny building that is the Sutton Post Office with its own zip code. Those places take up the four corners and then, of course, there are homes and farms up and down the hills off the main roads. Some of the old families that worked in Mundy moved out there."

I vaguely remembered something like that as I went into Tylerville, but it was one of those places that you miss if you blink or have your mind elsewhere. I hoped I wouldn't have to deal with someone who liked to rip off women or people from away. Out of self-defense, I had learned how to do oil changes, tune-ups, and other assorted work on my truck. Finances were also a consideration. I was tired of having men try to scare me into getting work done that wasn't necessary. Like the time I went to get new tires and they tried to tell me I needed shocks because mine were dangerously worn out. I nailed them on that one, because I had a warranty on them, and they would have had to pay out. I got a perverse sense of satisfaction out of playing the dumb broad and then naively whipping out the paperwork. It was still irritating. Maybe asking Hal what he thought of Charlie's would be a benign conversation starter.

Speaking of Hal, he was late. Wouldn't you know, when I wanted to see the guy; he'd be a no show. Josie was as puzzled as I was. At noon, Shirley showed up in a frenzy. She wasn't just on time, she was early. "Oh, Josie, have you heard the news? They found Bear out on the Wilcox Road."

"What do you mean they found him? I didn't know he was lost."

"No, silly, he's dead!" With that, she turned to me with an evil eye and then back to Josie. She obviously wasn't ready to go to work, and Josie wanted to get the lowdown, so they went back to the corner table and I kept waiting on customers. I was dying to know what was going on, but I wasn't about to give Shirley the satisfaction of knowing she knew something I didn't. I put on my best 'I could care' look but desperately wanted to hear what was being discussed. Josie would tell me everything later when she got the chance, but I didn't wait well.

At 12:30 I purposefully hung up my apron so Shirley could see it was time for her to get her ass in gear. She didn't want to pull herself away from the confab she and Josie were having. I went out in the kitchen and caught Dwight listening to a scanner. I'd forgotten all about the toys that people in this town all seemed to own.

Robby looked very serious. I glanced at Dwight who signaled with his eyes to be careful what I said. Don't tell me Robby was related to Bear. It would be best to exit the kitchen and find out from Josie what was going on. Shirley had finally pulled herself away from the corner and started work. I was just about to sit down next to Josie when Hal came in. Though his uniform was as starched as ever, his expression was haggard and his strut was missing. This wasn't good. I was having second thoughts about going to him with my little fender bender.

Shirley was waiting on tables across the room. As I was taking in Hal's arrival, I had lost track of my surroundings and wasn't aware of Josie's movements until she crossed into my line of sight next to Hal. She was waiting on him, and I was just standing there. What do I do now, sit down alone, go over to Hal, or just leave? I was in a quandary and rooted to the spot.

Saved by the bell. Josie was waving me over to Hal's table. I'd take my cue from her. "Margaret, why don't you join me for lunch?" Wow, maybe this wouldn't be so bad after all. I could console Hal. That had a nice feminine touch. I slid into the seat across from him and looked at Josie for some sign of what to do. "Josie tells me you've heard about Bear."

"I'm so sorry you have lost another friend."

"Yes. Well, Josie, could I have a cheeseburger and fries and a coke? Margaret what will you have?"

"I'll have the same but with iced tea." Josie took off with our orders, and I sat there feeling totally awkward. Comforting someone really wasn't my thing. Everything I had planned to use as a conversation starter seemed idiotic under the circumstances, which left me sitting there a total blank.

"Josie tells me you had some trouble last night. Why don't you tell me what happened."

For some reason, alarms started going off in my head. In the light of day it didn't seem like any big deal, especially compared to the death of Bear. I was suddenly uncomfortable discussing it but I couldn't just sit here and say nothing. With as few embellishments as possible, just the facts, I recounted what had happened. As I was talking, I became aware of a change in Hal. The deputy emerged as he abruptly started firing questions at me as soon as I had finished.

"What time did this happen?"

"I don't know, around nine maybe. I wasn't really paying attention to the time."

"Where were you headed?"

"I was just out driving, enjoying the night." There was that look, a rising rage just behind his eyes. What now? Why did that set him off?

"Alright, let's try something else. Where were you coming from and what direction were you going in? Can you at least tell me that?" This felt an awfully lot like an interrogation, and I was beginning to dig my heels in. The impatience in his voice was having an effect. I looked down at my hands. They were balled into fists in my lap. The heat was rising in my face and I could imagine the color I was turning. Now I was the one feeling angry. The difference was, I couldn't afford the luxury of anger because my answer had always been to reach for a bottle of booze or pills, whatever would turn off the world. There was a nagging fear in the back of my mind. What would he think if he knew I was an alcoholic coming from a meeting? I still hadn't gotten rid of the shame I felt at admitting to being an alcoholic. My mind knew it was a disease, but my gut or maybe my ego kept telling me it was only a matter of will power and I was a failure. It was a very uncomfortable feeling that I had been working on with Cat.

"Let's see. I was coming out of the Old Grange Hall parking lot. I flipped a coin to decide whether to go home or go for a drive. The drive won, and I turned right out of the parking lot and just followed that road. I wasn't going very fast, and I didn't take any side roads. I don't know how far I got or what road I was on when I was hit and run off the road. There were no houses or lights that I could see. Once I got my truck unstuck, I came right home."

At the end of my second recitation of what had happened, Josie showed up with our food. "How's it going, you two?" She had a concerned expression but gave no hint that she was going to stick around. "Hal, I didn't have a chance to fill Maggie in on the situation with Bear."

"Okay, I understand. It slips my mind that Margaret's not from around here. I apologize if I came on a little strong, but I've never seen things this bad before. Margaret, the road that runs in front of the grange hall is the Wilcox Road. It's the same road that some cross-country bikers found Teddy Cox's body on. We think it was a hit and run that happened some time last night. I don't believe in coincidence, so there is a distinct possibility that your accident and Teddy's are related."

Here we go again! "Maggie, you could be in danger." Well at least he wasn't accusing me of having caused Teddy's death like he sort of did with Sheila. "After we eat, I'll need to go look at your truck." We ate in silence. I didn't even taste my food; I just wanted to be done. Too late I realized I had gobbled down everything in a very un-ladylike manner. I was batting a thousand in how *not* to impress a guy.

Once outside, I got my composure back. I knew what the truck looked like so there were no surprises there. Hal concentrated on the front of the truck even though I'd told him that most of the damage was to the back. Questions like, "Is this all new damage or is some of it old?" and, "Have you run into any wildlife lately?" were all that came from him, and they were pissing me off. He was scrutinizing some blotches on the grill that I hadn't paid much attention to. Did he think it was Teddy's blood? The hackles were going up fast on the back of my neck.

"Maggie, I'm going to have to call this in. The state police will want to go over your truck."

"You're going to impound my truck? You can't do that! It's my only transportation. It's not like I can call a cab or hop a bus to go anywhere."

"Calm down. They can probably come out and go over it right here and finish in a couple of hours, tops." Had I been screaming? I didn't know, but the way Hal looked and sounded, he must have thought he was dealing with a raving lunatic.

Suddenly I knew I was going to cry and I'd be damned if I'd let him see me. I ran up to my apartment leaving Hal by my truck.

Great! Run away, that always helps. I was so confused. What was this place, the Village of the Damned? There must be some sane people with normal lives around here someplace. I heard pounding up the steps and Josie burst in.

"Hal said you were upset and I'd better look in on you."

"Oh really, was that an order?"

"Oh, come on, Maggie. He was worried about you. He's just trying to help."

"Josie, I feel like I'm trapped in a great big conspiracy. Besides, I don't want his help. I'm tired to death of being blamed for every problem in this burg."

"Look, why don't you give Margaret a call and go see her?"

"Right, I can't use my truck until the state police go over it."

"You like to walk, right? Margaret's place is in walking distance for a youngster like you, and there is a nice view of the harbor and the bay on your way up."

"I suppose. It sounds like more of a plan than I've got right now. Maybe she's someone with no connection to Sheila, Bear, or Hal for that matter. I'll give her a call. I'm sorry about all this cop stuff. It's as much of a puzzle to me as anyone. I hope it doesn't screw up your business."

"Stop worrying. A little local excitement is always good for business."

"That's kind of cynical, Josie. You say something like that to the wrong people and they'll run you out of town on a rail if they don't run me out first."

"Then we'll just keep it between us New Yorkers. Now I've got to get back downstairs. Business will probably pick up when the police arrive, and Shirley will be flapping her gums more than working. It doesn't take much to draw a crowd in this town."

Margaret was very amenable to me dropping by. She gave me directions to her home, which did sound like a pleasant walk even if it would be uphill, and so we set a time. I walked down the front stairs to the street in front of the diner to avoid seeing the police investigators and the local vultures who were peering at the goings on, eagerly waiting for a chance to grab a scrap of juicy gossip that would elevate them in the eyes of their fellow vultures. I was feeling very cynical about this place right now.

I was wearing a ball cap with my hair pulled back in a ponytail sticking out the back. I told myself I needed the visor for the sun, but

I was going in a northwesterly direction with the sun at my back. I was really hoping to be less conspicuous to the local populous.

The walk looked more like a hike as I gazed up at the promontory that was High Head. The name was certainly appropriate. Smuggler's Neck stuck out to the east, and though it was a hilly peninsula of rock and spruce forest, it was dwarfed by High Head, which surveyed the whole harbor and the waters of Fundy Bay running up the eastern coast of Maine. It was understandable that the wealthier members of the community had chosen this spot to be their home. I had the impression that Margaret was well to do— in an understated way, not an ostentatious one— but I never dreamed that she would live in High Head.

I took my time, savoring the many stimuli to my senses. This was like an English writing project I used to assign. I'd have my students go for walks, taking in the different sights and sounds, and then convey what they'd experienced in words. Today there was a cool salt breeze that filled my nostrils and tickled my skin with damp fingers. Bees were busy buzzing around, pollinating a magical carpet of wildflowers that laced the edges of the road. The remnants of lupine with their stalks of seeds ready to be harvested painted a picture of this road in June, a royal array of purples and pinks that had now given way to waves of yellow and orange like a sunrise of flowers. Not a speck of debris could be seen on the roadside as if it was indeed a royal pathway. The diner, the police, the things of everyday life drifted away, and I found myself thinking I had walked through a portal of time.

I was fascinated with the architecture of these big houses with their manicured lawns and exquisite landscaping. Someone had found a niche and was making a pretty penny taking care of these places. I hadn't noticed many business opportunities in the area, with all the fishing and packing being closed down by government regulations.

I had my fingers crossed that I'd be able to find a teaching position for the fall, but right now I didn't need to go there. It would ruin the moment.

There were different styles and periods but no contemporary homes. One of the first places I passed on the way up the head was a newly restored Victorian with freshly painted gingerbread bargeboards. The colors told me someone from away had recently purchased it. I wondered how many others besides Margaret's were owned by the old families who had built them.

I imagined I was on a field trip with my students to record some oral history. I wasn't worried about what to talk about with Margaret. She wasn't as old as the people my class had compiled oral histories from, and definitely not as frail. The focus could be on her life and memories of Mundy, a switch from the questioning I had been undergoing the last couple of days.

Margaret's home was unique. I wasn't up on my historic architecture, but something told me this was an eclectic collection of special features all rolled into one place. It was three stories tall including the round turret at one corner. There was no widow's walk like many of the old sea captain's homes along the coast. Instead there was a veranda that almost completely surrounded the first floor with a portion glassed in as a sun porch. The main part of the building appeared to be constructed of brick that had been painted a cream color, and accents including shutters were painted a dark green. Surrounding the immediate grounds was a matching cream colored wooden fence, not a picket fence but something classier. Inside the fence, a walkway of brick curving up to the front steps of the veranda was lined with tea roses. The veranda looked out on a rolling garden of perennial flowers and grasses that undulated in the sea breeze sweeping the head. I had been right about the gardening. This place had a personal touch that landscapers alone couldn't bring to it.

I looked out at the view from this hilltop as I stepped up onto the veranda. To the east the Atlantic shimmered in the sunlight. To the south below lay Mundy, with comings and goings of boats, cars, trucks, and people working or enjoying their vacations. To the west were rolling hills dotted with forests and fields. It was breathtaking, and I wanted to drink it all in.

Before I could knock, Margaret opened the door. "How do you like the view?" I turned to her in a daze. "It's magnificent!" She was wearing a cool willow green shirtwaist dress - green was definitely her color - and her hair was swept back with combs. Suddenly I felt self-conscious about the way I was dressed. The feeling was dispelled by Margaret's hospitality.

"Maggie, I'm so glad you could come today."

"Thank you for having me on such short notice. It's a little hectic down at my place right now."

"Well, come on in. We'll have tea out on the sun porch. Do you like tea or would you like something else?" She was so polite. "Actually I prefer tea, but I do like my morning coffee." I wondered if she were lonely. Didn't she have better things to do than play hostess to a young stranger? *Don't look a gift horse in the mouth, Margaret. It got you away from the mess at your place didn't it? Just say thank you.* Was that Catsy in my head or my conscience?

I stepped over the threshold like Alice in Wonderland. The house was immaculate. Classic white cotton curtains with ball fringe and tiebacks graced each window. Delicate flowered wallpaper gave the rooms a breezy spring feeling. We walked through to the kitchen which was an old country farmhouse style with glass paned cabinets painted white and a kitchen table with a red checkered tablecloth. All spotless. The sun porch was off the kitchen and all set up with tea and cookies; I was guessing home baked. It was soothing. We sat down in comfortable padded wicker rockers. I sank into mine like I was nestling into a cloud.

"It's quite a hike up the Head. You must be exhausted." It wasn't the walk so much as the whole day preceding it that had worn me out. Actually, the walk had given me a new sense of energy - it always did. It was those other events that had sapped my strength.

"The trip up here was worth it just for the view. I think I could stare out to sea for hours."

"I have to admit I haven't always appreciated the view, but these days I do enjoy looking up from gardening and seeing something special in all directions. We get high winds here during storms, but we've weathered them. How are you finding our quaint little harbor town?"

Did Margaret have any idea what a loaded question that was? How bluntly honest could I or should I be? "The bright spot of my summer so far has been meeting people like you, Kenny, Josie and Dwight. So, Margaret, would you be willing to share with me about your family and Mundy?"

Margaret had a mused expression for just a moment. "Are you here doing research for the summer on our little town? Mundy has a fascinating history. Was that why you chose here?"

Now this was some lady. I'd never had an interview go quite like this. She had neatly turned the tables and was asking me the questions, the same questions I had been ducking from others. For some reason, I didn't mind sharing with her. I told her that I was a teacher and about my visit to the library and my talk with Sarah Carter, the librarian I had met. She nodded and told me about the library and some ancient history of Mundy. Her great, great grandfather had come over from Ireland and settled here. His family had been through the Civil War in which he'd lost a son. After the Civil War, Mundy had experienced a boom in canning, fishing, and global shipping. Listening to her recount those bygone years was like listening to a living history book. She made it come alive.

"Margaret, were you ever a teacher? You have a gift that I wish I had."

"Oh, I've never taught school. What subjects do you teach?"

"I've taught social studies and English, but I prefer history. It's been a favorite of mine since I was little." Before I knew it, I was talking about my childhood. More like reliving it, as I recounted my pilgrimages to sites of the French and Indian War and the Revolutionary War. This was fun. It had been eons since I'd had someone to share my passion for the past. I didn't know if it was my imagination or not, but both of us had neatly leaped over the immediate past of family and submerged ourselves in distant impersonal history.

I was brought back from this trip when Margaret asked me how I got my name. "I think my father was partial to M's. His name was Martin Murphy and he married Mary Cavanaugh. I'm not sure where the name Margaret came from, but they had friends whose children were named Agnes Mary and Mary Margaret so I just got pegged with Margaret Mary. Thank goodness, because it beats some of the alternatives. Mom and Dad could have called me Marty after him but they didn't."

"You were close to your father, weren't you?"

"Mom died when I was young, so it was just the two of us against the world."

"That's an interesting choice of words. My brother and I often felt the same way."

"That's strange; I didn't get the impression that Kenny had ever felt that way."

She laughed. "Heavens no, that's not at all like Kenny. He's always been quite the optimist." Her countenance changed. Did I see regret or sadness in her eyes? "Kenny is the youngest of the boys in my family, but he's the only one left. There were four of us children. Murphys have always been prolific. Kenny has six children, my nieces and nephews. Robert, my husband, and I never had any children, but then if we had, they would have been Doyles, not Murphys."

There was a pause in our conversation. It didn't feel right to pry into her personal life. There was a wound there that had not healed. I don't know why I knew that, I just did.

All at once the events of this week seemed a safer subject to explore. "Speaking of families, have you heard about the accident with Teddy Cox?"

"Yes, Kenny gives me the news if I don't pick up on it around town. I don't get out as much as I used to, but church and the historical society keep me busy. We even have a garden club in Mundy. It's very sad about Teddy, but in a way it might be for the best. He would have been lost without Sheila. He was like a faithful puppy dog. They went everywhere together, and he always watched out for her. It must have broken his heart when she died. I don't understand young people today. Your lives are always in such turmoil. Now I'll be attending two funerals. It's all so senseless."

This didn't appear to be the best subject to be on either, but I needed to know the connections between people beyond the fact that,

122

in one way or another, everyone appeared to be related. "You know the Joneses? I thought Sheila was hooked up with Wayne McCarthy." I wondered if Sheila was involved in a threesome, but Margaret wasn't the kind of person I'd mention that to.

"Winnie, Wayne's grandmother, is a close friend of mine. Let's just say that the Jones family has been here almost as long as the Murphys." I detected an undercurrent to her statement but salted it away in my memory to be taken out at a later date.

We had talked for hours. Part of me wanted to stay and soak up as much history as I could, but it wouldn't have been polite, and I didn't want to offend this lovely lady. I hoped as I walked back down to my apartment that there would be no signs of the state police. I'd have to give Jeff a call to find out what was going on. Jeff knew me, and we both knew that I wouldn't ask him to divulge anything he wasn't supposed to. He certainly wouldn't even hint at accusing me of involvement with everything that had gone on, unlike some people I could mention.

It was late in the afternoon when I approached Water Street and the diner. Josie's was closed, but she and Dwight were still there cleaning up. I didn't see any signs of police. I peeked around the corner with my eyes scrunched up. Please be there, please, please! I opened my eyes. There was my poor little truck, thank you, God.

I went to the diner door and tapped on the glass, cupping my hands and peering in the glass window. Josie saw me and came jogging to the door. "Come on in. We're just finishing up." Here I thought I put in long days, but Josie and Dwight were here fourteen hours a day.

"Josie, do you know what the status is on my truck?"

"Oh, the state guys came, took lots of pictures and whatever else they do and then left. It did make for a busy afternoon. Shirley was in gossip seventh, although I don't know that she was able to pump any information out of those state guys. It's a lot easier to get locals to open up."

"So I can use my truck?"

"Of course you can. I think Hal mentioned something about an accident report, but you can make that out with the state police in Tylerville. I'd do it tomorrow though, because there is some kind of a time frame you're suppose to do it in."

"Great! If it's 24 hours, I'm screwed. Maybe the fact they got called to come out might count." I really, really needed to talk to Jeff.

"Aren't you going to tell me how the visit went?"

The memory of the walk up the Head and the view nearly sent me back into rapture. "I had a great time. Margaret and I have a lot in common, like a love of history. I told her she should have been a teacher."

"Was anything said about Sheila and Teddy?"

"Not much, but from what she said she'll be going to their funerals." I was wiped and could tell Josie was too. Dwight was giving me the wind-up sign. He wanted to get this show on the road and get home. Tomorrow would come early for us all.

I dragged my sorry ass upstairs. I needed to eat something but I had no desire to cook, so I rummaged around for something that would qualify as finger food. My dad would accuse me of grazing when I'd get like this. Going from one thing to the next but not really finding what I wanted, I settled for a bag of chips, a chunk of cheese and a glass of ice cold orange juice; plopped down in Dad's chair; and hit the remote.

Just my luck the local news was on. "Twice in as many days, bodies have been found in Tyler County. Cause of death has not been released but police are calling both deaths suspicious." There behind the bobbing blonde bimbo was a map of Maine with that telltale yellow dot. They cut to an interview with the state police spokesman, that pompous ass, Jonathan Turner. Jonathan and I had had a run in when I was teaching down in Southern Maine. There had been a situation that Jeff and I were working on involving one of my students and drug sales. Jonathan wanted to use it as a political soapbox for promoting an anti-drug program and didn't give a hoot about how he might affect the immediate families involved. I never did find out how Jeff managed to side- track him, but he did. It probably would have ruined my career as a teacher, not to mention my credibility with my students, if what had been going on had been made public. It was one of those difficult times when I had wanted to bolt but Catsy and Jeff had held onto me and kept me grounded.

I'd give Jeff a call on my break in the morning. There was so much I wanted to ask about that I started a list of questions and things I could take care of with a trip to Tylerville.

Chapter Twelve

When the alarm went off, I was ready to start a new day; I even had the urge to start baking. It had cooled off overnight and was looking like it would be an overcast day. I'd have to ask Josie to give me pointers on where I might find some curtains and other knickknacks to make my place more like home, and I wanted to go grocery shopping for some things that just weren't available in town at any price. They'd have to be the last thing before I headed back. Even an overcast day would be too hot for fresh food in a truck with no air-conditioning. I was just a-humming with no worries.

Josie had me baking up a storm and I was happy. When we opened there was a pile of newspapers on the front steps of the diner. Josie brought them in and put them next to the cash register but nabbed one for herself, which she promptly took back to the corner table with a cup of coffee before things got going. Business was brisk and time flew. At break time there was no sign of Hal again, but today I could have cared less. Josie motioned me to the back corner, paper in hand.

"You better read this, and then we'll talk." What the hell? I couldn't read Josie, and I definitely wasn't in the mood to read the local gossip sheet, but I took it and sat down. Sheila and Teddy's deaths made the headline. "Drugs Bring Death to Tyler County." No shit Sherlock. The byline for the story was John Driscoll's. He knew how to spice things up so that you thought you were reading the *National Enquirer* instead of a rinky-dink weekly newspaper that barely covered one county. His "death toll rises in war on drugs" was over the top. There were some interesting facts stuck in about the autopsies on Sheila and Teddy which showed they'd both had a high drug and alcohol content when they died. That must have been what made Sheila's death suspicious. The hit and run still could be an accident where the driver just panicked and left the scene. But Driscoll couldn't allow the possibility of an accident to linger in the minds of his readers. That wouldn't have quite the flair of the dramatic that murder held.

As I read on there was my name. Oh, no! In my mind's eye it was pulsating in bright red letters. Of course it wasn't, but that's how I saw it and it had that effect on me. He gave me credit for finding the first body and then said that the police had spoken to me in connection with Teddy's death. Where did he get off printing that? Now I was ready to strangle the son of a bitch. I was muttering to myself as I read on. Josie came up beside me to see where I was in the scandal sheet then murmured; "It gets better. Check out the Op Ed section under Editor's Note."

"I can't wait for more surprises. And this guy is a *friend* of yours?" I know I had an accusatory tone, but I was spitting mad. The Editor's Note was worse than I could have imagined. Driscoll had done some digging and someone had blabbed about me. I didn't want to contemplate who, but I had a pretty good idea it was that worm, Turner. There for all the world—or at least Tyler County— to see was the innuendo that I was linked to drug trafficking in Southern

Maine and had been involved in a sting operation there. The source was anonymous, of course, and the story was written in such a way as to be easily misinterpreted in many ways, all bad for me.

The 'sting' that Driscoll alluded to was no such thing. It involved one of my students who had gotten in over his head, and I tried to help out while being a buffer for him and his family. We'd kept it very quiet, and his family had been very appreciative. Jeff had kept Turner in the dark, but I guess it hadn't been dark enough.

In his Op Ed piece, John Driscoll called for authorities to act more decisively about the drug problem in Tyler County and promised to keep digging and keep pressure on until something was done. I wasn't the only one that got skewered; the cops came out looking like imbeciles. They wouldn't be pleased.

When I finished reading I looked up at Josie. "What?" She was looking at me as if she were trying to decide what kind of a person I was. She sat down next to me and put her hand on my arm.

"Maggie, I've got to know if you're mixed up in this thing like the paper says. I'll believe whatever you say, but I've got to know."

"Josie what are you asking, if I'm a drug dealer? Well, I'm not, and if you don't want to believe me then I'll just have to ..." Tears were welling up in my eyes, and I didn't have any tissues. Here was someone whom I had come to feel comfortable around in a short period of time, and it hurt to think she thought that about me.

"I don't think you're a drug dealer. That's not what I meant. Don't be silly." I started to try and pull myself together while she handed me a wad of tissues. "Don't worry, they aren't used." We both giggled and it lightened the moment.

She leaned in confidentially and whispered, "I meant are you working with the police, like an undercover agent or what do they call them? Narcs? I swear it will stay between us."

Oh lord! That question sent me rocketing into the past. The label 'narc' was etched in my mind. Dead bodies and nasty and embarrassing things went with that label along with a level of Dante's *Inferno* that I never wanted to visit again. There had been a time when that's exactly what I had been called. It had started off innocently enough, or perhaps I had been very naive. I was teaching and drinking too much, then balancing it out with speed, and I was in the right place at the right time to get information on a drug operation. Of course my head wasn't screwed on right at the time, but that didn't make any difference. The poor guy I'd found floating had been mistaken for the narc when, in reality, I was the one feeding information to the cops. Even drugs and alcohol hadn't blotted out the horrors of what I had gotten into.

Josie was shaking my arm. "Maggie, are you all right? Is this getting you in trouble? I swear I won't tell a soul."

It took a few seconds to focus on Josie and process what she was saying. It wasn't making any sense to me. Eventually I found my voice. "Josie, I'm not a narc." She looked a little disappointed. "I am not working with the police on anything and I know nothing about Sheila and Teddy. You probably know more about what's going on then I do."

"You're sure?"

"Yes, Josie, I'm positive." My voice was hoarse from all this forced whispering. "You've got to believe me."

She patted my hand. "Okay, Maggie, whatever you say." She didn't seem entirely convinced, but there was nothing I could do about that.

I was determined to stick to my schedule of things to do. This entailed a trip to Tylerville. The entire drive I kept going over everything that had happened, trying to find the lightening rod that Driscoll had talked about. My mind is like a ghetto, a dangerous place to go alone and here I was dwelling in it all by my lonesome. I tried to think positively, mentally composing a gratitude list: I had a place to live, a job, new friends, and old friends. When I concentrated on those things, there wasn't a whole lot of room for the negative. I thought about what Catsy would say. *Don't rent space in your head to people. Don't feel resentment. It is better to give than to receive, so let the other guy get mad.*

On my way over to Tylerville, Haggarty's Garage looked busy as I slowed down to take a gander at the premises. All those trucks and cars lined up were a good sign, especially in this sparsely populated county. I could handle the truck business later now that I knew where I would be going.

When I pulled into the state police parking lot I was praying that Jeff would be there. Thankfully he was. On the corner of his desk was the *Tidewater Times*.

"I wondered when you'd be in."

"I had to wait until I finished work. You heard about my little accident? The truck is all banged up and I feel like things are racing out of control. What is it with this part of the world?"

"Margaret, it isn't this part of the world. We have a big drug problem here in Tyler County, but then, so do a lot of other places.

It just seems more concentrated because of the small population and the close relationships between people. You of all people know what this disease does to everyone."

"Yes, I know, but do you know how this John Driscoll guy found out about Southern Maine?"

"He didn't get anything from me. He was asking questions, but I didn't say word one. Margaret, he talked to Turner."

"I figured that, and I buy the bit about this place being closely related. So what am I suppose to do about this Sheila and Teddy business?"

"You don't have to do anything about it. We just need to get a report of the traffic accident on the books and we'll take care of that right now. As far as the other two cases, the Drug Task Force is handling that. They play it pretty close to the vest."

"I just want to stay out of whatever they're doing."

"That should be easy enough. Just keep doing what you've been doing, and let us handle this other stuff. I know you, Margaret. Don't go sniffing around trying to figure things out."

"Jeff, you sound like Catsy."

"Have you talked to her lately? Beth and I miss her. She's such a character."

"As a matter of fact, I have called her and, of course, I got the proverbial tongue- lashing about not calling sooner. I needed to talk about the Sheila Jones thing. I'd really like to talk to you too but not here at work."

"Hey, why don't you come for dinner tonight? Talk about a tongue-lashing, Beth gave me holy hell for letting you get away last time. I'm not making the same mistake twice. I insist."

"Tell you what: after we finish up this report stuff, I'll go shopping. I need to get some things that aren't in Mundy and I can cruise around Tylerville until you get off work. When do you want me to come back?"

"Come back around five. That's when I get off duty. I'll give Beth a call to have everything ready."

When Jeff got off the phone with Beth, we got down to business on the report, and then I headed out. Jeff joked about how it might be harder to kill a couple of hours in Tylerville than I thought, but I could spend that much time just walking up and down the river's edge or watching the osprey.

Tylerville's library was as modern as Mundy's was ancient. I hit that last after spying a Career Center where I got some good leads on teaching positions. Shopping had been surprisingly successful, even without any major chain discount or department stores. Of all places to find curtains, I found them in a little second-hand shop called Twice Nice. I admired the creativity and imagination that went into the businesses around here. It must be a struggle. You had to be creative and imaginative just to adapt to what resources were at hand, but I was up to the challenge. Due to the time of year and the condition of my vehicle, perishable groceries would have to wait for another time. I'd adapt.

I was surprised when Jeff led the way across town and into an older housing development. It was a quiet place, but for some reason, I had expected the family to have a big log cabin out in the middle of the wilderness as far away from people as possible. Or maybe that was my version of the perfect hiding place.

The house was a garrison style building with white vinyl siding and forest green shutters. I parked out on the street and followed Jeff up to a side door. The boys tumbled out and Brian, the younger, muckled onto me before I could reach the steps.

"Maggie, are you going to live here too?" Brian looked up at me with his big hazel eyes out from under a mop of golden brown hair cut sharply across his forehead. He was a miniature version of Jeff. Todd was the elder and took after Beth with dark blonde hair and blue eyes, but he did have Jeff's large straight white teeth that you got to see smiling out at you on occasion. Todd was much more reserved in his welcome, probably because, by my reckoning, he would be thirteen, an official teenager. The boys ushered me in to a wonderful smelling kitchen with Beth busy at the stove concocting something that had my mouth on full drool.

"Brian, let go of Maggie and give her a chance to catch her breath. There will be plenty of time to talk at dinner." Beth grabbed the handle of the cast iron skillet she was working over and moved it to another burner, then wiped her hands on the apron she was wearing. She hurried over and threw her arms around me. The first words out of my mouth were "Look at you, Mrs. Domesticity herself. This downeast living seems to agree with you. Let me in on the secret."

"Maggie, it's so good to see you. Please excuse the mess. I've been out straight with Little League and church fundraising. We're trying to raise money to get the steeple repaired. Right now it leaks like a sieve."

"Beth, for crying out loud, we haven't seen Maggie for over a year and here you are talking about fundraising." I wasn't bothered a bit. It was as if the time and distance had melted away. Beth gave me another hug, then stepped back for a head to toe inspection. "Well you don't look too bad considering what Jeff said when you got into town." I looked over at Jeff who had a sheepish look on a face that was starting to turn bright red.

"I must have looked pretty bad. It hadn't been one of my better nights and I can't say that they have gotten much better, but I have looked worse, and I'm looking forward to some improvement."

"Let me give you a tour of the house and you can fill me in." We weren't that far apart in age—Beth was 35—and we had always gotten along great, even though there weren't that many similarities in our lives. She did aerobics and kept in shape with help, I was sure, from Todd and Brian who kept her running. I filled her in on my encounters with the locals and finding Sheila's body. I had never shared my past with her or Jeff in any great detail, so she had no idea that it wasn't the first time I had found a corpse. It just isn't something that you want to talk about in casual conversation. She thought it was just awful, what I had been through, and she didn't know how I could be coping so well. Beth wanted to be sure that I wouldn't judge everyone up here by the behavior of a few louts, as she called them.

The kitchen opened into a dining area with a familiar round table that could be expanded to seat a dozen people. The table was surrounded by antique hip-rest chairs with caned seats. If I remembered correctly, Beth had taken a class and re-caned them all herself. The walls were festooned with counted cross stitch that Beth had done, and all were professionally framed and sported non-glare glass. A matching side boy held sea glass candle holders and a blue patterned soup tureen and platter. The upstairs had four bedrooms, one of which was for guests, and Beth berated me for not having stayed at their place when I had gotten into town. I apologized and explained that with Dad's passing, my brain hadn't been functioning up to snuff. She was determined to make up for the lost opportunity to help me out.

The downstairs had a fireplace with floor to ceiling bookcases at one end. Over- stuffed love seats and Queen Anne wingback chairs with coordinating upholstery intermingled with wrought iron floor lamps. She was using blanket chests as end tables; I'd gotten the blanket chest coffee table idea from her. The remaining rooms included a den with a washer/dryer alcove—novel idea actually having a washer and dryer in your home, it sure beat the Laundromat.

Beth was really easy to be around, even though we were such opposites in so many ways. She was a stay-at-home mom and attentive wife to Jeff, giving him a place of refuge after his daily dealings with the more unsavory aspects of life. She had always extended that graciousness and hospitality to me and anyone else she could. I was a loner with a miserable track record of commitments. At this moment, I envied her life, but it wasn't in the cards for me.

Actually sitting at a table to eat was different. The kids were chattering about going to the lake as serving dishes were passed around. I soaked up the atmosphere of normality and enjoyed eating someone else's cooking and I had always been a sucker for grilled meals. After dinner the kids tore out into the yard and we went out on the deck. As we sat there gazing at a sloping lawn and wooded area, I could feel each muscle strand relaxing. My belly was full, and I felt safe and content. Even with homes on both sides of them, the Chandlers had a quiet privacy. Beth had a healthy-looking vegetable garden, flowers were blooming along the bit of privacy fence that separated the Chandler's yard from their neighbors, and blossoms walled in the deck in pinks, whites and yellows. I could only guess at the names of the varieties she had planted.

As we sat sipping iced tea and watching the boys play ball, I told Jeff everything I could think of about what had happened in Mundy. Jeff listened but didn't really say much of anything beyond his earlier warning to just stay clear of it. That off my chest, Beth and I got talking about the schools in the area.

From my conversation with Beth and the pickings at the Career Center, it was looking like I'd have to broaden my search for work beyond the narrow scope of high school social studies teacher. My certification was for seventh through twelfth grade and, since it was a professional certification, I could always get a transitional certification for another area of study and take courses in that to be certified.

It was time to make my exit, so I said my goodbyes and thanks for a great meal. "Don't be a stranger and let me know how things are going in the job search. You know you can use Jeff and me as references. It helps if they know you have connections in the community. They like to hire their own, and then newcomers only as a last resort. You already found out that everyone is related, and they don't believe in nepotism rules. Half the schools would shut their doors if they couldn't hire their relatives." Now that was a comforting thought...not.

"I'll keep that in mind." I hated to leave, and it was with reluctance that I climbed into my truck and set off for the next best thing to family. I'd still have time for part of a meeting tonight, and it would round off a very good day. I had to draw the line at actually calling it perfect.

Chapter Thirteen

When I showed up at the Grange, the parking lot was packed with cars and trucks. I found a spot to park and rushed to the entrance. As I ran up the steps into the meeting hall, the people parted like the Red Sea and conversation stopped. Was I being paranoid again? I practically fell across the threshold, desperately seeking a familiar, friendly face. Kenny and Del were sitting by the coffeepots in deep conversation. Kenny saw me coming toward them and got up to greet me. He reached out and grabbed my hand. "Margaret I'm so glad you came. I was afraid you might not be here tonight. Del here helped set up. Winfield is feeling a little under the weather and couldn't make it." At this Del got up. "Good to see you Margaret."

Alright, I was back to sanity. Relief swept over me, but I knew I needed to talk about what had happened the last time I'd been here. I also knew that probably most of the people here tonight, or at least those from Mundy, had heard it through the grapevine. Maybe that was too self-centered and grandiose. *Remember, Margaret, the world does not revolve around you. Other people have their own lives.*

"Margaret, I heard about your accident. Are you all right? Was there much damage to your truck?" Kenny looked concerned.

"It runs, but it looks a little more like yours now. It took it in the rear end. I have to find a place to fix the turn signal just so I'm at least street legal."

"Haggarty's is where you want to go. Charlie will take good care of you; just tell him I sent you. He's out at the Corners in Sutton."

"Yeah, I know. I drove by there this afternoon on my way to Tylerville and noticed the place was really jumping. I had to go in and file an accident report. It's not like I have any kind of insurance to cover anything but liability."

We chatted for a few minutes until the meeting got started. The discussion got around to what happened to Teddy and Sheila, not using any names, of course, but everyone knew who was being referred to. "If you're an alcoholic you end up in an institution, AA, or the grave, and the institution can be a nut ward, jail, hospital, or prison. This disease wants to kill you. You can't forget that." Well, I guess it had killed Teddy and Sheila with a little help from person or persons unknown.

After talking about where the disease of alcoholism had taken us, someone I didn't recognize spoke up. He sounded like he had a hair across his butt. "What about anonymity? You know this isn't a place to get the goods on addicts and alcoholics. What's the point of coming if someone is going to rat you out, go to the cops, or get you in trouble."

One of the old timers said something about resentments and that he should keep coming back. From the sound of him, he had probably been sent by the court and didn't want to be here. He was looking for any excuse to miss meetings, but they're a condition for staying out of jail. I had seen a lot of people with the same attitude. They wanted to blame their problems on others. They usually didn't stick around, or they bounced in and out of the program until they changed their attitudes or ended up in jail or dead.

There were a few others who mentioned how they thought their anonymity had been broken and about how people from town would drive by meetings to check out whose car was here. That's when I heard the bit about 'drunk school' again. People who didn't know anything about the program thought of it as a place to learn how to drink safely, hence 'drunk school.' I had heard old-timers share that they came to AA to learn how to drink sociably but eventually surrendered to the fact that they couldn't take one drink in safety. It's the first drink that gets you drunk. Many times I had hung onto that thought in early sobriety when I really, really wanted something, anything, to make the hurting stop.

I was disappointed that Tina and Joanne hadn't shown up. I was hoping we might get together after the meeting for an ice cream; strange how I could look forward to such simple things. I suppose there was always the possibility that they had gone back out and used again. It happens. I wished I had taken the time to call them, but I hadn't.

I helped clean up after the meeting. It was the least I could do. Del stayed with me, and we had a nice talk, just the two of us. He told me about the crazy family situation he had grown up with and how he came into the program. I found myself sharing more about my own story of getting sober than I had in a long time. As we were locking up, Del got all serious. "Margaret, Sheila's funeral is Saturday afternoon. I thought you should know."

"Are you going to it?"

"I'll be there, and I imagine half of Mundy will be there. It's in the late afternoon, so most people will have a good buzz on by then. Her old drinking and drugging buddies will be there and people there to show support for her family. They're getting together at the Spiny Urchin for the reception afterwards."

"The Spiny Urchin's a bar, isn't it?"

"It's a bar and grill. They actually serve some good food, but you're right, the emphasis is on bar. I don't go in there much, and when I do, I have to be in the right frame of mind. It's *the* place to hang out for a lot of the fishermen. They make these really meal-sized sandwiches that we get to take aboard the boat."

I wanted to be with people, but did I want to go to a funeral just for company? Margaret was going and Del was going. *Get real Margaret. Going would be the most ridiculous thing you could do. Remember, you are staying out of this whole mess. Your real reason has nothing to do with going to the funeral to be supportive. It's just your morbid curiosity again.* I could find better things to do with my afternoon and there wouldn't be as many prying eyes around because they'd all be at the funeral.

After the meeting, I made a decision to go right back to my place, and I didn't even have to flip my medallion. Del waved as I left, and I had a pang in my gut for some reason that I couldn't or wouldn't put a finger on. I wondered if he was married. There went my flights of fancy. I couldn't believe my warped mind. I wasn't supposed to be going to meetings to pick up guys. Catsy would have a field day with that. Better to pick up a stray cat, less trouble down the road.

The phone was ringing when I walked through the door of the apartment. I had to stop and think what I was hearing. Who would be calling me at this hour? Come to think of it, who had my number? "Hello?"

"Is this Margaret?" It was a girl's voice but strange, as though she was whispering, and it had a hint of familiarity to it. I was wracking my brains over who it could possibly be.

"Yes, this is Margaret. Who's calling?"

"It's me, Tina." I could barely make out what she was saying between the hoarse whisper and the hitching sobs. She was definitely crying.

"Tina, what's wrong? I missed you at the meeting tonight. Are you drunk?"

"They're going to take my kids. I don't know what I'm going to do. He's going to kill me."

"Tina, calm down and slow down. I can hardly understand you. Catch your breath and start from the beginning." I'd gotten hysterical calls before from pigeons -people I sponsored - who were stoned or drunk. I called them phone drunks because the first thing they did when they got wasted was pick up the phone and start calling anyone and everyone. The sobs had slowed down on the other end.

"Tina, I can't help you if you're drunk or high."

"No, really, I haven't had anything, but it's looking really tempting. I'm scared. I couldn't go to the meeting tonight 'cuz he might 'ah seen me. He warned me to stay away from you." She was still racing but she stopped long enough to take another hitching breath. "I gotta know, are you a narc?" This conversation was getting stranger by the minute. Hell, the whole day just kept getting crazier and crazier.

It's amazing how calm I can be when I'm dealing with someone else's hysteria. This was going to take a while to sort out; so much for going right to bed.

"No Tina, I'm not a narc. What in the world gave you that idea?" As if I didn't know. "I'm just a drunk trying to stay sober like you, one day at a time." When you stay calm and don't feed into their hysteria, it helps take the drama out of the situation. That was what Cat would say. It always worked on me.

"Now let's see if we can start from scratch and you tell me who they are and who he is and what's going on."

There is a new three-county task force trying to make a dent in the drug trade going on in Tyler County. This much I knew from Josie and Driscoll as well as Jeff. Because it was so hard to infiltrate these local operations—everybody knew everybody else and who they were related to—the police would try to recruit or flip people they had leverage on. The perfect patsies were mothers with kids they didn't want to lose - even if it was the welfare check they were more interested in - or those facing prison time rather than jail time. From what I had picked up in the short time I had been here, jail time was commonplace, almost a right of passage into adulthood.

Tina had decided to clean up her act. We had never discussed why she had made this particular decision when she did. Bottoms are different for each of us. I had just had enough and could see no point in living. I tried to do myself in, but I couldn't even do that right. I couldn't live and I couldn't die. It really sucked. No one threatened me with jail or anything, but that wasn't the case with Tina.

Tina had been one of those people singled out by the task force to put pressure on. She was vulnerable in several areas. They wanted her to turn in her former dealer by pretending to go back out and make a buy. She would have to wear a wire in order to have evidence that would stand up in court. There might have been a little fear of losing her supplier if sobriety didn't seem quite worth it, but from what she was saying and how she was saying it, she genuinely feared for her life. Because of what had happened this week, I could appreciate where she was coming from.

I hadn't figured out how I fit in. Apparently the guy she was afraid of thought the cops were bringing in someone from outside the area to get the goods on him. Thanks to Driscoll's article, I was tagged as that someone. This was just great. How was I supposed to stay out of this mess if I was the only one who knew I had nothing to do with it? For a second time today, I wanted to strangle Driscoll and Turner. Tina wouldn't tell me who the guy was that was threatening her, but I really didn't need to know.

I wasn't sure what to tell her. I had no idea what could be done. I asked her if she thought she could stall the police about the setup, and she said she'd try. Then I told her that I'd stop going to meetings in Tylerville and points south but that she really should go to those and stay in the program. If she went back out, she'd be toast. Things would only get worse. When we finally got off the phone she had calmed down. I, on the other hand, was all keyed up again.

I spent a very restless night. I couldn't help but wonder if everything going on was all connected. Visions of Sheila's dead body mingled and blurred into the sailor with the sound of lapping water tying them together. Narc! The terror that word struck in my heart made me gasp for breath. I'd been told to hide out and make sure that if anything happened only one story came out, this from an NCIS agent. The island was small. I'd slept with a 9mm and wore it on my hip as I waited to be discovered.

I'd say I was having those awful nightmares again, the ones I had tried to drown with booze and drugs, but I wasn't asleep. They were real memories of my visit to hell. Fear was creeping back into my life. I was *not* a happy camper.

Morning finally came and with it time to go to work. After the night I'd had, I was looking forward to the everyday drudgery of waiting tables. I got lost in baking, but I guess I looked like shit because Josie made a comment first thing. "Late night?"

"It's not what you think. I just couldn't sleep, is all." I had promised Tina I'd talk to someone about her dilemma with the police. I figured I would ask Hal, without using any names, if he had any suggestions. That was, if he came in today.

I was feeling lonely again. Maybe Josie was right; I needed to stop being so damned independent, trying to handle everything myself. It wasn't working very well. Maybe Hal really did just want to help. Why did I always pick a fight when I got around the guy?

Hal walked through the door back on his usual schedule. My heart started to pound. *Get a grip girl. He's just a guy you're going to talk to.* It was hard dealing with Mr. Perfect, but this time I rushed over to wait on him.

"Good morning. We missed you yesterday." I set down a mug of steaming hot coffee and a glass of water. I was trying to be perky and hoped I didn't look as rough as I had when I came in this morning. Hal looked up in mild surprise, first at me, and then scanning the diner for Josie. She had gone in the kitchen to replenish the goody case, and I was relieved. This would work better without Josie for an audience.

"Good morning, Margaret."

Okay, we'd gotten through that without an opening salvo. Now what? Let's keep it businesslike. "What would you like this morning, anything besides coffee?"

"What would you recommend? Is there any more of that raspberry cake?"

"I think so. Josie just went in to bring more stuff out to fill the case. Would you like a piece?"

"Sure." He was giving me an odd look, like, 'when is the bomb going off?' but we were still making nice. I had to get to the point of asking him a favor but I decided to wait until I brought him his cake. I set the plate down in front of him, and he looked at me with those gorgeous, intense brown eyes. I was getting all gooey inside. *Open your mouth, Margaret, and talk to him, for crying out loud!* "Hal, I'd like to talk to you about something but not here, not now."

He cocked one eyebrow in a Rock sort of way. "Can it wait until I get off duty?"

"Yeah, sure. When are you off, 4:00?"

"Yup. I'll stop by then, that is if you'll be here." Oh here it comes. Don't bite. You sort of deserve that. Remember you're going to be asking for a favor, so don't screw this up.

"I'll be here; actually I'll be upstairs." I was vaguely aware of more customers coming in and Josie bustling around the other side of the room. It was time to stop making nice and get back to work. I had to remember that I was taking my truck out to Haggarty's, which I'd have to do right after work if I wanted to be back here at four. It wouldn't be wise to keep this guy waiting again. I didn't sense a whole lot of tolerance or patience in him.

I told Josie that I was headed out to the garage to see what it would cost me to get the truck fixed. She asked if I needed an advance on my pay but that wasn't necessary. I'd barely touched my teacher's pay. Between tips and the money that Dad had left me, I wasn't hurting, but paying for the truck still rankled.

Haggarty's was just as busy today as it had looked on my way into Tylerville. I pulled my truck into an empty space between two big boys, an F150 extended cab and a Sierra. My little baby looked like a miniature in comparison. I hopped out and sauntered inside. It took a moment for my eyes to adjust to the change from bright sunlight to the dark interior of the squat building that housed the office. I was the only female in the place. There were two guys behind the counter who looked like brothers. Listening to them converse with customers with that marvelous dry wit and downeast drawl was like music to my ears. I was enjoying it so much that I was caught off guard when one of them spoke up, "What can I do for you, little lady?" The man had 'Charlie' embroidered on his overalls. He was very compact and reminded me of Santa Claus with his round nose, cherry cheeks, and twinkling eyes.

"I had a little accident the other night, and there's some damage to my truck that I need to get fixed."

"Well, we'll take a look at her and see what we can do." He came around the corner with his thumbs in his overalls and waited for me to lead the way to my truck. "Ayuh, don't believe I've seen this vintage for awhile. Best I can do is used parts; don't think they've made parts for this model for a time. The grill don't need to be replaced if the looks of it don't bother you. It's just cosmetic damage that would run you more to take care of."

"I'm all for leaving the grill just the way it is; I just want to keep her road-worthy so I don't get in any hassles."

Charlie looked at me and grinned, nodding his head. "I can order the parts from a guy over in the next county. It won't take long to get 'em if he's got 'em." We went back in to finish up business. He pored through these enormous books of parts and started scribbling down numbers with a pencil stub on a scrap of paper. I gave him my name and number. "Oh you must be one of Kenny's kids." Just as he was saying this, Kenny walked in with a guy I hadn't seen before. The guy looked haggard - like a bum, to be more exact. Deep circles under his sunken eyes told me he hadn't slept for days. It was hard to tell how old he was. I don't think he had washed for days either.

Kenny waved with that big impish grin; "Did you tell Charlie I sent ya?" Charlie looked over at Kenny. "I knew she was one of yours. I lost track after your fourth." Kenny blushed. "Naw, I can't take credit for this one, but you better take good care of her."

"Come on, Kenny, she's the spitting image of Terry but with redder hair, and you know I always take care of my customers, whether they're related to you or not." They both started laughing, and I started feeling a little uncomfortable about being discussed while I was standing right there.

One glance over at the guy who'd come in with Kenny took care of that. He looked like he was trying to focus on me and concentrate on the conversation between Charlie and Kenny at the same time. Apparently, in his condition this was one thing too many.

The conversation moved off me and on to why Kenny was here. "Wayne's truck got all stove to shit. What can you do for him?" They headed back out to the parking lot with me trailing behind. Wayne's truck was a late model Ford 150 in dark green. All I caught was something about insurance and Charlie with another chuckle saying "It's been a bad week for truck grills." I waved goodbye to Kenny as I surveyed Wayne's truck. Could this be Wayne McCarthy, Sheila's companion and Winnie's grandson? He was such a mess, it was hard to tell.

Before I could get back to my truck, Kenny called out "Margaret, wait up. Where are my manners? When men get talking about their vehicles, everything else goes by the wayside. I didn't make introductions. Margaret would have my head for being impolite. Charlie and Wayne, this is Margaret Mary Murphy. Margaret, this is Charlie Donovan and Wayne McCarthy."

"Come on, Kenny, you're pulling my leg. I thought you said this young lady wasn't one of yours."

"Maggie's from New York originally. She just came up from Southern Maine. She's met my sister, haven't you, Maggie?"

"I've run into quite a few Murphys since I moved up here."

"Oh, you say you've moved up here; for the summer or year round?"

"That's still up for grabs. It depends on work."

"It usually does for all of us."

"Charlie, pardon me for asking, but if you're a Donovan, who owns the garage?"

Kenny and Charlie started laughing while Wayne just stared at me with dead eyes. He wasn't finding any humor in this. He gave me the creeps. When Charlie caught his breath he explained that he and his brother Walt owned the garage, but since everyone knew it as Haggarty's, they'd kept the name. No relation to Haggarty except they were Irish. It was a confusing name game up here and I didn't think I'd ever learn how to play.

I did another sidelong scrutiny of Wayne's truck, wondering if it could have been the one that had run me off the road. Maybe I should say something to Hal? But then I stopped myself. I was going to stay out of it and let the police handle it. But Hal *was* the police.

I still had time. It hadn't taken as long as I thought it would at the garage, so I decided I'd head over to the library and do some more research on Mundy and maybe check for more teaching positions. Until I landed something, job hunting was going to be an ongoing process that was one of my least favorite things in the world to do. Falling into the job at Josie's for the summer had been a great gift that I had best be grateful for. Still, I was a procrastinator, and getting lost in history was much more enticing than job hunting.

Sarah was busy at the front desk with library patrons in all shapes and sizes asking questions. She was helpful and professional as she fielded them all and answered each one with a personal touch. The library was a very popular place today which made it a little too crowded for me. I gave Sarah a wave and a smile and headed downstairs to the local history corner. I was in luck. This part of the library didn't seem to be as popular. I had my choice of overstuffed chairs and was all by myself. That's the way I liked it, and I could just start in where I left off the other day. Of course, I promptly lost track of time. When I looked at my watch it was almost four o'clock, and if I didn't boogie, I'd be late again for Hal.

I tore out of the library and across the mall, jogging with my backpack flapping in the breeze. When I got to the foot of the stairs there was no cruiser in sight, so somewhere in my panting, I breathed a sigh of relief. Once in the apartment, I couldn't decide what to do or say, and I couldn't sit still. I was standing in front of my bedroom closet thinking about changing clothes when Hal knocked on the screen door and called out my name.

My heart started doing tell-tale tap dancing as I let him in. I was feeling really awkward, but what else was new? We moved to the living room, almost bumping into each other, and I got all tingly. Hal sat in Dad's chair, and I sat on the futon curling my feet under me. Hal seemed relaxed, but I felt like he was observing me in some official way which did nothing for my comfort level.

"What did you want to see me about?" I was glad he'd started the conversation, but where did I go from here?

"Well I need to ask for some advice for a friend." That sounded lame even to my ears.

"Oh?"

"Yeah, she's sort of in a bind with the authorities and others, and she asked me for help, and I wasn't sure what to tell her." His look had changed to one of curiosity, but I was betting he thought I was talking about me instead of a 'friend.' "This person has a problem with drugs... and has a couple of kids and... ah... The cops want her to help them nab a dealer and they have threatened to take away her kids if she doesn't help 'em, and her dealer is threatening too. She just wants to stay clean and sober." Hal appeared to get even more ramrod straight than ever, and he had a guarded, officious expression on his face that stonewalled my ability to read him.

"Is she using?"

"No! At least I don't think so."

"Did she tell you the name of her dealer?"

I was not going there! I drew the line at getting sucked into that arena, plus Tina had either been too scared to part with that information or she didn't want to burn her connections if this sobriety thing didn't work out. I could honestly say I didn't know. Hal was staring at me. "No, she didn't tell me, but that isn't important, is it?"

Hal took a moment. "Look, if she isn't using and she isn't doing anything else illegal, the police can't make her do anything, and they can't take away her kids that easily either. But if she's on probation or out on bail and she violates any conditions, her ass is grass."

"So what do I tell her?"

"Tell her to keep her nose clean and just say no. She might want to get a lawyer if she can afford it, or she probably has one if she's been in trouble before. I probably shouldn't be saying any of this. You certainly have interesting taste in friends." That remark cut to the quick. "What is it with you and druggies? You seem to have a history with them. Have you gotten me here as some sort of setup?"

What the hell was he talking about? My temperature was rising, and I felt like I was going to blow. "You should know better than to believe what you read in the papers." I knew I must be turning red, but I couldn't stop myself.

"Margaret, I'm just trying to figure out what side you're on."

"Why do I have to be on any side?" My voice was rising. *Calm down. Please, God, I don't want to get into a fight.*

"Okay, okay, maybe it's just my suspicious nature. It goes with the job, but you got to admit you do manage to get yourself in some weird situations, and you've been kind of secretive."

He was right. I was holding onto secrets, and they were making me sick inside just like Cat had warned me they would. His openness made me want to jump his bones, another indication of how sick I was. Half the time I wanted to pound the shit out of him, and the other half I wanted to make mad passionate love to him! So here I was trying to stay on the fence, and it was getting mighty uncomfortable. Could I be honest with him?

"Hal, you're right about me not exactly being forthcoming about myself. I've had some difficult times and gotten burned, so it's not easy opening up to anybody." I felt the sobs starting to roll up my throat as I tried to maintain control. I was not going to resort to feminine waterworks to get Hal's attention if I could help it, even if the emotions were genuine. What was I going to tell him?

"Let's just say there is a history that I'd rather not get into, but I'm trying to stay clean and sober in a new place, and it's hard." There was an excruciating moment of silence—more like an eternity—before Hal said anything. I still had a very hard time telling anyone I was an alcoholic. The word formed a knot in my throat, and it wasn't like it was anybody's business but mine—that's what I liked about anonymity.

"You're going to AA, aren't you?" At least he didn't call it 'drunk school.' "My brother goes."

My mouth fell open. I was totally shocked. His reaction was not what I had expected. Who was his brother? Had I met him? Did he know that his brother was telling people he was in the program? My mind was whirring and I thought I might have an emotional meltdown on the spot. I put my head in my hands. I wanted to shrink into nothingness totally out of sight. I started to sob. I was vaguely aware that Hal was beside me as he reached out and put his arms around me. I was rigid. It wasn't that I didn't want to be cradled in his arms, but it just wasn't part of my plan. "It's all right, Maggie." Neither of us said any more. I pulled myself together as best I could and stood up, resorting to comedy to break the spell.

"Do they prepare you for being a shoulder to cry on at the Sheriff's Department? How to Handle Emotional Women 101? I guess with all that has gone on, moving and all, I've gotten a tad unraveled." I had to change the subject quick. "Do you know if they have any leads on who may have run me off the road? When I was out at Haggarty's to get the truck checked out, I met Wayne McCarthy. His truck was all smashed up in front and it's a dark green. Do you think he might have…?"

Well, that certainly killed the moment. Hal practically turned to stone with that comment. "No, I do not think Wayne hit your truck. Wayne ran into a deer, if you must know. I think it would be best if you let the police handle the situation. There's no need to go looking for someone to accuse. It could get you in some pretty deep trouble. Not everyone would take kindly to it."

"Okay, I promise to stay out of it." How could I repair the situation? "I really appreciate you being here and all that you've done. Can we be friends?"

He towered over me in this small room. He was sizing me up like some inanimate object. I stood my ground. "I'll tell you what, I won't tell you how to cook that wonderful raspberry cake if you won't tell me how to catch crooks, and then we can be friends."

"When did you know I was the one who made the cake?" The heat was coursing between our bodies.

"I'd like to claim it was my policeman's intuition, but Josie set me straight from the get-go. Well, I've got to go. I want to get out of these clothes and kick back." As he said this, he moved toward the door. Going through my mind was the thought that I'd like to take off his clothes and help him kick back. *Don't go there. Just let him leave on a fairly civil note. No rash decisions or he'll think you're a slut.*

I had to give Tina a call before she left for a meeting; at least that was what I hoped she would be doing. It made me uncomfortable vouching for someone else's sobriety, but Hal had put me on the spot. Thank goodness I had Tina's number since I wouldn't be seeing her at meetings for awhile. Hopefully, the predicament she was in would end soon so we could get together.

She said I'd just caught her. She and Joanne were going to an early meeting south of Tylerville and then heading to a movie at a little theater not far from the meeting. I had a fleeting pang of jealousy and resentment. Last night she had called me hysterically, and now she was going to a meeting and a movie while I had spent a sleepless night, gone out on a limb for her with Hal, and now was alone. I couldn't dwell on it. I told her what Hal had said, but I didn't tell her where I got the information. I assured her that I hadn't broken her anonymity either. I might have been holding back, but Tina was newly sober and shaky. If she went back out and used, I didn't want to get dragged into anything else.

I had done my good deed for the day and was now at loose ends. Being alone in my own head was not the smartest move, but I was drained. I ate dinner in Dad's chair and flipped through the channels. I had no desire to watch the news, and there was nothing on that caught my interest.

I missed Dad more than ever right now. It's never a good sign when you start talking to yourself, but I'm not sure what it means when you start talking to someone who's not there. I needed to blame someone for feeling miserable right now, and Dad was the only one I could think of. In my heart, I knew he wasn't to blame for what I had done to my life. I could hear him as plain as day. "Maggot, with your mother gone it's just you and me against the world, but everything will be all right. We have each other and we can stand on our own two feet. No one can put us down unless we let them." Then I would go and do something stupid, and he would just shake his head and say, "Maggot, what have you gotten yourself into now? You have so much potential—why don't you use the brains God gave you?" I would try to make him proud of me. I thought he'd be pleased when I got my teaching certificate, but then the putdown would come. "Those who can, do. Those who can't, teach." No wonder I'd grabbed at the opportunity to go to Alaska to teach. It was as far away as I could get. I'd show him. That turned out to be another disaster, and I turned up back home with my tail between my legs.

Things had started to change when I got sober. Of course, then I'd found out that he was dying, and my tendency to run away and drink myself into oblivion was no longer an option. It didn't work anymore. For the first time, I'd felt he really needed me, and I was happy to be there for him, but I'd turned in one way of escaping for another. Everything revolved around taking care of Dad. It became my excuse for keeping everyone at arm's length. He would say, "Jesus H, Maggot, go out and have some fun. You don't need to hover over me all the time." So I'd go out with Catsy and a group of us from the program, just hoping to please him. I had to admit it hadn't been all that satisfying.

As I sat there and ran this morbid rerun of my life, I looked over at the filing cabinet that I had hauled with me. It was a project that I could start and that would keep me busy. I rummaged for the keys to unlock it. I had assumed that the key would be with my dad's things. Now I thought what a crock it would be if I couldn't find it.

After several tries with keys of all kinds, I found the one that fit. Voila! She was open. I pulled open the top drawer, took out a pile of stuff, parked myself on the floor cross-legged, and started to go through what was there. Now I had pictures and memorabilia of my life to go with the reruns in my head. This was definitely a trip down memory lane. My baby book was here with a lock of my red hair, comments on my first words, and pictures of me eating and crawling. There was one of Dad holding my hands for my first steps and another of Mom spooning vegetables into my mouth where I appeared to be more interested in wearing my food than eating it. That had certainly changed.

This was going to be an emotional roller coaster that would take some time. I had been so fixated on Dad that I had forgotten about Mom. It had been so long. I suddenly realized that Mom must have felt a lot like I was feeling right now. First she was adopted, then her adoptive parents were killed in a car accident. When her parents died, she had only been a few years older than I was when I lost her. There were wedding pictures of the two of them, my drawings from school, and my report cards. There were little notes clipped to some of my awards from school. "That's our Maggot." "My girl, she's the smartest lassie of them all." I started to cry. I never thought I had done anything good enough to warrant high praise, but here in his handwriting were all the little words that I had been starving for.

I didn't even finish going through the first drawer before I started to doze off. The discomfort of lying on the floor woke me just enough that I got up, put the pile of things back in the drawer, locked it, and headed for bed.

Chapter Fourteen

The conversations of the locals at the diner were all about Sheila's funeral and what the police did or didn't know about the circumstances of her death. The air was positively thick with it. Even the tourists got roped into conjecturing on the state of affairs in Tyler County in general and Mundy in particular. Nothing like a homicide to get your town its fifteen minutes of fame. Teddy's death was left on the back burner. It had been less spectacular—as if hit-and-run deaths occurred every other day—and therefore not discussed with as much fervor. Even Josie and Dwight were talking about the funeral as if it was some gala event that everyone who was anyone must attend. The Spiny Urchin would certainly be doing a great deal of business today.

The Waylands were closing the diner at noon so they could go. Josie had already placed a neatly hand-lettered placard in the window to let her customers know the change in plans. I could imagine the businesses up and down the street doing the same because she was 'one of their own'. It wasn't the best way to become a tourist hot spot, and it amazed me how laid back businesses were up here. A sign in a store window said it all, 'Customers by Chance or Appointment.'

The upside was that I wouldn't be waiting for Shirley to show up, since she didn't have to come in at all. She probably needed the whole morning to get ready for a two o'clock funeral. Meow! If the truth be known, I was suddenly feeling lonely and left out again.

When Winfield and Margaret came in, I was hoping the mood might lighten up, but it didn't. I went over to their table to take their order and mentioned that people couldn't stop talking about the funeral. Margaret's expression was downcast. "Winfield is taking me. It's being held at the Sutton Methodist Church. You know, Sheila and Wayne had a place out in Sutton."

"I didn't know that, but I do remember seeing the church on my way back from Tylerville. I really feel bad for the kids. I wasn't planning on going, but Dwight and Josie are going. Maybe I should go with them and pay my respects to Winnie."

"No, dear, I think it would be best if you didn't go." Winfield nodded in agreement and turned to Margaret. I hated it when someone pointed out that I wasn't thinking logically or using common sense. No matter how nicely it was done, I took it as a personal slam, and my pride was hurt. Or maybe she sounded like she knew something I didn't. Either way, I was hurt and angry.

"Margaret, you don't think I had anything to do with what happened to Sheila, do you? I just found her, that's all." I realized I was practically whimpering.

"Maggie, of course I don't think that. You aren't responsible for what happened to her, but this is a small town with a long memory and a great deal of history. Once people get something in their heads, no matter how misguided or flat out wrong, they simply can't let go of it. Some people are ruled by emotions and incapable of behaving in a civilized manner under any circumstances. Maggie, what I am trying to say as delicately as possible is that it's best not to give them a target to latch on to. I would hate to have anything happen to hurt you, and I would like to be the first to apologize for anything that may have caused you pain." She was very sincere, but I didn't quite know what she was talking about. I was in the dark again, and that seemed to be happening a lot lately.

"You told me you like bird-watching and nature. It's going to be a beautiful afternoon. Why don't you enjoy some of our many nature trails? There are some spectacular views overlooking Sail Rock Light out at the park across the river. You might even get to see a whale or two."

Well, I guessed Margaret was just worried about me in a motherly sort of way. It was kind of nice that someone cared about me like that. The idea of seeing whales was much more enticing than going to a funeral with a bunch of people I didn't know. "Do you think I really might see a whale? It would be a first for me."

"We have a very active pod of minkes off Sail Rock, and humpbacks like these waters too, so it's very possible." Winfield sounded like a professional tour guide.

I resolved to play it smart for once in my life and follow their suggestions. Winfield wasn't going to let me off quite so easily though. As I was leaving, he mentioned Wilcox and steps in a veiled reference to the Stepping into Sobriety meeting that I had missed last night. Instant guilt assailed me, and I promised myself that I would try to get to one tonight if I could find one north of Tylerville. There was no way I would be able to explain my agreement with Tina to Winfield, and especially not in front of Margaret. Besides, Catsy had told me repeatedly to stop explaining myself because I always dug myself into a hole that was impossible to get out of.

I decided to go on a picnic at Sail Rock Park and blend in with all the tourists. I even got a weekend paper to check for more possible job leads, although I had no high expectations of finding anything new. My backpack was crammed with all the paraphernalia that a bird watching geek would need. I had a beauty of a camera with a zoom lens and special attachments for photographing wildlife that I was still learning how to use, my binoculars, snack food, and water. That was just for the hiking part. Then there was the actual picnic supper and dining materials that I placed in a ratty old Styrofoam cooler. Hey, as long as it kept things cold, I didn't care how it looked. You would have thought I was going on a month long safari instead of a day trip.

In order to get to the park you had to go upriver and down the other side. The crossing point was a tall arched bridge that had a miniature Stonehenge along each side. It was unique but kind of spooky. I suppose if you had a boat you could make the trip from Mundy to Sail Rock Park in about fifteen minutes, but by road it took almost an hour. The drive was interesting, and there were some intriguing turnoffs that I salted away for further exploration at another time.

The park overlooking the lighthouse was busy with people of all ages, and dogs of all breeds ran around barking. It wasn't exactly what I had in mind for enjoying nature, but then I might be rushing to judgment. After parking the truck I went over to the information kiosks that described the trails and the possible wildlife one might be lucky enough to see.

One trail that looked particularly promising wound around the headlands of the coast. I'd take that one first and then see about the more wooded trails later. My binoculars went around my neck and I strapped my backpack on, something I rarely did, but I wanted both hands free.

There were a few people on the trail at different intervals but nothing like the crowd in the parking lot. That was nice. I could go at my own pace in semi-privacy. As the trail began to climb and wind there were even fewer hardy souls willing to go the distance. The views of rugged rock formations were magnificent. The striations in the rocks that had been exposed by the ocean waters slamming against them creating thunder holes resembled bold brush strokes of color put down by a powerful artist. The trees at this height and proximity to the coast had been swept and bent as if they were in a forest of carefully sculpted bonsai. Their trunks were driftwood gray and their branches sported tufts of green, while at the base were mounds of moss and lichen in a palette of soft shades of green and red. It was a veritable fairyland.

At one point I stopped to sit on a bench in a clearing and gaze out at the crystal blue water. It was still; even the breeze singing through the trees had stopped. I heard a strange huffing sound every so often. Could it be a person having trouble making the climb? What could I do if it were an emergency? I looked on both sides and didn't see anyone; then I noticed movement in the water in time with the sound. Using my binoculars to scan the horizon, I finally pinpointed the movement. I had actually sighted a group of whales, and they were breaching intermittently causing the sounds I was hearing. This was so exciting. The only time I had seen anything close to this was on one of those nature shows you run across when you're looking for something to watch on TV. I couldn't stop watching them. Seabirds followed above like groupies. I said a little prayer of thanks for Margaret and Winfield's suggestion. This whole place was beautiful and relaxing. I don't know how long I spent watching the whales. There were porpoises, too. I did take time out to eat some gorp and chug some water.

Back on the trail I moved into the woods as I hiked around the head and away from the ocean. I could hear different birds singing in the treetops but spotting them was tricky. There were warblers and a common redpoll. I was trying to see how many different kinds of birds I could identify. While I was watching the whales, I had spotted guillemots and dovekies. They were black and white, but it was their diving, not their plumage, that was fun to watch. The warblers, on the other hand, sounded great but were harder to see, despite their varied colors.

I followed the sounds to give me a starting point. The most prolific were the yellow-rump warblers. I think I spotted a blackburnian warbler. The Audubon Society would have a field day here. Come to think of it, they had discovered this place before I did! Ego again.

By the time I got back to the parking lot, I was famished. I pulled out a blanket, my little cooler, and the weekend paper. I found a picnic tabled nestled in a grove of balsam fir trees that were giving off a marvelous perfume in the midday heat. The bugs hadn't found me yet, but I took precautions and slathered on repellent. Too late I realized that now I would have to find a place to wash my hands, or my wonderful food would taste like poison. There was a water spigot up by the latrines that looked like my best bet.

I don't know what startled me into looking over my shoulder, maybe it was movement or sound. I glimpsed a shape in the afternoon ripples of warm air. At first I didn't pay much attention, but as I went back to my table I felt like I was being watched, and goose bumps started popping up. It was a strange feeling in the middle of a hot summer day.

As I ate my dinner and went through the paper, my senses were on high alert for any sight or sound that might be out of place. I couldn't concentrate on the want ads in this state of mind. This was the cost of picnicking alone. I tried to convince myself that I was being ridiculous and that I should go back to enjoying the day. The sound of a cardinal had helped me change the focus back to birds when I caught sight of the same guy I had seen watching me at the water spigot.

He was hanging off the tailgate of a dark colored truck looking at people milling by him, but his head kept returning to my location. There was something very familiar about that figure, but I couldn't place him. Obviously there was only so much peering through binoculars I could do before I started to look conspicuous. He was lounging around looking out of place, and he didn't seem to be with anyone else at the park. I wondered if I, too, looked out of place because I was by myself.

Let it go, Margaret! But I couldn't. I went back to the paper with no intention of reading it, but as a cover for my surveillance of this person I had fixated on. If he was going to watch me, I was going to watch him. I started to feel silly. Jeff and Hal's words came back to me. I'd promised I was going to stay clear of intrigue. I'd come to enjoy the park, and that was what I was going to do. I picked up all my things and put them back in the truck. The guy made a move, not toward me but toward the cab of his truck. So much for melodrama.

Everything tucked away, I swapped my binoculars for my camera and checked out the trail plaques for my next jaunt. The trail was more wooded but shorter, which was fine because the day was moving on. Who knew? I might be able to get some really neat photos that I could frame for the apartment so it would look like somebody actually lived there.

Between the flora and the fauna I had used up almost a whole roll of film. If they came out, I had a couple of really great shots. It was getting late, and I would need to leave here if I wanted to make the meeting I had found listed. As I crouched down for one last photo of a clump of wildflowers, I was conscious of a shuffling sound. Was it more wildlife? I stared through the bushes in several directions and then caught movement. The trail was full of loops that imitated petals of a flower. From where I was, I could make out someone on the trail on the opposite side of one of those loops. Big deal, there had been people in the park all day, but this was the same guy I had seen by the truck back at the picnic area. Watching him move up the trail, it came to me why he seemed so familiar. It was the lizard man from one of my excursions into the woods, the guy who didn't look like a nature lover. Could this be a coincidence? Maybe I'd misjudged him. Just for the heck of it, I focused the camera and zoomed in for a couple of shots as he went past a clearing. Now I was out of film and getting nervous.

It was definitely time to go. I finished the trail at a trot and went right for my truck. Before I headed out into unknown territory, I had to know if the guy was following me. I didn't want to play another round of bumper trucks. Was I getting paranoid or what? My mind said I was justified, but a little voice added, *but your mind has a miserable track record.* I never claimed to be a bastion of mental health.

I pretended to be reorganizing my things as I watched him emerge from the woods behind me. He made for his truck, but he was definitely watching. I just knew it. *Okay, Margaret what are you going to do now?* There were still plenty of people around. Did I have the guts to confront him? It was either that or run back to the apartment and hide out.

Slinging my backpack over one shoulder, I walked toward his truck. He hadn't gotten into the cab yet. He wasn't moving very fast, but he looked startled and curious as I approached. On closer examination of his face, the lizard aspect was even more pronounced. His eyelids had no lashes to speak of, and they kept opening and closing in a rhythm that was almost hypnotic. His tongue flicked over thin cracked lips as he gave me a leering grin. Oh brother. I couldn't believe I was getting this close to the creep. Here goes, "Do I know you?" That threw him but he recovered. "Naw, but we could get to know each other real fast, babe." Oh gross! He thought I was coming on to him. Now I was the one getting the once over. *Nice going Margaret. How do you plan to extricate yourself from this situation?*

"Sorry, you sort of reminded me of someone. Guess I was wrong. Have a nice day." With that I whipped around and forced myself to walk, not run, back to my truck. I didn't look back, got in and revved up the truck, then spit gravel tearing out of there. My heart was racing, and sweat was pouring down my face. I was keeping an eye in my rearview mirror. I was hoping that if he had been following me I had spooked him, but I was the one acting spooked. In any case, I wouldn't have to make a decision about whether to go to the meeting or home until I got back to the bridge. By then I should know if he was following me.

The ride was tense, but by the time I got to the bridge I hadn't seen hide or hair of him and I could go to the meeting. By the time he got to the bridge, he wouldn't have a clue as to whether I'd turned down toward Mundy or kept going straight.

I probably drove faster than I should have over unfamiliar roads, but it helped relieve the tension, and there was still enough daylight to give me a sense of security. The meeting was well worth the trip, and luckily there was no one I recognized from the other meetings. My ride home was a leisurely one with no rude encounters. I was looking forward to a good night's sleep, and as I tallied the pluses and minuses of the day, they weighed heavily on the plus side. I had a better perspective on things now. Obviously I had been overly anxious about being followed and had gotten an adrenalin rush from worrying about it. I still tended to look for that high even if it was fear based.

Coming into Mundy all seemed quiet, but as I crested the hill at the center of town, I noticed a commotion on Water Street almost in front of Josie's Diner. I couldn't figure out what was going on, but I wasn't about to go driving right into the middle of it. I turned down a side street above the town common that paralleled Water Street to get a better glimpse of the goings-on. The Spiny Urchin was the hub of the activity. The funeral reception must still be in full swing and the drinks had been flowing for quite awhile. My survival instincts were screaming to stay away, but I was bushed and not thinking clearly. I had to get some sleep, and who knew how long this revelry would last. *Think, Margaret, think.*

After driving around town for what seemed like an eternity, I decided to find a secluded spot to park the truck and walk to the back of the apartment, hopefully unobserved. On the third trip down another side street near the mall, I caught sight of the Wash Tub sign and the dark driveway next to the building. Perfect. Even in the daylight it would be obscured from prying eyes. Pulling in was easy. I hugged the side of the building just in case someone else might be thinking of parking there. I could get the truck in the morning or before if things quieted down.

The only thing I'd bring with me was my backpack. I'd leave the rest till I brought the truck back. I realized I had no flashlight. Who knew where it was now after I'd left it in the rocks by Sheila's body? Oh well, I'd just have to make do without it. I knotted my hair up and tucked it under my ball cap, then put on my big ratty hooded sweatshirt over the backpack. It probably made me look like the hunchback of Notre Dame, but it made me feel invisible.

Maneuvering around town with street lights was no problem as long as I stayed out of the direct light. Getting to the back road to the apartment and following it to the stairs was a little trickier. The crowd noises got louder, and I could just make out the tone. It sounded like a lynch mob. The sooner I got off the street the better I'd be. I was stumbling over gravel, through bushes, virtually slinking in search of stairs. Even as I did this, I thought how ludicrous it must look.

I skinned my knees on the way up, but I barely felt it as I fumbled for the door latch. It was dark out, and I hadn't left the porch light on. The windows of the apartment were all wide open with sounds from the street filtering into the stifling hot air. Well here I was standing in the hot darkness. I couldn't turn on the lights; that would defeat the whole purpose of my stealthy journey here. I did turn on the fan to get the air circulating, then slumped down in the rocker out of sight, just sitting, thinking, and listening. I wished they would go back to the bar. Drunken mobs were unpredictable.

No sooner had this thought crossed my mind than I heard the racket outside escalate. What the hell was going on now? I peeked out the window to see if I recognized anyone. The street lights worked in my favor. I didn't see anyone I knew at first, but as I kept staring and listening to what was being said, it dawned on me that Howie Jones was down there and so was Wayne. From their stance I could finally make them out. Howie obviously was distraught over his sister's death, and it looked like the crowd was willing and ready to commiserate with him to justify their behavior. Enough of this shit! The picture of Sheila on the beach was seared into my mind and I had no patience or tolerance. The emotional roller coaster ride that went with finding a body had left me with a need to do something.

I walked over to the phone, turned on the light and started to punch in 911. Shit! There was no 911; when was I going to remember that? Great! Now what? I looked through the phone book. I hadn't written down any emergency numbers in the front like they suggest you do. It wasn't one of those things you really think about unless you're obsessive compulsive or something. Rage and frustration were creeping up my spine, and I wanted to scream. Fine, I'd call the

Sheriff's Department, so I punched in that number. They picked up on the second ring. In as calm a voice as I could muster I explained what was happening outside my window. It was after ten pm so it qualified as disturbing the peace. Could they send someone out before it escalated to property damage? The dispatcher assured me that a deputy would be right there and wanted to know my name and address. I wasn't sure how ready I was to part with that information. My silence elicited a "Ma'am, are you still there? I need your name and address please." What could I do, hang up and have them think it was a crank call or give them my name? I pulled out my medallion and flipped it. Heads I had to give them my name. That got me a relieved thank you, and I hung up.

My need to know prevented me from going to bed. I turned out the light and went back to my rocker to wait for the police. The sounds and the group down below ebbed and flowed with spurts of loud cries. I tried to sit back and look at this objectively as a third party. I wasn't very successful. At last a cruiser came slowly down the street flicked on the blue lights and chirped its siren. The rowdies got back on the sidewalk and started to meander down towards the Spiny Urchin, all accept Howie and Wayne who tagged behind. They went to the patrol car window and had a nice chat with the deputy on duty. After some finger pointing, the cruiser's spotlight went on and swiveled to illuminate the diner. I wondered what that was all about. I had no idea how long the police would be there, but I knew I needed to hit the sack. I was not getting up early tomorrow unless the place was on fire.

Chapter Fifteen

I slept like a log. The tension and lack of sleep had finally caught up with me, and only noises from the street and bright sunlight streaming in my bedroom window had roused me from my slumber. My clock said it was nine am. I hadn't slept this late in years and it was difficult to wake up. I needed caffeine, the sooner the better. I pulled my sticky t-shirt down, slid into my mules, and headed out to the kitchen to put on a pot of coffee. While I waited for that, I gulped down water and orange juice. I was so parched, I would have thought I'd gone on a bender last night.

I was startled when the phone rang. I couldn't get use to the rude interruption of incoming calls. I hope it's not Tina with more problems. "Hello?" I could barely get out a croak.

"Oh, Maggie, did I wake you? Are you okay? You sound funny." I didn't feel funny, and I wasn't up to twenty questions just yet, even from Josie.

I cleared my throat and tried again. "Hi Josie, I just woke up. What's up?"

"There was a little trouble here last night. What time did you get in? I didn't see your truck."

Oh shit, I had forgotten all about leaving the truck next to the Wash Tub. "Josie, where are you calling from?" I was trying to get my bearings.

"I'm down here in the diner. I didn't want to disturb you if you had company."

"What are you talking about?"

"Have you seen the diner this morning?" One of us wasn't making any sense and at this moment, I wasn't sure which of us it was.

"Josie, I'm not awake, and I'm really confused. Who in the world do you think would be up here at this hour? No, don't answer that. I don't want to know. What's this about the diner? You're not open today are you? I thought you were closed on Sunday."

"We are, but the sheriff's office gave us a call because of the vandalism."

I was suddenly awake. "Can you hold on? Are you going to be downstairs for awhile?"

"Oh yeah, we'll probably be here the whole morning."

"Let me jump in the shower and grab some coffee and I'll be right down." We hung up, and my adrenaline was taking the place of the coffee I needed to pull my mind together. I poured a cup and took a few sips as I hit the shower. I can be fast when I have to be. Except for a mop of wet hair I was dressed and on the move in a matter of minutes.

As I rounded the corner of the diner my whole body felt like it had been slammed over the edge of an abyss. There scrawled across the front of the diner was **MURDRING MURPHY MAGGOT!** The red spray paint stood out in stark contrast to the meticulously painted white clapboard front of the diner. Dwight was on his knees with a drop cloth and bucket of paint preparing to cover the grotesque message. I could barely breathe. It was like a ton of bricks was sitting on my chest. Josie came barreling out of the diner as I burst into tears.

I couldn't begin to talk, let alone try and explain how I was feeling, but there was more to that message than simple poor spelling and vandalism. It was personal. Josie had her arm around my shoulder ushering me into the diner. I don't know whether Dwight even acknowledged my presence, which compounded the guilt I was feeling.

"Josie I'm so very sorry about all this, really I am."

"Maggie, you don't have anything to be sorry about unless you did the paint job, which I highly doubt."

"But if I wasn't here this wouldn't have happened."

"Don't be silly. If it's not one thing it's another around here. It keeps life interesting and gives people something to talk about in their dreary little lives."

"I feel so bad with Dwight out there painting on a Sunday, his only day off. The least I can do is help."

"Don't you dare! Now you're making *me* feel guilty. Dwight can handle a little painting; besides this way he gets to do some socializing. You just wait. There'll be all kinds of sidewalk supervisors here this morning. Remember, we're from the City. This kinda brings back fond memories of home."

"Oh, Josie, you've got to be kidding. Thanks for trying to cheer me up, though. I wonder when they did it. That must have been what the spotlight was on."

"Look, while Dwight is out socializing, you need to catch me up on a few things. Like for instance, what spotlight and where's your truck?" She made coffee, and we sat in the back while I told her about my day and even about lizard lids following me. I ended with my trying to call 911, only to be reminded that there wasn't any and having to resort to calling the Sheriff's Department. I didn't leave out the characters in the street scene below my window, Howie and Wayne.

We broke into girl talk and laughing as Josie pointed to the outside where a small crowd had gathered. We went out to join Dwight's entourage. He had covered the words with a coat of paint but they were still painfully visible.

I saw Terry Murphy, Kenny's youngest from the hardware store, come loping down the street. "Morons!" Terry was in a tear. Her outburst surprised me. She was taking this almost as personally as I was. "I see the Jones gang must have been shit-faced last night. They're incredible morons. How Howie stays on as deputy sheriff beats the hell out of me. Don't let this bother you, Margaret. In this town it's every opportunity to keep the Murphy curse going. It rates right up there with Murphy's Law." Her scowl had changed to a wicked grin. She was a girl after my own heart. We chatted awhile about things in general, but she wouldn't say anything more about the curse part that intrigued me. She gave me a personal evaluation of the male species in town that didn't include much high praise and seemed terribly cynical for someone her age. I wonder if that's the way I'd come across when I was younger. I had the experience now to back up my opinions, but did she? Winfield had arrived and was tsk, tsking and shaking his head at the goings-on as he conversed with Dwight and Josie. Even Robby showed up with wide eyes and his mouth agape to check it out.

With all this hoorah, it dawned on me that I hadn't eaten anything and that I had no plans for the day. As far as I could tell, most places were closed. There wasn't much retail business to begin with, but you really felt the pinch on Sunday. Oh lord, I had forgotten about my truck again. I had the odd sensation of waking from a drunk dream or just coming to after a night out and wondering where I was and how I'd gotten there. Then there was the spying out the window to see if my truck was in the dooryard and racking my brains to remember what I had done the night before. I didn't want to go there again.

I asked Dwight if there was anything I could do. He said not to worry, he'd get it taken care of. I said hello to Winfield, then told Josie I was going upstairs to grab a bite to eat and then get the truck. She invited me for dinner at six at her place, and I said it sounded great.

The truck was right where I had left it, unmolested. Since it was my day off, I had time on my hands with no clue what to do with it. Six o'clock was a ways away. There had been a few more positions in the paper that I could kill time preparing packets for so I could drop them in the mail on Monday. One of the positions opening up was right here in Mundy, but in my travels I hadn't seen any schools in town. I would have to ask Josie where it was and maybe get some more background on the town and its school system. I was compiling quite a list of questions.

I debated with myself about whether I should bother to apply for a position in Mundy. The first rule of teaching that I picked up was, never live in the same town you teach in. There were a number of good reasons for that, and all appeared to apply in my case. First, it was hard to ever actually leave work, because—and this was especially true in a small town—you were always running into students or parents who latched onto you so you could solve a problem or continue with an issue from the school day. Second, it was difficult to maintain any privacy, which was a big thing for me. And third, going along with lack of privacy, were the entanglements with other people's problems that I would invariably get drawn into. My Alaskan experience brought the dangers of that home to me really quickly. Just look at the mess I was in now, and I wasn't even teaching.

It was bizarre that I would seriously contemplate staying here after all that had happened in two short weeks, but I had formed an attachment to the place. Maybe it was the story of my life, always love/hate relationships with people and places. It could just be a matter of inertia. I was here, and I was too lazy to move on. Fate might take that decision out of my hands. I'd just have to wait and see while practicing that dreaded virtue of patience.

My job seeking duties completed, I was looking at the rest of the afternoon. I decided to do what I always did when I wanted to clear my head: go for a walk. A leisurely walk around town and down by the river took care of it. My stomach let me know that the little bit of brunch I had crammed down wasn't cutting it. I didn't want to show up at Josie's house famished and make a pig of myself. The Icebox was open, so I strolled over to peruse the menu. A crab roll, onion rings, and a chocolate milkshake sounded good so I placed my order and went to scout out a comfy lawn chair down by the water. I pulled out my binoculars and scanned the harbor. There were people milling around, seagulls foraging the grass for dropped food, and children playing tag or hide and seek. My thoughts went back to the Fourth and Hal. Wouldn't it be nice if he happened along and we could laze away the afternoon? But he was probably working, and I had no desire to see a uniform right now, no matter what kind of a hunk was in it.

My order was up. The seagulls acted like dive bombers as they circled me on my way back to devour my afternoon snack. They were aggressive feathered rats, which was our nickname for them in Southern Maine. I was hungry so I wasn't about to share. I savored every morsel and didn't feel sorry about not tossing them so much as a ring.

At this moment I couldn't think of a thing I needed. I was carefree sauntering back to the apartment. There were cars passing by as they circled the town out for a Sunday drive, mostly older couples but some younger groups stuffed in cars looking for something happening or killing time until the evening.

I was so caught up in this time to myself that I didn't think twice about walking past the Spiny Urchin Bar and Grill which happened to be open on this lovely day. I had no desire to go inside and have a drink. The compulsion to get wasted wasn't there, and I was very grateful for that. I was taken totally by surprise in my own little world when someone called out "If it isn't that Murphy Slut." I swung around to see Wayne McCarthy propped up against the Urchin's door jam. The dark cavernous interior behind him echoed with the click of billiard balls and an indeterminate kind of music. The smell of stale beer assaulted my nose.

Wayne was plastered. Blurry bloodshot eyes stared out from dark sunken eye sockets. There wasn't much to him but blotchy skin and bones. He looked as though he had aged ten years in the little time since I first met him out at Charlie's. He didn't flinch when I stared back at him, and his eyes didn't move from mine. It was like he was possessed. "Why don't you get out of town before you get anyone else killed? You Murphys are killers—always will be—and you get away with it, but not this time."

For someone looking as crazed as he did, he was managing to speak his mind loud and clear, not that it made much sense. I was dumbfounded. I wanted to say something, a biting retort that would slap him down, but he looked so miserable and pathetic that I couldn't find the words. I couldn't even ask a question about why he had such a personal vendetta against me just because my last name was Murphy. He seemed to get along with Kenny. It was this name game all over again, and I still didn't know how to play.

I pivoted and walked away and, believe me, that was one of the hardest things for me to do. There was something buried in this town that was beginning to stink. Someone had to have some answers, and I wanted them. Maybe Josie and Dwight could shed some light on the subject.

Josie and Dwight lived in an old colonial place that was in a state of ongoing renovation. The wallpaper layers had been peeled off the walls, and the woodwork had been stripped and sanded around all the doors and baseboards. The kitchen area held a huge old wood stove that was spotless, but I wouldn't have a clue how to use it. Dwight told me it was more for looks than everyday use, but when the power went out it was heavenly because you could cook, bake, and heat the house all at the same time, and it would smell some good. What used to be the original pantry now housed apartment-sized modern appliances. Since they were city folks, it was hard to picture them doing the rustic routine. In a corner of one of the front rooms, which all had fireplaces, Josie had collected swatches of fabric and wallpaper and pieces of wall board with paint samples all over them. "When I go into the city I load up," she commented as I took in the decorating supplies. "I don't get as many chances to get away as I'd like, but come winter we'll be closed from after Thanksgiving until March, and that's when I'll be able to do more. It's a work in progress." As she waved her arms to encompass the house, her giant earrings glinted in the light of a chandelier that looked incongruous in the current state of upheaval of the room.

At dinner Dwight regaled us with the local gossip. Most of it went over my head because I didn't know most of the people he and Josie were talking about, but I nodded politely. It did give me an opening to ask about the Murphys, their position in the general scheme of the town, and the so-called curse.

"That's ancient history, and we don't know exactly what the basis for it is, but the Murphys still retain a strong influence on the community, and there is the assumption that at least Margaret is loaded, but most of that may be her husband's money. I guess the Murphys are considered one of the founding families of Mundy."

"Yeah, that old adage, 'the sins of the fathers,' is taken literally here."

"Well, what are some of those sins?"

"Dear, that would be something you'd have to take up with one of the locals like Winfield."

"Maggie, don't you go getting drawn into some of the lunacy of this place. The location is beautiful but some of the inhabitants act like they would be right at home in the Bronx Zoo."

"Dwight, you are such a card." It was clear that out-of-staters were not the people you wanted to ask about old gossip, but as taxpayers, they might have some sense of the school system, so I decided to take a different tack. "What can you two tell me about Mundy's school system?"

"Now there's a hot bed of intrigue! You don't want anything to do with the school board. They're robbing us blind hiring all their relatives. It's like their personal employment agency." Josie was giving Dwight a warning scowl. "Now I'm not saying they don't have some good programs and good teachers, but it isn't because of the school board. They wouldn't know a qualified person if they got a pronouncement from the president."

I was taken back by Dwight's vociferousness. I don't think I had heard him say so much in such seriousness in all the time I had known him—granted that hadn't been all that long. I must have hit a nerve—or was it a hornet's nest?

"Oh, that situation has calmed down somewhat, Dwight. You're going to scare Maggie. Are you planning on applying for a position over at the school?"

"There's an opening that I'm qualified for." When I said this, I looked at Dwight. "It might not be a good idea with what's been going on and what you were saying, Dwight."

"Oh don't pay any attention to him. See, I told you you'd scare her. That's in the past, and it's just a lot of political mumbo-jumbo. Besides, we have a new superintendent, and the high school principal seems like a nice man. I'd go for it, and you wouldn't have to move."

"It's probably a moot point, since I'm 'from away.' I guess I won't know unless I try." I picked up a lot of scuttlebutt, and once Dwight had gotten over the school thing, he was his old self. I was still apologizing profusely about the vandalism done to the diner as if it were my fault, then it was Josie's turn to tell us to move on, life was too short. I had a great time, and I was determined to find out what secrets Mundy residents were holding onto so tightly.

Chapter Sixteen

At work, I zeroed in on Winfield when he came in. "Winfield, I need to talk with someone, and I think you could help."

"Now Margaret, you know it's best for the women to be with the women and men with the men."

"No, Winfield. This isn't about the program or sobriety. It's about Mundy and the Murphys."

"Oh well, then you best talk to Margaret; she's the historian and a Murphy."

"That's exactly why I can't talk to her. She's too close, and I get the impression that there are things she'd rather not talk about, especially to me. You two are friends, so I thought it might be easier to talk to you, and Josie says you know all the stuff that goes on around here."

"She does, does she? Does this have anything to do with the paint job yesterday?"

"It might. I'm not sure, but I have some questions that have come up and situations that are really confusing me. Would you have time this afternoon to get together?"

"I like to have an afternoon ice cream down at the Icebox. It's something I do for myself. If it meets with your approval, we could talk down there, say one o'clock?"

"Great. You're a love, Winfield. I'll even treat you to that ice cream."

I got back to work, but I felt lighter. It would be great to sit and pick Winfield's brain, and I was sure the conversation would get around to the program, but that was okay too.

The next person in my sights was going to be Hal. He'd better come in today. I had a few things to say about his buddies, and I also wanted to tell him about being followed. Maybe he'd have some ideas about what to do.

When Hal walked through the door of the diner, it was just like the first time I'd seen him in daylight. I wanted him, but at the same time I was irritated with him. Maybe that was because I wasn't getting the kind of attention I wanted from him. I started to doubt my motives. Did I dream up this stuff just to have something to talk to him about?

Here I was, dying to talk with him, and I could barely put down his coffee without spilling it. The heat was rising in my face, a dead give away that I was excited about something. Let's hope he couldn't figure out what. As I tried to get my mouth set in the right gear, Hal started the conversation.

"How's it going with your friend? Is she taking the suggestions?" That threw me off track. I hadn't even thought about Tina and her problems. It took me a moment to think about who and what he was talking about. How soon I had forgotten and gotten tied up in my own little world.

"I guess everything is alright for now. I passed on your advice, but I haven't really been in touch; besides I don't know if anything could be done over the weekend anyway."

"A person can get into a lot of trouble over a weekend."

I didn't know how to take that comment, especially considering the weekend I'd had, but I was going to stay calm. "Speaking of trouble and weekends, I have a bone to pick with you about your friends." One good jab deserves another. I just couldn't keep from getting in the ring with this guy.

That look like 'I haven't the foggiest idea what you're talking about,' came into those deep brown eyes as his long lashes dipped over them. Geez, he was making it extremely difficult for me to keep from dissolving into a puddle right here on the spot. "I'm sure you heard or saw what happened to the front of the diner Saturday night. Howard Jones and Wayne McCarthy were part of the group responsible for it."

"You witnessed them painting the front of the building?"

"Noooo, but they were in the street with the rest of the hoodlums."

"I read the report. They were trying to break up the crowd." Oh puleeease, I was there. "Do you always go around accusing people you hardly know? And what is it with you and Wayne McCarthy?"

Both of our voices had gone up a notch, and I was suddenly conscious of customers beginning to look in our direction. In a whisper I said, "Wayne threatened me yesterday outside the Spiny Urchin, and some guy has been following me even out to Sail Rock Park."

Now he was hunched over looking up at me. "Are you serious or just seriously paranoid?"

"I'm serious, and I'm not paranoid, just seriously scared."

"I'd like to help, but you keep pushing me away. It would work a lot better if you would trust me, Margaret. What do you want me to do?"

"Don't be condescending. If you think I'm some sort of a nut, fine."

"I don't think you're some kind of a nut, and I am taking you seriously, but I still don't know what you expect me to do."

"I'm sorry, Hal. I don't know what I expect you to do either. I seem to be caught in a nightmare, and I just want to wakeup."

"I can think of a number of ways I could help you wake up." There was something salacious about that comment.

"It's really strange, like everyone wants to get rid of me, and I just got here."

"Hmm…I thought you were trying to get rid of *me*." Now he was grinning. At that moment Josie broke in, "If you two love birds have so much to talk about, why don't you go out on a date? We've got customers to deal with right now." I knew I was blushing, but was that a little color in Hal's cheeks as well?

"You want to get together tonight?"

I hesitated. I was meeting with Winfield, but that was this afternoon, and I wasn't planning on going to a meeting, although I was sure Winfield would bring that up. A little male company for the evening would be a pleasant change. What the hell, why was I stalling? It was what I really wanted wasn't it?

"You know, Hal that sounds good to me."

"I get off work at four and I can swing by about five thirty. Would you be offended if I took you to dinner somewhere?"

"I think I could handle that. I'll try to be on my best behavior."

"This I've got to see."

"Don't start!"

He had to get back to work and so did I. Maybe he took off before I had time to change my mind. I don't know, but I did know that I owed Josie an apology. "I apologize for goofing off on the job, Josie. It won't happen again."

"Did you two make a date or what?"

"I'm not sure how it will work out, but I think you could safely say we made a date. He wants to take me out to dinner."

"It's about time you two moved on. You go and have a good time tonight and leave the past in the past."

"Yes ma'am!"

The day had gone quickly. Shirley was back to her normal schedule of tardiness, which didn't give me much time to get cleaned up before meeting Winfield. I was panting when I jogged up to Winfield sitting at a picnic table near the order window. I'd have to start getting in shape. I had slacked off and was feeling it.

"Glad you could make it. It's not every day I get treated to an ice cream by a pretty young lady."

"Let's order and find a more comfortable place to sit." I wanted some privacy. We placed our orders. I'm a sucker for soft-serve, so I ordered a large chocolate cone that I could get my tongue around. Winfield ordered a small dish of vanilla. I told him I'd spring for a sundae but he said a dish of vanilla was his limit. We laughed.

"What was so special that you needed me for answers?"

"There are so many comments, innuendos, and things like the paint job on the diner, and things Wayne said yesterday and Terry Murphy said, and they're all piling up and driving me crazy."

"Slow down, dear, you'll run out of breath. Can you give me something a bit more specific to work with?"

I told him about Wayne's comments about getting out of town before anyone else got killed and how Murphys were killers who got away with it. I told him about Terry mentioning something about a Murphy curse.

"I see." He rubbed his arthritically gnarled hand over his stubble-laden chin and looked right into my eyes. "I'll tell you the story of the Murphys. It goes back to when Margaret was only eleven or twelve.

Actually the envy went even deeper, but that's really ancient history. You have to understand that the Murphys were very powerful people in Mundy. Margaret's father, John, had a finger in almost every pie. He was in banking and owned fish packing plants that his grandfather had started. That meant he had an impact on almost everyone's life in one way or another.

It was in June and the school children and their families all went out to Bolton Lake for an end of the year picnic. It was a tradition. John owned a hunting camp on the lake and a boat. It was there that the accident happened. Back in those days, people had large families, and the Joneses and McCarthys each had a sizable brood, mostly boys. They were rambunctious as boys often are. During one of the boat rides later in the day, a group of boys decided to swim out to the boat as it puttered around the lake. There would have been no harm done, but the boys decided to try and climb aboard the boat, which was already packed with children, mostly girls.

"That's when tragedy struck. The boat capsized, spilling out everyone. The children were all ages, and they didn't all know how to swim. The ones that could swim made it back to shore. By the time people on the beach realized there was a problem, it was too late. Some of the men and older boys, including Thomas, swam out to try and rescue the children. John had been hit on the head when the boat went over but he managed to pull one little girl to shore. Margaret was on the beach and saw all of it.

"Six children died that day, among them one of the Jones girls and two of the McCarthy boys. You can imagine the devastation to the whole community, especially considering how tightly knit they were. It was ruled an accident, but that didn't sit well with the families who lost children."

"Who were the boys who caused the accident?"

"Well, there's the rub. It made it even more difficult for the Jones and McCarthys to accept. Their own boys had been part of the group that caused the trouble. They couldn't blame the boys, so they turned on the one prominent figure that they envied to begin with, John Murphy."

"Was it because he had taken the kids out without life jackets?"

"Oh no, there was no big to-do over things like that back then. No, they said John had been drinking and it was because he was drunk that the boat capsized."

"But that makes no sense. If he was drunk, why would people let their children go with him in the first place?"

"Remember he was a powerful man, and he was known to be a hard drinker, but the police cleared him of any wrongdoing. Of course, there was always talk about him using his influence to get things hushed up. The whole thing left a deep scar on Mundy that John could never live down. They aren't very forgiving here, as you have found out. Margaret knew what the sentiment would be like when a Murphy and a dead Jones girl were put together. She was trying to protect you and that's why she didn't want you going to Sheila's funeral. It would have opened old wounds."

"Hold on, Winfield. All this happened, what, fifty years ago or more? Are you telling me that somehow the Joneses and McCarthys are still holding a grudge and I'm guilty because my last name is Murphy?"

"In a way, yes. You see, everybody is related around here by blood or marriage, and people—maybe because they lead sheltered lives or because there is nothing in their lives to talk about—hold on to those gruesome events. They build on them, and it makes for a rotten foundation. Margaret, in case you haven't noticed, there are also a lot of drunks around here and only a few in recovery. You know what that life is like."

"All right, maybe I can buy some of this, but it doesn't explain the curse bit that Terry talked about."

"Terry's father, Kenny, might be considered the first victim of that curse."

"You mean something besides being an alcoholic? I considered that quite a curse near the end of my drinking and the beginning of sobriety. I always hated it when people would introduce themselves as grateful alcoholics."

"Don't you mean grateful recovering alcoholics? I hope you have a different outlook on that now. But that's not what I'm talking about. Mary, Margaret's mother was pregnant with Kenny and was due in September but it didn't work out that way. He was born shortly after the accident. He was premature and was always a sickly child. You've noticed how he walks? That was some kind of problem he's had since maybe birth. Mary was getting on in years and having another child would have been hard enough, but the accident just made it that much more difficult."

"I have to admit it's hard to believe that Kenny is so much younger than Margaret."

"Let's just say that the Murphy family, at least the males, didn't fare so well in the next couple of years. The sins of the father seemed to have been visited on his sons or so the story goes." It was surprising to hear that analogy from Winfield after hearing it from the Waylands.

"I feel like I've stepped back in time or into the Twilight Zone. Can you tell me more about Margaret's family, her brothers? What were these sins of the father anyway?"

"I'd rather not say. If you two want to get together and talk about it, that's one thing. It's not my place to go into all that. I try not to indulge in gossip or criticism to the best of my ability. It's how I practice the principles in my life. I will tell you one thing, if the old newspapers are still up in your apartment, the ones on the accident are probably there. They can tell you the official story."

"I appreciate that, Winfield. I hope you don't mind me saying you've got some pretty sick cookies around here."

I had enjoyed our conversation and said I'd probably see him at the meeting tomorrow night. I told him about the meeting I had gone to on Saturday and he said it was a good group but a little further than he felt comfortable traveling at his age. Because of poor eyesight, he didn't like driving at night anymore.

The information about the newspapers was tantalizing. Now I wished I hadn't made a date with Hal. I could be spending the evening going through old newspapers. *Right! Get a grip. Date with a scrumptious guy or alone with a bundle of moldy old newspapers? That was a no-brainer!*

Back at the apartment as I tried to figure out what to wear, I found myself muttering to Dad. "The Murphys in this place are as screwed up as we are, Dad. You'd be proud of me, I've got a real live date and he's not a drunk or a druggie. Can you believe it? He's a cop. Go figure."

Here I was, a grown woman trying to please her dead father. Maybe I was more screwed up than the Murphys I had met here.

I knew I needed to talk with Catsy. She'd warned me about trying to live up to someone else's expectations. It's a no win, big losing situation. "Please God I just want to have a normal good time."

I had just gotten out more stuff from Dad's filing cabinet when Hal showed up at my door. I jumped up, left everything where it was, and grabbed my backpack.

Some girls think uniforms are sexy but Hal looked more luscious in civvies and more obtainable. Yum!

Hal was smiling and then he looked down at the backpack. "Do you always carry that thing with you? I thought we might travel light tonight. There's this nice place up by Bolton Lake I thought we could go to, but it's not an overnight trip."

I couldn't believe it. We hadn't even gotten out the door and already I was riled. *Count to ten and don't be so oversensitive. Remember this is supposed to be a date and fun.* I know I was blushing but I tried to laugh it off by pulling out my wallet and leaving the backpack on the kitchen table. I felt naked without it. Imagine a grown woman with a security blanket in the form of a backpack.

Hal had a pickup just like everybody else in town. It looked brand new with an extended cab that was quite roomy, and the truck rode like a luxury car. The color was a bright cranberry that I could fall in love with. I asked Hal about it, and he said it was a Chevy Colorado, which started us talking about places we'd been or wanted to go. So far, so good.

Hal told me that the Fin, Fur, and Feather Lodge used to be a hunting camp that slowly morphed into a place where people from away could come and do their Downeast thing and have a base for dinners with the appropriate atmosphere. The lodge was a giant log mansion. The restaurant had cathedral ceilings and a big stone fireplace. The décor was pure L.L.Bean with hunting camp paraphernalia and trophies. It was a taxidermist's dream. I wondered who had decorated first, Beans or the lodge. Fishing gear, hunting gear, even a canoe in the rafters reminded me even more of the Maine retailer. The fireplace sported the cliché moose head with a huge rack of antlers. Wherever a bare spot might have been, there was a hide of some kind or an animal's head to cover it up.

I could imagine this place as a ski lodge and wonderfully cozy in the winter with the fireplace crackling. There was no fire at this time of the year, but you could still smell that campfire aroma in the warm humid air. The clientele, mostly tourists, were getting lobster dinners. Hal and I slid into a wooden booth next to a small nine pane window.

As we waited for a waitress, I took in all the sights. "Do you come here often?"

"Once in a while it's nice to get out of town."

Hal ordered a steak, rare, and a glass of beer. As an afterthought, he asked if I minded. The only thing I minded was having him say something in front of the waitress. I said "no problem" and ordered fish and chips with iced tea. The food was good, and we continued our talk about places other than Mundy or Tyler County. Then I asked Hal about his plans for the future.

"Actually, I'm getting ready to move on. I don't intend to stick around here too much longer. There isn't much here, and I have bigger plans in mind then being a sheriff's deputy for the rest of my life. California or Colorado sound like good places to start."

"So look who's going west. You better be careful or you'll become a real cowboy." That probably wasn't the smartest crack to make, and I wanted to bite my tongue after I made it.

"I suppose you used to live out there."

I wasn't ready to have the focus on my past, so I neatly switched the subject. "I'm sure it's different growing up in Mundy. What was that like?" He answered my questions with minimal enthusiasm and a quizzical expression. Hal was as noncommittal about sharing his past as I was about sharing mine, so I switched the topic to Hal's job. I knew he probably dealt with stuff I was all too familiar with, plus I thought it would be a good way to show him how interested I was in him.

At one point in the dinner, Hal put his hand over mine and fixed me with those penetrating brown eyes. I felt a tingle run up my arm and down my spine. Perhaps it had worked; at least I was beginning to loosen up. The moment was broken when the waitress came by to see if we would like anything else. Hal ordered another beer and I ordered another iced tea, only this time I didn't want it to drink but to hold onto. I recognized the signs and knew it was time to stop the stampede of my emotions, something easier said than done.

Like an idiot, I was beginning to panic. I wasn't sure what kind of commitment I had made with this date. My mind was saying one thing and my body was saying the opposite. After dinner we were trying to decide what to do next. There isn't a heck of a lot to do in Tyler County, as Hal had already pointed out. "My place is just up the road. Do you want to grab a movie and go back there? It's still early." That seemed like a dangerous place to go in my state of mind. My body was saying, hell, who needs a movie? Let's just get down to it. We were standing outside with the sun setting over the lake. The air was still, and I could just make out the scampering and rustling of the nocturnal animal life. Could Hal hear my heart beating in my chest?

"Do you know where the old Murphy hunting camp is?"

There was a strange look in his eyes. I suddenly wished I could read people's minds. "Where did you hear about that?"

"Oh, I have my sources. Call it morbid curiosity, but I'd like to check it out." "It's way back in the woods, and the roads aren't that great. I don't think anyone has been out there in years. I don't think I could even find it in the dark. You sure you wouldn't rather come back to my place?"

He was certainly saying no in a lot of ways. "The offer sounds all too tempting, but I start work a couple of hours before you, so I guess I'd better take a rain check. Tell me, would there be time to go to the public beach on this lake?"

"You're just full of strange requests."

"I know, but could you just humor me?"

Hal drove halfway around the lake until we came to an open area with some picnic tables and those old fashion pole grills. There was a small broken-down dock sticking out into the water that, together with the orange and purples of the sky, gave a jack-o'lantern smile to the flat surface of the lake. Both of us had been quiet for the ride. The view was so peaceful that it was difficult to fathom that a tragedy had taken place here. I thought of Josie's warning to leave the past in the past, even if she was referring to my dealings with Hal, but I just couldn't let it go.

"What's going through that pretty little mind of yours?" We had moved close and Hal's arm had come off the steering wheel and was resting on my shoulders. It felt warm and electrifying. I moved closer. "Oh, I was thinking how sad it is that such a beautiful spot should be surrounded with sad memories."

"Where is your head? I thought you were a stranger here, and then you come up with that."

"My job requires doing research, something I really enjoy." It was probably a cop-out. The ancient past always seemed safer to me.

"Oh yeah, which job is that?"

"Teaching, silly. I'm hoping to find a job up here, and it helps to know some of the background of the place. I'm also trying to understand some of the attitudes of those people you think I judge too fast." There was just a slight tensing in his body. Darn it, I did it again.

"Right now I'm enjoying good company and digesting a great meal." Hal smiled down at me, put his other arm around me and drew me close. In a soft voice he said, "I would have preferred great company and a good meal, but I'll take the compliment." At that moment he kissed me, and I wanted to disappear right into him. His firm lips enveloped mine, and the muscles in his chest and arms were a welcome protection. I wanted him inside me so desperately. It had been a very long time. Every nerve in my body was screaming as his fingers caressed my arms and moved up my thighs. What was I doing? Here we were in the front seat of a truck, acting like a couple of teenagers in Lover's Lane. I throbbed to his touch as he explored my body and his rose in reply. I was whimpering like a child, ready to come at any moment. Where was my resolve?

Hal gently pulled away. "Margaret, I don't want to rush you." I almost choked like someone who has been dying of thirst and has been given a bottle of water, only to have it jerked from her grasp. Ugh! Once the torch is lit, it isn't that easy to snuff out. He was in control and I was not. A strangled "thank you" was all I could muster.

"It's getting late. We'd better be getting you back. Morning will be here before you know it." Damn, why did I have to mention getting up early? I felt like a schoolgirl with a curfew.

The drive home was another quiet one as I wrestled with my emotions in an unsuccessful attempt to gain control. I was horny and let down, and that was an understatement. The little talking we did was soft, and there was a growing sense of anticipation on my part that I just might start to have a life again. At the door, he held me in his arms and gave me a parting kiss that I didn't want to end. It sent me floating into the apartment with sweet dreams. Yes indeed!

Chapter Seventeen

Josie scrutinized me with a penetrating stare and danced all over the place in an attempt to find out how the date went. I was having fun torturing her. "I can't stand it any more. Aren't you going to tell me how it went?"

"It gets mixed reviews. We had a great meal at the Fin, Fur and Feather. That place is wild with all the stuff everywhere."

"I'm not interested in where you ate. How did it go?" Josie wanted all the juicy details, but I was still savoring them since they were all I had with perhaps a promise of more to come...hopefully. "Let's just say we didn't kill each other, we parted on a good note, and I wouldn't mind seeing him again—soon."

Josie didn't know whether to be ecstatic or irritated, because it was obviously not a detailed enough accounting to satisfy her need to know. "You are a tease. You're not going to give any more than those meager crumbs?"

"Nope."

I'm sure my face lit up when Hal walked in. I had made some apple pie muffins and was waiting for the real apple pies to cool.

"Good morning, Margaret. I smell something absolutely mouthwatering. It smells suspiciously like apple pie."

"I made some apple pies but they're not ready yet. I have the next best thing though, apple pie muffins."

"That sounds great. Why don't you bring me two?" I hustled over the muffins and dutifully waited for his reaction. "You weren't kidding about these being the next best thing. They're one of your creations, aren't they?" I blushed at the compliment but it didn't bother me a bit. I needed to cook more often. I could get used to compliments, especially coming from him. "What are you doing tonight? I thought we could get together." My spirits fell. I had promised Winfield I'd be at the meeting and I didn't exactly want to blurt that out.

Hal was looking confused over my silence. I had to say something but not a lie. "I already have plans for tonight."

"Well you take care of yourself and we'll get together some other time." I felt like I was being dismissed, but I didn't want to leave it on a sour note. "Thanks Hal, I'd really like that."

At that moment, I hated being a sober alcoholic, which was totally insane thinking. I needed to get a hold of myself and change my attitude. This guy was not healthy to be with if I was so willing to throw everything away just to get laid. The rest of the morning crawled by. I had decided to try and get in touch with Catsy for a reality check after work. I didn't want to contemplate the idea that I had traded one obsession for another.

I took my time with a leisurely lunch before I gave Catsy a call. Once we connected, she could tell by the sound of my voice that something was up. "I'm not here to give you advice, but I will share my experiences and observations." With that I had a quick 'this is your life' lecture about my past relationships and discerning between lust or physical need and an actual relationship with another person. "What can you bring to a relationship when you haven't buried your father yet?"

That really hurt. What did she mean I hadn't buried my father? Didn't I handle all that and then moved as far away as I could? But she was right. He was still with me and I was even still talking to him. It was a wrenching conversation with Catsy that lasted over an hour. I didn't even want to think about the phone bill I'd get slammed with, but Catsy was my lifeline to sanity right now, a friendship I could count on. Her parting words were again a suggestion that I try out a cat for companionship, and if I could handle that, I just might be able to handle having a man in my life.

After the phone call, I thought I'd better check in with Tina and Joanne to see how they were doing. Miracles of miracles, I got ahold of them both. They were having coffee at Joanne's and regaled me with the meetings they had found south of Tylerville. It had done them good to get away from their old stomping grounds. They were both in good spirits, and once again I was jealous that they had each other and were having so much fun experiencing new people and different types of meetings.

The afternoon was just about over, and I had some grocery shopping to do for the diner and for myself. I also needed to check the mail, although I didn't relish the prospect of rejection letters from places I had applied to, but Catsy's talk had given me some small courage to go and do what needed to be done. Procrastination was another of the character traits that I was working on. I grabbed my backpack and went down to the post office on my way to the grocery store. The post office box pickings were meager but there was an overstuffed envelope from the Mundy Consolidated School System. It figured that the one school I was hesitant to teach at would send me an application form. It didn't mean I'd get an interview, but it was better than a rejection letter.

Driving into the parking lot of the grocery store, I was astonished to see a row of outlandish vehicles, most covered with mud, and a group of guys hanging out that included Howie and Wayne. Just off to the side of this group of macho-emoting guys was a lurking figure I recognized immediately, Lizard Lids himself. Who was that guy? Some day it would come to me. I guess I had been staring because I realized that the group was suddenly staring back at me in a decidedly unfriendly manner. The hell with this, I dropped my gaze and almost ran into the store.

I was taking my time hoping that they'd be gone by the time I was finished but no such luck. At the check out I peered through the windows and although there seemed to be fewer standing around, Wayne and Howie were hanging in there. Wheeling my cart out to the truck, I gripped it like a shield and kept my eyes on the pavement. My heart started to race when I noticed Wayne and Howie, the gruesome twosome, approaching me. What did they want with me? Suddenly I felt small and vulnerable. Wasn't there anyone who would come to my rescue?

Howie was strutting like a pompous little prick. Wayne had that same sunken dead look in his eyes. The two of them got between the door of my truck and me.

"I thought you might like to know. My sister was murdered and so was Bear. I *will* get the person responsible."

"We know who's responsible, don't we Howie and you're going to pay." I think my jaw must have dropped a foot. I had difficulty closing it. Howie's eyes were riveted to mine. Did he really believe I caused his sister's death? I couldn't tell what was going on in his head.

"Murderers run in your family, you fucking bitch. Don't play this Miss Innocent crap with me. Why'd ya hav'ta come here?" Wayne was definitely losing it. I couldn't tell if he was going to break into tears or slug me. I clutched my backpack, ready to swing and run. Just when I thought I'd have to act, a sheriff's cruiser rolled up behind Howie and Wayne with Hal behind the wheel. My knight in shining armor had arrived just in time. I could feel my shoulders drop.

"How's it going boys?" Howie whipped around to see Hal but Wayne either couldn't or wouldn't take his eyes off of me. "You know what we gotta do." This came from Wayne but it was a mystery who he was talking to. I sure as hell didn't know what he meant by it, but it didn't sound good.

"Howie, why don't you see that Wayne gets back to his place alright? Wayne, when's Charlie going to have your truck done?"

This must have jolted Wayne out of his trance because the look in his eyes changed as he turned to look at Hal. "Howie's takin' me out now. It's ready."

"I'll let you two get to it then." Hal nodded to them and they moved off as if nothing had happened. I walked over to Hal. "It was a good thing you showed up when you did, I was getting a bit nervous."

"Well we can't have you taking out any more of our men with that lethal backpack of yours, can we? Don't worry about Wayne. He's harmless."

"Well he doesn't seem harmless to me. Every time he sees me he threatens me, and he comes out with the weirdest things."

"Let's just forget it, okay? I've got rounds to do. You take it easy." He left me standing there more confused than ever. It was impossible for me to forget what Wayne had said, but who was there I could talk to?

I pulled myself together and climbed into my truck. My mind would not shut off. I needed a meeting. I was relieved when I had finished dinner and was on my way to the Grange. Even a couple of old codgers like Winfield and Kenny were looking good to me.

Winfield and Kenny drove into the parking lot, one right after the other. I couldn't really talk to Winfield about the situation with Wayne until after we had set up the meeting, and I didn't know how much I wanted to say in front of Kenny. After all, Kenny was a Murphy, and he had also been trying to help Wayne out. I didn't want to offend anyone else in this tight little community. When I finally got a chance to get Winfield off to one side and tell him what Wayne had said, he was silent for what seemed an eternity.

"Margaret, I'm not sure what you want to hear from me, and I'm not sure what kind of connection Wayne was trying to draw between you and past events. You have to understand that, due to the use of drugs and alcohol, he is a very sick individual. He has no coping skills, and you know how we drunks can build resentments out of thin air. Whatever is in his mind, it has no bearing on your life today. There is no point in dredging up old hurts to try to analyze his train of thought."

"So basically you're telling me just to forget it and mind my own business. I'm not sure I can do that, and I don't think this will be the last go-round with him."

"Ask yourself what you hope to gain from going into this. What's more important, figuring out what's going on in another sick and suffering alcoholic's mind or your own sobriety and serenity? Pray for him, Margaret."

I felt sufficiently chastised. I'd pray all right, but for me and for acceptance, not for Wayne. I wasn't ready to pray for him. There was something more that Winfield wasn't sharing with me, just like there were things left unsaid by Margaret. I hadn't wanted to open old wounds with her, but now my need to know was getting the better of me.

The meeting didn't have my full attention. I was vaguely aware that Del said something that I needed to hear, but I wasn't really too receptive. I had hoped that the meeting would somehow magically remove all the garbage that was floating around in my head, but it didn't. I wasn't ready to go home and sleep. Maybe I could literally drive it out of me. When I headed out of the parking lot, I turned away from town. I wasn't even in the mood to enjoy the moonlight that showered the highway with an iridescent glow.

I don't know how far I had gone when I noticed another set of headlights on the road behind me. It was amazing how easily I had come to expect having the road to myself up here after living in Southern Maine where there were traffic lights every fifty feet and multiple lanes of bumper to bumper cars and trucks. It gave me a sense of freedom, but there was that guardedness that had come with being run off the road that kept me checking my rearview mirror.

Shortly after spotting the first set of lights I could just make out another set that was gaining on the first set. In a way I felt reassured now that there were two other people on the road. I continued mulling over the meeting, Winfield, Wayne, and Howie. It was like trying to play a game of connect-the-dots when you didn't have all the dots.

The committee in my head was getting noisier instead of quieter. How could I let go and shut down the committee?

I glimpsed the two sets of headlights again, only now they were side by side. They sure had some peculiar road habits up this way. I picked up speed to give them room for passing even though I knew I should be finding a place to turn around and head for home. I could hear horns honking behind me. I could only go so fast. Couldn't they manage to pass on this empty stretch without all the commotion? One vehicle had dropped back but the other was coming even faster than before. Keeping one eye on the road and the other in the rearview mirror wasn't easy, especially since I didn't know these roads. I didn't even want to contemplate the possibility of having any of the local wildlife jump out at me.

There was yelling from the vehicle that had sped up close behind me and then a jostling crunch as my backend was smacked. My hands slipped from the wheel momentarily and I was slammed against my seatbelt. My foot crammed down the accelerator and my truck shot forward as I grabbed the wheel. Just when I thought I had regained control, the vehicle came back at me but this time it was right beside me. Here we go again. My hands were numb from gripping the wheel and my heart was racing as the side of my truck was struck a glancing blow. The sound of scraping metal drowned out whatever the driver of this other vehicle was screaming so I had no clue what was happening. Before I could adjust the vehicle pulled ahead. The last thing I remember was a set of taillights coming at me like a flyswatter, and then there was pain before everything went black.

Who knows how long I was out, but my first sensation was that of dangling sideways staring at the glove compartment. The dizziness made it hard to get my bearings. *Where am I? Am I drunk?*

"Margaret! Margaret!" Oh don't shout it hurts too much. Who was shouting at me? "Margaret can you hear me?" Hear you? Of course I can, you're screaming in my ear. "Margaret, say something." I thought I just did. I opened my mouth. What a strange sensation! My mouth tasted like copper pennies and my tongue didn't seem to fit. "Whaa…" was all that would come out.

"Margaret, look at me." Okay, okay. I tried to move my head. Pain shot through and around my skull like an electrical current. This was not good. I managed to pick my head up and rest it on the back of the seat, which made looking at whoever was talking a little easier, but it was hard to focus.

"Del?"

"Yes, Margaret, it's me. Can you tell if anything is broken or where it hurts?" *My eardrums, if you don't stop shouting.*

"My head, what happened? Where am I?" I was getting panicky hanging here. "Help me I've got to get out."

"Hold on, it might be dangerous to move. You could do more damage." My head was starting to clear but with clarity came more pain. I could move my fingers and toes, arms and legs. My chest still felt crushed by the damn seatbelt and sitting sideways against gravity wasn't helping either.

"Del I can move everything but I can't hang here much longer. Please help me get out."

"Okay, but real easy." He swung the door open—thank God it wasn't stuck—then reached over me to help me unlatch the seatbelt. He grabbed me as it let go and pulled me from the cab. We were on the side of an embankment. The truck had gone off on the shoulder and slid down on its side. The motor was still running until Del reached in and switched off the ignition. I dragged myself up to the road and just lay there on my other side for a minute.

Del came up and sat beside me as we both took a breather and stared down at the truck. "How are you doing? Do you want me to call an ambulance? You're bleeding. You could have done something to your insides."

"I think I just bit my tongue from the way it feels, and now that I'm out of that seatbelt I can breathe. My head is killing me. What happened?"

"You got run off the road."

"Did you see who did it?" There was a hesitation, but finally he said yes without saying whom.

"I'll call for some help. You stay here—or would you rather sit in my truck?"

"I think I'll stay right here for the time being." He went back to his truck, which was pulled to the side of the road, and I sat rocking back and forth. I was a mess. When Del came back, he sat down beside me again.

"I called the Sheriff's Department and I called Charlie. He does towing. They should be here shortly. You sure you don't want to get checked out at the hospital?"

"I'll survive. Besides, I don't want to go to Tylerville tonight without transportation, and I've got work tomorrow."

"Well when you get back I'd suggest you call Josie and pass on work tomorrow. You'll feel worse once the shock wears off and the bruises set in."

"You're probably right." I took him up on his offer to sit in the truck while we waited for help to arrive. Del had a CB radio, which I assumed was how he called for help. I hadn't noticed too many cell phones up this way and no towers to speak of.

Charlie showed up first. He nodded at me, and then he and Del went down to the truck to see what needed to be done. Charlie hooked onto the front bumper and I watched from Del's truck as his winch hoisted my truck up out of the ditch and set her on the shoulder of the road. Del got in and fired her up. Well at least the engine worked. I couldn't make out the damage in the dark.

Charlie came back to Del's truck wiping his hands on a rag. "I was going to give you a call to tell you I had those parts in, but it looks like she's going to need more now. She's runnin' so's you can get her home, but bring her out tomorrow and we'll take a look at her in the daylight."

"Thanks, Charlie. What do I owe you for the service call?"

"Del and Kenny both vouch for you so I'll just add it to the bill for parts and labor."

"Thank you so much. I don't know what to say."

"You know, I'm not so hard up for business that you have to give me somethin' ta do." With that he gave Del a slap on the back and headed to his truck.

"He seems like a real nice guy and thanks for vouching for me. I'll make good on all the repairs and stuff." I started getting out of Del's truck just as a sheriff's cruiser pulled up with lights flashing. They didn't help my headache any.

Oh lord, it was Howie looking officious and resembling a thug that brought to mind Nazi Brown Shirts. The last person I wanted to deal with right now was him. Del and I walked over to him as he got out of the car. He had his notebook out, nodded to Del, and stared at me. It was apparent that he wasn't any happier to see me than I was to see him. "I'll need to see your driver's license, registration, and proof of insurance; then you can tell me what happened here." I had to go to my truck and get my backpack and the paperwork from the glove compartment. It was a relief to be away from him, so I took my time. When I handed him the information, he examined it as if I might be handing him forgeries, then went back to his car and did whatever they do.

"Del, I want to thank you for staying with me. I don't think I'd do too well by myself. If it wouldn't be too much to ask, could you kind of give me an escort home once we're finished here?"

"No problem—that's what I'm here for." He looked a little sheepish and I was puzzled but grateful.

"What do you mean that's what you're here for?"

"I probably shouldn't have said anything, but Hal was concerned about you so he asked me to keep an eye on you."

"Hal? I don't get it. What's your connection to Hal?"

"He's my brother. I thought you knew." How could I know? We never exchanged last names.

Howie came back with a little box in his hand. "I'd like you to take a breathalyzer test."

"Oh come on Howie, she's not drunk."

"Then she won't mind taking the test. I'm just doing my job."

This was humiliating. "Hey! I was the one who was run off the road by a lunatic, and you want to test me?" I was indignant. The truth was that even with my past behaviors before I got sober, I had never been pulled over for drunk driving—not that there weren't times when I should have been. I tried not to dig myself into a hole. *Catsy, what would you tell me to do?* It suddenly dawned on me that I should be grateful that I hadn't been drinking, that I was alive, that I had someone else here with me…the list could have gone on and on. Getting all riled up was making my head pound, so I tried to calm down and detach from it all. I submitted to the test and passed. Whoopee! Then I told Howie what I could remember before the lights went out and then Del told Howie what he had seen.

"Did you recognize the driver or the vehicle?"

"Yes. It was Wayne. He was acting crazy, hoot and hollering and honking his horn. He passed me and was definitely out to get Margaret."

I was astounded. "It was Wayne?" So much for calming down, "That son-of-a-bitch tried to kill me! I'd like to put his lights out. Why don't you people do something about him?" I forgot who I was talking to, and Del was probably part of the childhood boys club too.

"Calm down Margaret. That doesn't help anything. Remember we can't afford the luxury of anger." This was between Del and me, but I wasn't in the mood to hear program jargon. I was past anger and into rage and it showed.

Howie's parting shot was that he'd be in touch and to make sure I got the damage repaired to my truck. What an asshole! I really felt like strangling someone. I wanted to be out of here and the hell with all of them.

As Howie pulled out, Del put his hand on my shoulder. I almost recoiled but my energy level was taking a nosedive and I didn't have any more resistance left in me.

"Margaret, are you sure you can drive back? You know I can take you home and you can get your truck later."

I didn't want to be indebted any more than I already was. I wanted control back, and I thought if I had my truck, I'd have that control. "I'm sorry Del. I didn't mean to blow up like that. I guess I'm not myself. I can make it, but I'd appreciate knowing you were behind me just in case I lose it." I tried to laugh, but what I really wanted to do was cry and sleep.

I pulled into the apartment after what seemed like an interminable cross-country journey, waved thanks to Del, and climbed up the stairs dragging my backpack behind me. Del was right. I wasn't going to be in any shape to work tomorrow, so I gave Josie a call. I didn't wake her, which was a good thing, but she and Dwight had heard the call over the scanner so they knew more than I had been ready to share. Josie understood and said they'd make do. I thanked her and hung up. Before crashing for the night, I took a nice hot shower and surveyed the damage. I had bruises on top of bruises, and they'd look worse in the morning.

Chapter Eighteen

I didn't want to get out of bed, and then I wasn't sure I *could* get out of bed. My body was agonizingly stiff with aches in every major muscle group and some minor ones. Most of the bruising was caused by the seatbelt, but it had probably kept me alive.

It wasn't easy to get moving, but the truck would need to be looked at. When I noticed the time, I couldn't believe I had slept that long. It was ten o'clock and I was just barely conscious of the sounds and smells coming from the diner. As delicately as I could, I moved to the kitchen and got out cooking utensils to make breakfast without too much clatter to add to my headache. Even with the headache I felt like eating a horse. After downing two aspirins, the coffee, pancakes, orange juice, an egg over easy and a piece of leftover ham steak, hit the spot. The pain was now tolerable but definitely still there.

During the night, thoughts had whirled through my head accompanied by faces from present and past. I needed to talk with someone about all that had gone on so I could get a better picture and lay to rest all these nagging thoughts. I hated to impose on Margaret and dredge up old hurts, but she was the only one who came to mind. She had a calming influence on me, too. She could always say no if I called and asked to talk with her. It was worth a try.

I made the call to her. She sounded puzzled on the phone but agreeable. I knew she would be. I couldn't tell her when exactly I would get there, what with the truck and all, but we left it at sometime in the afternoon. That settled, I slowly got ready to go out to Charlie's. I took my crammed backpack and steeled myself to go and look at the truck in the light of day. There was no bouncing down the stairs this morning, but tentative steps while I clung to the railing. The sun was bright and the glare cut into my skull with a painful vengeance. I pulled the visor of my hat down and donned my sunglasses for a bit of relief.

My poor truck—I could hardly bare to look at her. With all the dents and scrapes, she resembled a demolition derby contestant. It was amazing that the driver's door still opened. I'd need help getting her back in shape—and that was putting it lightly. With any luck Wayne's insurance might pick up the tab—then again, what were the odds he had any kind of real insurance? I had the impression that some people tended to skirt the regulations in this part of the world. I only had the minimum required to register a vehicle which didn't pay for repairs so why would I think he would have anything more? Collecting on insurance could be its own kind of nightmare. Of course leaving the scene of the accident was a crime that might carry some jail time, so he'd probably deny everything. I'd have to get pictures of the damage. All I was going to be able to swing were the essentials to make her road-worthy. I was willing to bet that Howie would be on my case about it just because it gave him the perfect excuse to hassle me. Boy did he irritate me to no end!

The drive out to the garage was uneventful and actually quite relaxing, even though the anticipation of the bill I was running up weighed on my mind. I was amazed when I pulled up to the garage. A field of muddy vehicles had sprouted up beside the garage. This time there wasn't a group of guys hanging around so I could get a good look at these curious contraptions.

Charlie wanted to put my truck up on the lift to check out the undercarriage for damage. While he was busy doing that I took the time to stroll out to the trucks. Though the drive was nice, I had managed to stiffen up again so I kept moving to get the kinks out. There were certainly a lot of muddy trucks here in one place. They weren't street legal, but they had seen some pretty rough terrain and were built for it. Besides the muddy covering that most had, they also had names emblazoned on their sides or fronts or both. It was like looking at a wrestling match lineup: The Claw, Terminator, The Beast, and Big Mudder.

Charlie came out to find me perusing the cavalcade of vehicles. "You thinking of entering your truck in the mud run? I might have time to get her fitted out."

"I don't have a clue what a mud run is. I just want to have legal transportation."

"Well I'll order the rest of the parts and put them all together at the same time. She runs fine and she'll get you where you want to go. I'll have to get back to you on when to bring her in. I'm booked right solid with the mud run coming up."

"What's this mud run stuff all about?"

"It's a local summer event around here, second only to the Fourth of July, a big competition that has all ages and types of vehicles. You know ladies, teens, and the guys. They give cash awards. The Beast, here, has won the last three years, but Big Mudder gave him a run for his money each time. Big Mudder is running the favorite this year."

"And who owns these two behemoths?"

"Craig Wilson runs the Big Mudder and Howie Jones runs The Beast." For some reason I had difficulty picturing Howie Jones in this big hulking truck. It was easier to accept him in a sheriff's cruiser.

"When is this big event anyway?"

"The last weekend of July so you can see how my schedule's a bit tight, but we'll squeeze you in. Here's your truck." Just then my truck was backed out of the garage bay. I didn't recognize the guy driving it but he parked my truck right across from the row of muddy trucks. The cosmetic damage to the side of the truck was again glaringly apparent. I thanked Charlie and decided the light was good for getting those pictures while I was here.

As I was reloading my camera I happened to catch a glint in my side mirror, a tiny reflection of the sun's rays. It was hard to believe that there were any reflective surfaces on any of those dirty trucks behind me. I sat there staring at the glint through the mirror almost hypnotized. *Hello! You have things to do Margaret. Try to focus.* Probably talking to myself again wasn't a healthy sign.

I started taking pictures of all sides of the truck. When I got to the back and looked at my mangled stickers, I felt anger welling up again. Who did they think they were, trying to scare me? I don't know why, but at that moment I turned around to come face to face with The Beast parked right behind me. A flashback to my childhood terror of big trucks went through my mind. As a child, I thought they were alive and huge monsters out to get me. Whenever one would come barreling down our road, I would run and hide in the bushes.

The headlights looked like eyes and the big mean grills resembled gaping jaws out to crush me.

I caught a glint again and it was coming from the Road Warrior style bars that had been attached to the front of The Beast's grill. I was drawn to them like a moth to a flame. There on those bars were bits of a shiny substance that looked like the missing pieces of my stickers, pieces of flesh in those terrible jaws. As I examined the front of the truck I noticed that though it was covered in mud, the headlights had been wiped clean (*All the better to see you with, my dear*). I looked over at my tailgate and back to the truck. My excitement was growing. It was like putting Legos together, my matching my dented tailgate to the bars of this metal cage on the front of this truck, *Howie's* truck!

What was I going to do? The ramifications of this discovery were enormous and almost incomprehensible. I needed to document this so I would know I wasn't hallucinating. Raising my camera and uttering a little prayer, I zoomed in on The Beast and took all kinds of shots including the telltale grill of The Beast lined up with the rear of my truck. I couldn't get enough.

Suddenly I felt very conspicuous and a little nervous. What if someone saw me and wanted to know what I was doing? What if Howie pulled in? How would I explain?

I figured I had enough pictures, but now I needed to get them developed, and I wanted to hightail it out of here. It would mean going into Tylerville, and I had promised Margaret that we would get together sometime this afternoon. Damn. The distance between everything up here was a pain in the ass. I'd just have to do my best.

I sped out of Charlie's toward Tylerville with an eye on the speedometer. I couldn't afford to get stopped for speeding, especially with the condition of my truck and Howie possibly on duty.

The national pharmacy chain in town had one-hour processing. I didn't like to use the quick developing because it always seemed like some of the quality was lost, but I didn't have a choice. I kept my fingers crossed that they wouldn't screw up the negatives and that the prints would show what I had seen. I ordered double prints even though I hadn't used a whole roll, but the guy behind the counter said he'd prorate the cost. I threw in the full roll of my park pictures. I knew it would take more time, but then again, I was here, and I didn't want to worry about coming all the way in just to have a roll of film developed.

I'm not a shopper, so passing time was agonizing. I walked up and down all the aisles checking out the merchandise. Unfortunately that didn't take much time. After cataloging everything they carried in the store, I ended up pacing back and forth in front of the developing center. I must have been driving the clerk crazy. Either he was really good at his job or he really wanted to get rid of me. He finished in record time and I was very appreciative.

In the truck, I sorted through the pictures and put each set in its own pile. As I did a cursory run through of the park pictures I came across the one of Lizard Lids. The nickname had stuck in my mind. I threw one of him in with the set of the trucks. Maybe Jeff could find out who he was. It was a long shot but what the hell. I was watching the time. Thank goodness the police barracks was on the way back to Mundy. I was rushing and feeling frantic. I had to calm down.

Jeff wasn't alone when I showed up at the barracks. I was flustered and didn't want to speak with anyone but Jeff. There was an air of intensity about this other officer. He did a detailed assessment of me as I kept my eyes on Jeff and waited for him to get off the phone. When Jeff saw me, he motioned for me to come and sit down with a look of concern. The other officer prepared to leave with a nod from Jeff.

"Maggie, what brings you here?"

"I don't know where to begin. Things are getting way too weird for me." Jeff smiled and was patient and encouraging.

"Just start somewhere and I'll let you know if I have any questions."

"Last night Wayne McCarthy ran me off the road, and I have a witness."

"Wayne McCarthy? Does he live in Sutton?"

"I'm not sure where he lives but he was a 'significant other' of Sheila Jones and possibly the father of her kids. He's a real screwball and he left the scene and …" My words were tumbling out of my mouth and I could barely catch my breath.

"Whoa Maggie, Wayne is dead. He was found this morning out at his place."

"What! But, but that can't be. How?"

"We don't have all the details yet but our investigators are up there now."

I was in shock. The pictures I had been gripping in my hand fell to the floor. It took a minute for me to react and only after Jeff had bent down to scoop them up.

"Maggie, are you all right?" I wish people would stop asking me that. Wasn't it obvious that I wasn't? At this moment I wondered if I would ever be all right.

"What are all these about?" He was looking through the pictures he had picked up. I needed to regroup.

"Jeff I need to start over and now I'm really confused. When I was out at Haggarty's Garage to see what damage Wayne had done to my truck last night I saw something."

"You're saying Wayne ran you off the road last night? What time was this?"

"About nine-thirty or so. I was out for a drive after a meeting. I had to think some things through. Wayne had threatened me and said some wild things that really bothered me."

"When was that?"

"Well the most recent was yesterday afternoon."

"It happened more than once? Did you report it?"

"Yes. I told Hal, Deputy Grimes. He didn't seem to think it was any big deal but it bothered me. Then last night Wayne ran me off the road."

"You saw it was Wayne?"

"No, but Del did, and he told Howie Jones, who was on duty when I had to get pulled out of the ditch." The memory of the humiliating sobriety test still rankled.

"But that's not why I came here. The pictures don't have anything to do with last night."

"All right, tell me about the pictures." He was sorting through them again as I continued.

"I noticed a glint coming from this big muddy truck at the garage, and when I went over to look, I thought it was coming from pieces of stickers that had come off my truck when I was rammed the first time. You know, the same night that Teddy Cox's hit and run happened. The more I looked at the front of that truck and the back of mine, the more it looked like this truck had been the one that hit me." I pointed to the pictures with the bars and the dents.

"You say this truck is out at Haggarty's?"

"Yes, it's called The Beast, and I guess it's for the mud run competition but guess whose truck it is?"

"You know who it belongs to?"

"Yeah—it's all very confusing, but The Beast is Howie Jones's'"

"Are you absolutely sure about this?"

"Yes, that's what Charlie Donovan told me, before I noticed the stickers."

"Did you talk to Charlie about this?"

"No."

"Wait just a minute." Jeff went to the phone with his back to me and called someone. I couldn't make out what was being said and I gathered I wasn't supposed to. He was still holding the photos when he came back. "And who is this person?" It was the park shot of Lizard Lids.

"This may sound silly, but the guy looked familiar and I had the creepy feeling he was following me. I was kind of hoping you might know who he was or could find out." I tried to put on my lost puppy dog expression, which didn't usually work with Jeff.

Jeff tapped the picture rubbed his chin and made a hmmm sound. "He looks familiar to me too. Can I keep these?"

"Sure. I got double sets. Jeff, I feel kind of silly bothering you with all this. I didn't think moving up to the back of beyond could be so complicated. I'll let you get on with your work. I'm just relieved to get all my suspicions out in the open. They were renting entirely too much space in my head. Say 'hi' to Beth and the boys for me. Tell her I applied for a job in Mundy and I'm taking her up on her offer to give me a reference." I was all set to be on my way.

"Margaret, I need to go over some more details with you first since you have so kindly dumped all this in my lap." Oh, oh, he called me 'Margaret' in a serious tone. My relief was short lived. Jeff saw me tense up and he tried to put me at ease by joking about paperwork, proper procedures, and CYA. After he got down all the information I could come up with, like who was Del, etc., he gave me a hug.

"Maggie I want you to keep in close touch. I trust your instincts. If you feel anything is out of place or hinky give me a call. I'll let you know about this guy you so fondly call Lizard Lids if I find out anything."

"Thanks Jeff. I need all the friends I can get right now."

I didn't speed back to Mundy even though it was getting close to dinner time. Wayne's death was beginning to sink in. I wished I knew how it had happened. I had a difficult time believing in coincidences. Three people had died—one right after the other—who were involved with one another. The news of Wayne's death would be upsetting to Margaret and Winnie. I know it was silly, but for some reason, I felt responsible for bringing this tragedy, though not because of anything Wayne or Howie had said. I didn't need to take on any more guilt today.

I hadn't been back in the apartment two minutes when the phone rang. It was Josie. "Where have you been? I've been worried sick about you what with what happened last night and Wayne's death. Have you heard about Howie's truck? The state police have impounded it because they think it was used in Bear's hit and run and boy is Howie pissed! How are you feeling?" The barrage of questions was almost more than I could handle.

"Are you going to let me get a word in edgewise? To answer as many of your questions as I can remember, I've been out to get the truck looked at and into Tylerville. No, I haven't heard about Howie's truck. And if you must know, I feel like crap, but I'll live. Is there anything else I can answer, Mom?"

"Okay, point taken. I'm not your mother, but that doesn't keep me from worrying about you."

"I understand, but I'm really alright, just stiff and sore, but if I keep moving I don't notice it much."

"So what do you think about this Wayne thing? They're saying it was an accidental overdose but the conspiracy buffs aren't buying it."

"I don't know any more about it than you do and probably less. As a matter of fact, you're way ahead of me." I hated lying to her but I could convince myself it wasn't really a lie. She didn't need to know I had been to the state police.

"Oh I almost forgot, Hal was asking for you this morning. I don't just think he has the hots for you, I *know* it. The signs are all there." Oh please! That was the last thing I could take on right now.

"Josie, I'll be at work tomorrow but right now I've got to make a call, so I'll talk to you later, ok?" We said our goodbyes, but I sensed she was a bit miffed at my abruptness. It was getting late, and I wanted to give Margaret a call before I went barging in on her.

"Margaret this is Maggie. I'm sorry I'm so late, but I just got back."

"That's all right, dear. Winnie is here. Did you hear the news?"

"Yes, I just heard what happened. I don't want to disturb you and Winnie. Would you give her my condolences? We can get together some other time." I really didn't want to wait, but I could imagine what Winnie was going through, not to mention the kids now that both parents were dead. It was a sorry state of affairs but in the back of my mind, I was ashamed to think that the kids might be better off.

"Maggie, if you don't have plans for dinner, why don't you come up here in about an hour and we'll eat and talk. You sounded like it was important this morning."

"Thank you, Margaret that's very kind of you, I'd love to join you for dinner. Is there anything I can bring?"

"No, no, there's no need of that. I'll look for you in an hour then."

I flopped down in the living room and started cleaning out my backpack. I set things out on the blanket chest I was using as a coffee table—or perhaps 'piling surface' might be a more appropriate descriptor. The pictures and papers from the filing cabinet were still strewn on the floor where I had left them days ago. A neat housekeeper I was not. The pictures I had just gotten developed held some promise for enlargement and framing. I perused them with an eye to grouping. Of course, the thought that I might not be staying long in this bewildering seaside community went zipping through my head. That's when I came across the shots of Lizard Lids and the truck. I decided not to focus on those and dumped them unceremoniously in a cardboard box by the computer. My first motto has always been, 'let no container go unfilled' and the second, 'let no waist-high flat surface remain bare.'

With that I lost interest and thought I might have time to whip up a batch of cookies if I had enough ingredients. I rummaged around in the kitchen and found the basics for chocolate chip cookies. I threw in some toasted almonds and dried cherries for extra tang. With the scoops I used, I could get about a dozen to a cookie sheet, which meant that I'd only have time to cook up a dozen, but that was more than enough. The rest of the dough I sealed up and put in the refrigerator for those little emergencies that called for warm yummy comfort food. I wasn't sure who needed the cookies more, but bringing something to Margaret would make me feel better.

Somewhere in among my few possessions, I had some of those paper gift bags for all occasions. After pawing through the third cardboard box in the extra bedroom, I had success. A pretty little bag with daisies across the top was just the right size, and there was even some pretty yellow tissue paper still in it. My third motto was 'never throw out anything that can be used as a container.' Call it just one of my many quirks. Who could remember what had come in this bag, but with wax paper for a liner, I carefully placed a dozen cookies inside and gently nestled the tissue paper on top. I had timed that perfectly. It was all I could do to keep from sampling the cookies. Once again I had skipped a meal and was ravenous.

Margaret was as welcoming this evening as she had been on my first visit. I suddenly felt guilty about intruding on her memories and prying into her past. I heard a little voice in the back of my mind saying *don't do this*, but it was drowned out by one that said I was past the point of turning back.

The dinner was simple and good, but the conversation was strained as we both steered clear of anything that might be emotional. We talked about my job hunting for the fall and the scarcity of opportunities. I didn't mention the fact that Mundy had positions open, but Margaret seemed to know all about the school situations. She was the one who brought up the positions available in town while we ate. I nodded and thanked her for the input.

After dinner we took cookies and milk out on the sun porch. The porch was situated perfectly for sunrises and sunsets but also got the brunt of the afternoon sun. Overhead fans kept the air circulating with a quiet swishing so the area didn't become an oven. We both settled in and gazed at the sunset. It was another spectacular array of colors and wispy cloud shapes. The silence wasn't awkward, but I felt Margaret was waiting for me to make the first move.

"Margaret, Winfield told me about the lake accident and the curse because I asked him. Wayne said some very strange things to me before he died and then there was that awful vandalism at the diner. I always thought of Maggot as a term of endearment but seeing it scrolled in red, well it was unnerving. I've been getting fallout because my last name is Murphy. It probably shouldn't bother me, but for some reason I get very defensive when people make derogatory remarks about my dad, even if they are totally ludicrous." Margaret nodded her head ever so slightly as I babbled this litany.

"Can you tell me what some of the comments were that bothered you so much?"

"Wayne said Murphys were killers and then just yesterday he said murderers run in my family. Obviously he was referring to Murphys since he didn't know my dad, but it was the plurals that stuck out so I figured there was more than just the boating accident."

"You made a curious remark yourself just now when you said maggot was a term of endearment. What did you mean by that?"

"It seems kind of silly now but Dad used to call me his little Maggot. It was my nickname. The kids in school would sometimes use it but it was really a family thing."

"Do you have family albums? I'd like to meet the family you are so protective of." I was suddenly getting the impression that Margaret was neatly trying to sidetrack me with her questions. I didn't want to get pushy but I was sticking to my guns to get some answers and if I wanted to be honest I was getting defensive about my family again.

"Our family wasn't much on photographs. All I have are a handful that Dad kept in a filing cabinet. I pulled them out and thought I might frame some to spruce up the apartment." Neither one of us was looking at the other now. We had turned to look at the dwindling light of the sunset as the intensity of orange and purple increased and moved down toward the horizon.

"I don't want to rake up a lot of muck, but whatever conceptions people have around here are being held against me and I don't get it. People aren't very forgiving. I think if I understood the history behind some of this stuff, I might be able to handle it better rather than get blind-sided every time."

"My faith helps me handle situations. I don't believe in curses, but I do believe we reap what we sow. There are always consequences to our actions. What did Winfield tell you about the lake and the so-called curse?" I was trying hard to be patient but it was extremely difficult. Did I honestly expect this woman to blurt out family secrets that she had kept bottled up for all these years? As gently as I could, I reviewed what Winfield had told me. There was silence as I waited.

Tears spilled from Margaret's eyes, and she suddenly looked old and frail. "I haven't spoken about this for years. Dear Winfield, ever the gentleman. That year just went from bad to worse. When it looked like Kenny would survive after his premature birth, my father was a relatively happy man. But then it happened."

"You mean you found out Kenny had birth defects?" I jumped in.

"No, that realization came later. Remember I told you Kenny was my younger brother?"

"Yes, you said there were four of you and Kenny was the only brother left. Is this about your other brothers?" Oh I could tell I had hit a nerve. Margaret had a faraway look. Tears were rolling down her face now as she rocked in her wicker rocker. What can of worms had I opened? Catsy's voice came into my head. *What are your motives? Are you being selfish at the expense of others?*

"Margaret, you don't have to tell me anything more if it is too painful. I'm sorry. I never should have come or brought this up. The last thing I wanted to do was hurt you. It seems I keep hurting everyone I care about." Now I was in tears and ready to run. Gone was my resolve along with my inquisitiveness.

Margaret turned to me and put her hand over mine, "No dear, it's time to get this out. It will be good to shed some light on it. Secrets are private little poisons, you know. You'll have to forgive an old woman for sounding confused, but there is so much emotion that I find goes with my memories. You were an only child and close to your father. I was an only daughter with older brothers. I was closer to my brother, Tommy, than I was to John or my father. My father was a hard man to be close to." I sensed there was more that she wanted to share but hadn't quite figured out how or how much.

"Tommy and I would try and stay out of my father's way. We did just about everything together, even though he was four years older. Tommy would always say it was just he and I against the world, but it was more like he and I were in our own world away from my father's." There was a melancholy to her voice that struck at my heart. Hearing those words that my father used to say brought my own loss back to me. I knew what it was like to lose someone you were close to.

"Tommy sounds like a keen older brother. I've had some friends that I sort of thought of as brothers, always there to protect you."

"Yes, great protectors. Tommy was my protector. He was always looking out for me." The tears started to flow again. This was excruciating for her. I didn't know how to stop it, and I don't think, at that moment, that I had the power to stop it. She would have continued down this road even without me.

"That summer at the lake was the worst time of my life. Things were done that no amount of praying could undo. Every year my father and John, my oldest brother, would go out to the camp by themselves, ostensibly to make it ready for the family outings and, of course, the hunting season. I don't have any really fond memories of that camp. You would have thought as a child spending summers at the lake, I'd have many memorable experiences. My father and then my brother John would turn into entirely different people. They drank." There was disgust in her voice. I wondered if she knew I was an alcoholic. I hoped she had a better understanding than Hal did about the disease. Obviously, having a brother in the program was no guarantee, if Hal was any indication.

As if she were reading my thoughts she continued, "I don't blame them any more than I could blame Kenny. It's a disease that robbed me of the most precious things in my life. To this day, I can't go anywhere near that wretched camp, especially after what happened there." I wanted her to finish quickly but I sat in silence as Margaret took her time in sharing what had happened during that tragic year.

"It was usually just Father and John who went to open up camp, but that year Tommy had graduated and he was invited along. Invited is probably the wrong word. Compelled or commanded would be better. I suppose it was some rite of passage into manhood. Mother and I never did really find out what happened, only that there had been a shooting accident. Tommy had shot John. John had been the apple of our father's eye—ran the packing plant that Father owned and was being groomed to take over all the family businesses. It had always been assumed that Tommy would take over at the bank after he had gone to college. He was the family bookworm. That was another thing we shared, a love of reading. We would escape into the make-believe world of books."

I felt Margaret had left a lot unsaid about her home life, and maybe that's another reason why she thought so highly of Winfield who kept silent about it. "When Tommy and Father came home, neither one would talk to us about what had happened. Tommy was shattered. The look in his eyes was indescribable. Father did all the talking to the authorities. There were many in Mundy who relished our misfortune and were furious when Tommy wasn't arrested. It wasn't just John I lost, it was my brother Tommy I lost that day. He never came back from that accursed camp!"

"Oh, Margaret, I'm so sorry. I can't imagine the devastation your family suffered." Margaret was rocking back and forth obsessively in her chair, the expression of desolation being supplanted by anger—but anger at whom?

"I thought I had mastered my feelings but apparently not. Tommy and I couldn't recover what we had lost in our relationship. I wanted to be supportive. We have no control over accidents, but I guess Tommy couldn't forgive himself for what happened. Of course the town folks wouldn't let up on him. It broke my heart as he tried to ignore the things that were said, but he was all alone. He wouldn't even let me in. Every day saw each of us in our own hell, pardon my language." I almost wanted to giggle at the absurdity of her concern about language when she was sharing such a horrendous story.

"The final blow came at the end of August. I never understood what was meant by the Dog Days of Summer but that year I developed my own meaning."

I couldn't help myself. "You mean more happened?"

"Oh yes. Mother had Kenny to the doctors and I was down at the school helping out with a youth program. You'd probably call it babysitting, but I loved anything that would take me out of the house. Well, that afternoon Tommy apparently found father in the basement. He'd hung himself. It was all very odd, so many questions. The police ruled it a suicide. I always wondered what happened, but I was still a child. Father's drinking had escalated after Johnny died, and he wouldn't even look at Tommy. They couldn't stand to be in the same room with each other.

Oh dear, I've rambled on shamelessly, but it does help to get it out. Tommy left after the police cleared everything up. He didn't even stay for the funeral. I've never seen or heard from him since. That was over forty years ago."

"You mean he left without saying anything?"

"He left me a note. I've kept it safe all these years."

My heart went out to her. To lose someone you loved and not know whether they were still alive was a torture I couldn't begin to imagine. This was Murphy's Law to the extreme. I felt very small at this moment, worrying about my pitiful little problems when this woman had held all this inside for so very long a time.

It was dark out now, and there were no lights on, because we had been sitting here talking. The darkness was a comforting blanket. Margaret roused herself from her memories. "Dear, let me get a light." She reached over and switched on a wrought iron floor lamp with a cut parchment lampshade that looked handcrafted. Even though it was a small light, it felt blinding when she first turned it on. "I must look a sight." Margaret dabbed at her eyes and blew her nose in a lace hanky that she took from her pocket. I felt like a snotty-nosed little kid that needed a sleeve to wipe on, but I had a tissue in my pocket and we both composed ourselves. As we did so, we looked at each other and started to laugh like girlfriends at a sleep over. Margaret's shared confidences brought relief as I realized that it wasn't all about me. She had given me a chance to have compassion for another person.

It was late, and I needed to get back. I was emotionally drained, and I was sure Margaret was as well. It was awkward leaving. "We must get together again soon," Margaret said. I enjoyed our time together. I have some family albums I'd love to share with you and perhaps you could bring your family pictures too." I told her I would love to and I made my exit. It had been a very long day.

Chapter Nineteen

"---me little Maggot, that's the way of the Little People. You hold onto them 'til they give you their pot o' gold. Never stop believing." It was just a dream but a comforting one when my alarm rudely went off. It took time to shake off the dream and settle back in reality. I really didn't want to, but then Catsy's voice came to me, "You haven't buried your dad yet."

It was too early in the morning to deal with that! Missing a day's work felt strange and going down to the diner was like the first day on the job. Josie and I talked just briefly about my visit with Margaret. My so-called accident was something else. She wanted all the gory details, and then she filled me in on what she knew about Wayne and Howie's truck. I had forgotten about the Beast. I was happy to talk about the accident because I was not about to share my conversation with Margaret—that was strictly confidential. Josie reiterated Hal's concern at not seeing me yesterday and then told me how pissed Howie was about the state troopers impounding his truck. He was planning on beating everyone in the Mud Run with it. Now that didn't seem likely. Apparently Jeff had sent someone right out. I didn't mention my part in Jeff's actions. There was no need to give Howie more reasons to try to kill me. He might be a slobbering drunk but I took his animosity seriously. While I was contemplating Josie's comments and playing scenarios in my head, there was a thump at the front door of the diner and I realized it was Thursday and time for the Tidewater Times. If I was in there again, I told Josie, I didn't want to know.

As the morning customers filtered in, it may have been my imagination, but I thought I was getting some pretty strange looks from the locals. It made me thankful for tourists who also tipped better.

I almost didn't notice when Hal came in. I was busy replenishing the pastry cases and putting on coffee. He caught my eye and signaled me over to his table. I was a bit out of breath. The heat and humidity were intense today.

"I missed you yesterday with what happened. Where'd you get to, anyway? Del and Howie filled me in on your accident."

"I wanted to thank you for having Del follow me. He was a lifesaver."

"I swear you must have nine lives, the way you pull yourself out of scrapes, but I'm glad I could be of assistance." There was a strange look in his eyes that had me baffled and I didn't know how to take his comment. After my evening with Margaret I was feeling less insecure about my predicament so I just said, "That's me, a real cat."

"I thought we could get together while you're still here, maybe go to Tylerville for a movie or something." While I was still here was an odd statement for him to make but I dismissed it as my paranoia acting up.

"Actually that sounds like a change of pace. What's playing?" With that we were just two ordinary people planning a—dare I say it—date. The morning flew by after that, and Shirley finally arrived so I got out of work only a half-hour late.

Margaret's family history still haunted me when I got back to the apartment. I was trying to tidy up the place and kill time before Hal would pick me up. There on the chest and filing cabinet were all the pictures of our little family that I had taken out to look through. "Dad, I think I'll take some of your pictures over to Margaret so you can meet her. She's a really nice lady. You would have approved." What in hell was I doing? I was weeping uncontrollably again. Margaret's loss had triggered thoughts of my own loss, and everything I had tried to dam up inside was pouring out.

I was going to look like a train wreck when Hal came if I didn't pull myself together. I piled the pictures in neat stacks on the blanket chest with the others from the park, took a long hot shower and then finished off with cold. The cold water on my face and body was refreshing, and I hoped it would take away the red swelling that came with my tears.

Hal was punctual as usual, and I had remembered to carry light with just a wallet, no backpack. Just as we were leaving, the phone rang. Now, I'm not strong enough to walk out and let it ring. My need to know is too great. Hal looked a little teed off that I went back to answer it.

"Hello?"

"Maggie I'm glad I caught you. This is Jeff. We got an ID on that fellow you think was following you. Turns out he isn't from around here, but he has a rap sheet a mile long and guess where his last little stint with local accommodations was."

"Where? Who is he?" I didn't know why, but I guess I was whispering or at least speaking in a low voice while I cradled the phone. Hal had sidled up beside me. It was ridiculous to be hiding, so I turned my attention back to Jeff.

"Jason Cleaves has a lot of aliases, no outstanding warrants but it's good to know he's in the area. We can keep an eye out for him."

"Where did you say he was in jail again? I missed that part."

"York County, he was part of the collateral fallout from that drug bust we did down at the school, so he might be up here on a personal vendetta. Watch yourself, Maggie. He can't be up to any good, and it's too much of a coincidence that both of you are here now. There's a drug connection written all over this, and with what's been happening here of late, he could be serious trouble."

"Thanks for the heads up Jeff. I'll watch my back. Gotta go, bye."

As I put the phone down and spun around I ran right into Hal's chest. "Whoa, didn't mean to run into you," but it was kinda nice nestled there in his arms.

With concern written all over his face, Hal asked, "Is there anything the matter? I couldn't help but hear you say you'd watch your back. Is there something I could help with?"

"That's sweet, Hal. It's kind of a mystery, and I'm not sure how deeply involved I am in it if at all. Why don't we get out of here and go have dinner before the phone rings again. Besides…"

"I know, you're starving!"

We went to Captain Black's. Even though I had been impressed the first time I had been there, it was much better with someone else. The conversation was sparse because it was so crowded and neither one of us felt like shouting. I was feeling more at ease than I had in a long time, and I was determined to savor the moment.

The movie was not due to start for awhile, so after dinner Hal drove down to the waterfront park on the river. There were trees for shade and benches along the walkway that wound along the banks of the river. I was so full that when Hal sat down on a secluded bench in the shade of the setting sun I was more than happy to take a load off my feet and park my butt next to him.

"So do you feel up to sharing a little more about your phone call? You worry me, Margaret." I was touched and maybe my contentment and full belly helped loosen me up as I explained about Lizard Lids and Jeff's take on the guy.

"Lizard Lids? That's a rather bizarre name."

"Oh you have to see this guy up close. Obviously he doesn't use that name. It's my way of tagging him so I remember what he looks like."

"That sounds pretty professional. So you got up close to the guy and Lieutenant Chandler came up with identification just from your description? I'm impressed."

"Hardly; I'm not that good and neither is Jeff. No, I got a picture of him when I was out at Sail Rock Park."

"Don't tell me he posed for you?"

"No. He doesn't appear to be the brightest bulb in the box, but he's hardly that stupid. According to Jeff, he's more hired help than an independent operator."

"So how do you know Lieutenant Chandler on a first name basis?" I couldn't tell if there was a hint of jealousy in that question but maybe that was just my ego again. It didn't bother me to give Hal a thumbnail sketch of working with Jeff down in Southern Maine. I even told him how Jeff had helped me with getting Dad the services he needed to stay at home until the end. It amazed me that I could mention that part without getting all teary-eyed. Maybe that was a side effect of sharing with Margaret or maybe just the healing process. By listening to her it helped me. Sort of like one drunk helping another, once removed. I liked that thought.

The movie theater was an old fashioned one in the heart of downtown Tylerville, not a Cineplex like I was used to. It was retro-showing old movies, classics I guess. I wasn't really tuned into the movie, *Sea of Grass,* except to notice that it was a western. Hal seemed into it more than I was, and he would glance over at me now and then as if he were checking for a reaction to what was on the screen. Instead, I was going over the past in my mind. I knew I was flirting with fire doing it, but I wanted to see things from a more objective light. I was enjoying this newfound feeling of confidence so I started to try it out by sharing my reminiscence with Hal.

The euphoria of the evening was making me very talkative. It was almost like having a good buzz on. In the back of my mind I could feel a little voice cautioning me to shut up, but I ignored it. When we got back to the apartment, Hal plopped down in Dad's chair and perused the stack of pictures on the blanket chest. "You took all these?"

"Well, yeah, the ones at the park. The pictures of my parents when I was young are all I really have left of our family." We went through them, laughing at some of the old poses and antics that children pull when they're being photographed. It's funny that I wasn't experiencing any embarrassment about how I looked then. I had been a terribly self-conscious kid. In my eyes I looked ugly with all that flyaway red hair. Now they almost seemed like pictures of strangers. The intense attention that Hal gave to the pictures of Mom and Dad was a bit disconcerting until he made an observation. "You look a lot like your dad except for your build." Of course I was crestfallen because in my warped mind I thought he was trying to make sure of my true parentage. Because I looked like my parents I was legitimate. It is sick, I know, but I suddenly felt I had put on the gloves and was ready to climb into the ring. My newfound confidence had been fleeting and had disappeared in an instant. I couldn't ditch the childhood trauma of feeling different because my family was different from the other kids. *When are you going to grow up, Margaret?*

Then Hal turned more serious. "Margaret, about this guy who you say has been following you, the one you told Lt. Chandler about— don't you think you ought to let me in on it so I can keep an eye out for this guy? Looking out for you could be a very enjoyable part of my job." His tone of intimacy caressed me, making me tingle all over.

"I didn't think you cared or even believed me."

"Look, it has been a long difficult summer so far, and if I seemed, well, distant…... I've lost people I've known all my life and, well, it may have clouded my judgment." This was as vulnerable as I had ever seen Hal. I was touched and that tingly feeling was getting more intense. I had a craving, but it wasn't for a drink!

I ran over to my box by the computer and snatched the photographs I had stored there, rifling through them to find Lizard Lids—Cleaves. With enthusiasm I handed him the picture. He studied it with a professional air and then looked at me. "You know you did a very dangerous thing when you got up close and personal with this guy?"

"You had to be there. I don't like feeling threatened, and some times I overreact. You know, a fool rushing in sort of thing. But I did get rid of him, which is what I wanted to do."

"What's done is done. I'll keep an eye out for this guy. Did Lt. Chandler say if there were any outstanding warrants on him? What's his name again, and I don't mean your nickname for him?"

"Jason Cleaves, but let's not talk about him anymore."

"You're right. We both have an early day tomorrow. I had a very nice time and enjoyed your company, Margaret. It's been awhile."

My jaw must have dropped. That was it? Nice time, gotta go? This was the second time he had done that, or was it the third time? Easy does it is one thing, but I don't know if I can stand this much longer. He was on his feet heading for the door when he turned as if he had just had a thought.

"Margaret, the Mud Run is next weekend, the 24th and 25th. If you like we could go. It can be a lot of fun. Have you ever been to one?"

"I really don't know anything about it except I did see some of the trucks at Charlie's garage. He tried to talk me into entering."

"Do you think you want to?"

"No, but it might be a hoot to go and observe."

"Great! We'll play it by ear. If nothing else catastrophic happens between now and then, I should have the whole weekend off."

"Oh, I just remembered, I work Saturday."

"No problem, it doesn't really get underway until two. You'll have plenty of time. But listen, Margaret, just leave when your shift is over. Don't wait around for Shirley to show up. Besides, knowing her, she's probably asked for the day off already. Oh, and don't let Josie talk you into working longer either."

"Yes sir!" And I saluted him. He looked a trifle sheepish and irritated at the same time.

"Tell you what. I'll stop trying to give orders if you stop trying to be brave and sassy. Is it a deal?"

"It's a deal and you've got a date." I still hated to see him leave. I moved closer, put my arms around his neck and looked up into those gorgeous brown eyes. "I had a really good time tonight." He put his arms around my lower back and pressed me to him. "You're a dangerous girl, Margaret." Before I could retort he had his lips locked over mine, and I was being pulled into his warm firm body. All I could think of was how I wanted to get even closer.

The moment didn't last, and Hal left me breathless at the door. The sting from his initial parting words had left. Things were definitely looking up, but a cold shower was a necessity!

Josie could tell that I was on cloud nine as I whirled in and out of the kitchen, waiting on customers. The morning zoomed by. When we took our break I told her some of the high points of the evening and about the date for the mud run. She looked impish with a phony crestfallen expression. "I was going to ask if you could work that

Saturday afternoon because Shirley's boyfriend is in the mud run, and she won't be coming in."

"I promised Hal I wouldn't let you wheedle me into working any more this weekend. You understand, don't you?"

"Of course I do. I was just practicing a guilt trip on you. You weren't buying any of it, were you? It will be really slow, and I've even thought about closing early or for the whole day so Dwight and I can go. That's one of the perks of being retired—you can be flexible."

"Trust, me Josie, you don't need to practice guilt tripping. You have it down to a fine art. For people who are retired, you certainly put in a lot of time working."

Josie watched with a knowing nod when Hal came in and I rushed over to him. I had to be a tease so I told him that he had been right about Shirley and that Josie would need help. It was hard keeping a straight face especially with Hal looking like he was going to blow a gasket. "I'm just kidding. I told Josie I had promised you, and she might close for the day." It was fun watching him defuse.

I had things to look forward to, which was always nice. Of course, as Catsy had told me time and again, it's fine to make plans as long as you don't plan the outcome. That was difficult to do. In my mind I'd rehearse what I would say, what others would say, how I would act and react, even what I would wear; though weather should have something to do with that decision. I forgot that I couldn't control the weather or anything else for that matter. The nice thing about a new way of thinking was that I didn't have to be perfect; I just had to practice being a little better each day. I had seven plus days to catch myself planning the outcome and step back; seven plus days to anticipate my date.

I was excited. I don't know why because it should have been no big deal, but I needed to talk to someone, so I called Catsy to share the news about my upcoming date. "Two calls in one week, I'm honored. You sound different, almost giddy, so what's up." I told her about everything that had transpired in the short time since we had talked last. I wanted her to be as excited as I was, but she just listened quietly asking an occasional question to clarify or maybe slow me down.

"Maggie, your life is starting to sound like a rollercoaster again. You're out of balance and I'm worried about you. Did you go to a meeting last night and are you eating three squares a day?"

If she were trying to be a wet blanket she was doing an exceptional job at putting out my fire. "No, I didn't go to a meeting last night but I have been going pretty regular. As far as the eating part goes, I'm trying to eat; it's just so hard and hectic."

"Maggie, 'try' is a drunk's word. You either do or you don't. I'm only telling you these things to help make your life more manageable."

"I know, and I'm glad that you care enough to do it. I need to be set straight when I get crazy in the head."

"Most of what goes on in your head is none of your business." I knew all that. This wasn't the first time I'd gotten this lecture, but I needed to hear it over and over again to get it to sink in. When the lecture was over, we continued to have a nice long talk. After I got off the phone with her I tried calling Tina and Joanne, but there was no luck there.

I decided to go to the Friday night meeting out of town and leave with everyone else, so there would be less likelihood of road rage situations. I had to admit I was getting a tad gun-shy about driving at night. My track record wasn't good, but my rebel streak was strong. I wasn't going to let anybody interfere with my life.

I walked down to the Icebox for some dinner and debated whether to sit there or take it home. I hated making decisions and had managed to avoid them most of my life; then if anything went wrong it wasn't my fault. It was cool down by the water, so I parked myself in a lawn chair and chowed down. A few brazen seagulls conned some fries and a crusty part of my fish burger out of me. "That's it guys. Go find another patsy."

Walking back to the apartment, I became acutely aware of someone staring at me from the doorway of the Spiny Urchin. The bar was on the opposite side of the street and the doorway was in the shadows. The last person that had accosted me from there was Wayne, but he was dead, and I didn't believe in ghosts. It was hard to act nonchalant, but I wasn't up for a confrontation especially after my talk with Catsy.

Those eyes were boring into me. I had to know. Just as I came to the corner of my building, I surreptitiously flung a glance over my shoulder. It was supposed to be quick and off hand but I locked eyes with Howie as he sauntered out of the doorway and blatantly stared back at me with a malicious glare. I was totally freaked out and fled up the stairs to the safety of my apartment.

I was not about to let Howie intimidate me, and I was going to a meeting! I still had some time before I had to leave, but I was not especially motivated to do anything but hit the chair and switch on the 'boob tube,' as Dad would say. I hadn't had time to watch much and no real desire to. The news was on, so I could find out what was going on in the rest of the world, but it seemed like the same old stuff, just different faces. If I had a teaching job lined up, I would be watching the news religiously because social studies teachers had to be up on current events, and it was nice to have background material to build on. The thirty second sound bites could have a devastating impact on young impressionable minds. It was almost impossible to decipher what kids were talking about when they gave their rendition of what was on the news. If I had to teach current events, I wanted them to have some substance, but I really hated that part of social studies. Right now that isn't my concern, because I don't have a teaching position and no prospects that I can see. A dreaded decision was speeding in my direction. If I didn't get a teaching job, I'd have to figure out what I was going to do about the next stage of my life. It was one of those things that I kept putting off. *Don't panic, there is still plenty of time.*

While I was contemplating my job prospects, I caught something about Mundy. "Police are ruling the death of Sheila Jones a homicide. Jones was found dead on July 5th in Mundy. A police spokesman said they have a suspect but would not comment or disclose any further information other than the case is ongoing. When asked if the case was connected to the Theodore Cox hit–and–run, police spokesman Jonathan Turner declined to comment." *I'll bet he did.* The worm turns! I guess I resent the hell out of Turner. Funny thing about that, he almost gets me killed or run out of town but that's my problem. Obviously I was not ready to forgive and forget his involvement in Old Orchard and his wanting to make a federal case out of a kid's indiscretion. Well I'd work on that another day.

After a bit of national news, I hit the road for the meeting. I was experiencing some major paranoia. I kept watch in my rearview mirror for any signs of someone following me. There were a few cars on the road, some with out-of-state plates that passed me or turned off. I couldn't go on like this, worrying every time I left the apartment. It was ridiculous. I tried to focus on the people in the program I might see at the meeting and what I could bring to the meeting, going over Catsy's words of wisdom. What I really wanted was to walk into the hall, be greeted by smiling faces, and feel safe.

The people at the meeting did not disappoint. Winfield was there and came right up to me. "I don't know what you said to Margaret, but whatever it was it made a remarkable change in her. Thank you so much. She has gone through such terrible times that it's nice to see her smiling." I didn't have a clue that I'd done anything that positive. If anything she had helped me. Going back with my family pictures to share as well as more conversation was rising on my priority list.

The meeting was on the fourth step, and acceptance, humility, and forgiveness were all words that had not been part of my vocabulary before I got sober. We laughed and shared, and I experienced a peacefulness that just washed over me. I never cease to be amazed at hearing just what I need at a meeting to help me with an attitude adjustment. Catsy had assured me that I was simply experiencing life and that eleven of the twelve steps were all about living life on life's terms, with a higher power replacing those chemical helpers I had always thought I needed.

Totally refreshed by the meeting, some of my paranoia evaporated and I was able to enjoy the ride back to Mundy. I wanted to be able to feel that it was home. I was tired of picking up and moving and starting over and over and over again. I parked the truck and bounced up the steps. I was way too keyed up to go straight to bed so I circled the apartment looking for something to do. The stacks of the old Tidewater Times were calling to me. After talking to Winfield tonight, I wanted to read up on all the things that Margaret had touched on. I had no idea if the right newspapers were here, but I was ready to begin the search. I wasn't sure how they were stacked. Were they in some kind of chronological order or just gathered and tied up in bundles? Looking over the banners of the top papers on the stacks,

I found some that were in the ballpark, so I took out my trusty little pocket knife and knelt down on the floor.

Cutting that first bundle open was exhilarating, but that moment wore off quickly. I wanted to be methodical with my approach so I gently lifted the top issue and put it face down on a clear area so I could reconstruct the pile after going through it.

When I got to the middle of the pile, I realized that I was off by a year one way or the other. The bundles appeared to be stacked according to years with a couple of years in each bundle. There were some gaps in the issues and it appeared that the paper had always been a weekly with no advertising inserts to take up space, which saved me time. The only thing left was to ascertain how many years were in each bundle. I decided on the easy way to find out by flipping the rest of the bundle on top of the new pile I had started and then I checked the date on the bottom issue of this pile. I'd need to find another pile, but there had been three years worth of papers in the first one I had chosen.

After scanning several piles, I chose another with the hopes that this would be the one. This was more tedious but I finally hit pay dirt. It was the right year but the end of the summer for that year so, being careful not to tear or crumple the papers, I set aside the ones I thought I would need, even going back to May's issues. By now it was getting late and my back and knees were killing me, so I scooped up the pile I was interested in and took it to the living room and settled on the futon.

As I skimmed each May issue, I cursed my lack of speed-reading ability. This might take all night, and I still had to get up to go to work in the morning. It was already past midnight but I was obsessing. I read the coverage of the lake accident including the editorial page. It was big news back then with several families losing children.

Familiar family names stood out from the page, Jones and Cox among them. John Thomas Murphy, Senior was exonerated officially but the editorial page gave the tenor of community feeling. If he hadn't been so powerful I could envision him facing a lynch-mob or at least being run out of town on a rail. It was understandable. Whenever kids are involved, feelings are at a fever pitch. My experience with my students' parents had borne that out, which was the reason why living in the same town that you taught in was a bad idea.

John Junior's death made front-page news with what looked like his senior high school picture. He was a hunk. I remembered what Margaret had said about his drinking. It figured—I was always attracted to drunks. Hal's face danced through my head. Maybe I was changing the kind of guys I picked to hang out with. I had never seen him drink to excess, and there was no scuttlebutt around town about anything hinky going on. Of course he had hung out with a bunch of drunks in his school days. Maybe that was why he was attracted to me. *We aren't going there tonight Margaret.* It was painful to read about the shooting, knowing how Margaret felt about her Tommy. There were no photos of him.

There wasn't much in the way of details about the accident at camp, although, there was a plug for gun safety. The editorial page wasn't quite as vociferous on the subject as it undoubtedly would be today under Driscoll's direction. The odd thing about the articles was that they weren't as intrusive as today's media. There were no wild speculations or conclusions drawn out of thin air. We could take some lessons from these older times.

The last thing I found to read about was the death of John Thomas Murphy, Sr. I almost missed it. His death hadn't made headlines. There was only an obituary in which his next of kin were listed along with his community affiliations. He came from a large family of boys, only three of whom survived him. If they'd all married and had large families we were talking a lot of Murphys. Many had probably moved away. There was a picture of the old boy that showed him to be of stern countenance with what looked like a tyrannical mean streak in his eyes, backed up by what Margaret had said. John Senior looked like it would be a cold day in hell before he would forgive anyone!

I looked at the time, two in the morning! I crawled off to bed dreading the alarm that would go off in a couple of hours. My imagination took over as I replayed everything I had read, heard and thought had happened.

Chapter Twenty

I was dragging when I went to work. Bleary-eyed didn't cover the half of it. "Look what the cat dragged in."

"Oh come on Josie. Can't you think of anything better than that old cliché? Besides, you've seen me look a lot worse."

"May I at least know what in the world you were doing last night to account for your present state?"

"No big deal. I was just reading and didn't want to stop. I lost track of time, but I'll be fine after one of your great cups of coffee."

We bantered back and forth while I baked. When I'm overtired, punning and sharp retorts just sort of flow out of me. Josie could take it and dish it out herself. Dwight played along with my verbal antics. He was better at it than I was, and Robby just laughed. I knew Hal wouldn't be coming in to make the morning go quicker and I could have used something to hurry time along.

John Driscoll strolled in like an arrogant bastard. I should be more careful what I wish for. He wasn't exactly what I had in mind. "Well Josie, looks like all hell is going to break loose soon, but you probably already know that." He glanced over at me and winked. Josie looked as baffled as I felt. What was this blowhard talking about? He was a piece of work.

"What'cha talking about, John?"

"Didn't you catch the news? They've got a suspect in the Jones girl's murder. I'm sure it's all tied into a drug cartel operation." Oh please. This bozo was so far out that he was on another planet. I had no intentions of entering a conversation with him, but I was interested to know if he was referring to that lame broadcast I had seen, or if there had been some further developments. As long as I was absolved of any connection I would be happy. Let nature and the police take their respective courses.

Driscoll went off with Josie, but he kept tossing weird looks at me. *Ignore him, he's just a dirty old man.* As a gift from God to take my mind off Driscoll and his outrageous opinions, Winfield and Margaret came in. It struck me that they were an odd couple, even more now than when I first saw them together here in the diner. Creatures of habit, they settled at their usual table. I brought them water, ready to take their order. "Good morning, dear. My, you look tired. I hope you aren't overdoing things."

I was so happy to see both of them. "Good morning. I stayed up too late last night reading. I can hardly say I'm over worked."

"It's hard to put down a good book. I've been known to stay up all night at times, but then as you get to be my age, you don't seem to need as much sleep." It wouldn't be a lie to let her think it was a good book I had been into. She was happy, and I liked seeing her that way instead of carrying the cares of the world on her shoulders. Winfield was very attentive to her, and it was kind of sweet watching the two of them. They ordered tea and Morning Glory muffins. As I brought them over, Josie was disengaging from Driscoll. I was sure she had picked his brain—pretty meager pickings if you ask me—and I would be sure to do likewise to her before I left.

Good hostess she was, Josie made the rounds with her regular customers, stopping here and there to welcome visitors, and then ended up at Winfield and Margaret's table. Margaret motioned me back over. "Maggie dear, I've just invited Josie and Dwight to a picnic that Kenny is having out at his home before the mud run. It's an annual gathering, and Kenny and I would like you to come. Have you met his wife, Penny?"

"No I haven't met her, but I met his daughter Terry over at the hardware store when I got a key made for my apartment."

"There are many Murphy family members, and most of them show up at the picnic. You could bring a friend. Josie tells me you have become friends with one of our local sheriff's deputies, Del's brother Hal. I think Del will be there as well." Margaret made it sound very inviting.

I turned to Josie. "So I've been invited to the mud run with Hal. I'll ask him, but are you going to be open on Saturday or not?"

"Seeing how most of my regulars will probably be at the picnic and the mud run, I might as well stop fighting it and join in. We'll be closed on Saturday. I'll go out and make up a sign for the window."

"Josie, are you going to bring some of your wonderful potato salad this year?"

"Of course I will. It's a snap to make, Margaret, if you'd like the recipe. Maggie, you'll have to whip up some special creation for the picnic, too. Speaking of which, what do you know about blueberries?" I looked quizzically at Josie because I knew there had to be more to her question.

"I've never raked them, if that's what you mean, but I've gathered them and eaten them. I've even made a wicked blueberry fudge. The ones I've picked were high bush blueberries that I'd get at Ferry Beach State Park. I wore a bucket around my neck so I could pick with both hands. I know when they're ripe and love taste testing them. Does that qualify me for whatever it is you have in mind?"

"Dwight and I have some property up the coast off Bolton Lake Road that is a blueberry barren was. I think they might be ripe enough to rake but Dwight and I haven't had the time to get up there. I was thinking…could you check them out for me? You like exploring. It's a great spot, and the coast at low tide is fascinating to explore, especially when you're young and agile. I'm getting a mite too old for rock climbing. You know the area don't you, Margaret?" There was a fleeting expression of pain that went across Margaret's face. Winfield looked over and rested his hand on hers.

"Are you all right Margaret?" I looked at Margaret, Winfield and then Josie in turn. Josie had a slight blush.

"I forgot that the Murphy's used to own that whole stretch of coastline and the other side of Bolton Lake Road as well. You still have some land out there don't you? Every parcel that was put on the market was snatched up. Now if any place has even a water view it's going for big bucks."

Josie sounded like she was about to go off on another tangent and I didn't want her to get carried away. It was obvious that there was a sensitive spot about that area for Margaret and my guess was that it had something to do with the Murphy camp.

"I'm not familiar with the Bolton Lake Road. You'd have to show me how to get there. Can you draw me a map?"

"Well, I'm not really good at directions. Dwight says I'm a typical woman who could confuse the bejeezus out of a Maine guide. Winfield, you know the area. Can you give Maggie directions?"

"I'd be happy to." Josie was off to wait on people just coming in, and Winfield flipped over his placemat and took out a pen. Margaret had become quiet, so while Winfield was drawing a map, I started up a conversation. "Margaret I went through some of the family pictures I was telling you about. I'd love to get together and show you."

She perked up. "Why don't you come by tomorrow afternoon? I'll be back from church and I'll dig out my albums."

"Promise you won't laugh at some of my pictures. I was a bit of a hellion, actually I still am. I just try not to have it show up on camera." We laughed.

Winfield's map was simple and to the point. I shouldn't have any problem finding Josie's blueberries. On the map there was a road off to the left almost opposite where Winfield had indicated Josie's blueberry barren. I spotted it as I was folding up the map to put it in my apron pocket. I looked up at Winfield and he gave me a wink… curious.

I was in a hurry to go exploring when I left work but, remembering Catsy's warning, I took time to eat lunch, then packed a snack and plenty of water in my backpack. My camera was loaded. I felt prepared for anything.

Following the map was a cinch. The road was deserted so I could take my time and gawk around. I was seeing a few camp roads with painted wooden family signs, some with nicknames for the places like *Gramp's Camp* and *Coyote Cottage*, nailed to trees, painted on rocks, or stuck on poles. On the other side of the road were 'no trespassing' and 'private road' signs with the obligatory gates across the drives even if they were overgrown and nearly impassable. What a difference! Then I saw what Winfield had traced on the map. There was a large rough wooden sign hanging from a rusty set of chains attached to a metal arm which was in turn attached to a tall tree. I slowed to take a better look. The growing tree had swallowed the metal arm. It looked like a grotesque prosthetic device for an amputee. The sign itself had been carved and painted and possibly shellacked at one time. In the Celtic style it simply said MURPHY'S.

I was so mesmerized by that swaying sign that I had almost come to a stop in the middle of the road and would have missed the right hand turn to Josie's place. I would have to go back and check that road out after I checked out the berries.

I took the dirt turn-off just past Murphy's and followed it out to the coast. Opening up in front of me was a small blueberry barren with shades of dusty blue ripening berries in patches that reached the blue ocean and cloud dotted blue sky. It was gorgeous and peaceful. I parked the truck at the end of the road next to trees and an abandoned house.

I couldn't resist. I got my backpack out and started by walking around the house. The windows were broken out and the door was hanging by a single hinge. Weather had taken its toll on the floors and walls. On the first floor, the rooms appeared empty of any furniture or appliances. There was a staircase off to the left with a broken banister. It didn't look very sturdy and I knew better than to try and go up the steps. I wasn't as foolish as I used to be. If I'd been drunk,

I would have thought nothing of plowing right in to check it out. It was a good way to end up dead.

A childhood memory of another house that I'd thought was abandoned came to mind. I was with my pals and we made our way through the whole place from the basement to the attic. I found some old books and an antique candle mold that I fancied. We each piled our finds in an old wagon and brought the treasures back to our homes. My mom had a fit and called a friend of hers in the Sheriff's Department. I was very young and easily intimidated at the time. I was marched back to the house with my mom and dad to return my treasures in my wagon. Nothing happened to my pals, Chris, Jeff, and Al.

As this old scenario rolled through my head, I was brought back to the present by the rustling sound above me. I nearly jumped out of my skin. *My, aren't we on edge? Is the big, bad boogieman out to get you?* When I realized how silly I was being, I had to laugh. It sounded like there might be a family of raccoons nesting up in the eaves. I called out that I had no intention of disturbing them and continued scouting around the premises. I came to a steep path and a brook that was trickling over the rocks and down to a beach with reddish soil. I slid down on my haunches and bounced on my feet when I hit the sand. As I peered back up at the cliff edge I admired the intricate patterns of erosion exposing rocks and the roots of cedars clinging precariously to the soil that was left by the ocean surf.

The rock formations were intriguing. The tide had worn away shelves of rock and dirt, creating caves and carvings that were surreal. I took pictures galore, explored the caves, and picked through the interesting debris left among the rocks. I couldn't keep from picking up some of the rarer gems and sticking them in my backpack.

It was so easy to lose track of time and tide in this wonderland that I had almost forgotten about why I was here in the first place. I was having a ball in my own little world. I found another way up to the top that was easier to maneuver, with brush for handholds and flat rocks sticking out of the clay, almost as if they were man-made steps.

When I reached the top, I found myself in a thick grove of trees bordering the far side of the barren from my truck, which I could make out from across the field of berries. I had come quite a distance. I decided to eat my way back to the truck because the berries were ready for raking and I couldn't resist.

It was suppertime now, but I was all set with the blueberries and the snacks I had packed. I was ready for another rigorous walk. Turning the truck around, I made my way to the Bolton Lake Road. Since I didn't know what condition the other road was in, it would be best if I left my truck in Josie's road and walked up the other road. I couldn't wait to find the infamous Murphy Camp.

The sky had turned an overcast steel gray, and there was a cool moist breeze beginning to ruffle the leaves of the massive oaks that lined the camp road. It didn't look that overgrown, though there were bent and snapped branches of underbrush and flattened grass running up the middle. I could have driven the truck down through here just like others obviously had, but not knowing what was at the end of the road or if there was a turn- around spot made me glad I was on foot. The ferns wafted a pungent scent. I filled my nostrils, sucking in the heady perfume as I walked.

After what seemed like miles but was maybe a mile in, there it was—a log cabin with shuttered windows and something shiny on the front that looked oddly out of place. I don't know what I had been expecting, perhaps something along the lines of the lodge of the Fin, Fur and Feather. It was nothing so impressive. At one time it had probably been a simple one room camp. Over time rooms had been added so it spread out. There was a great view of the lake and rough log steps leading down to the water's edge. It was very quiet with only the sporadic chirping of a few birds and the chattering of chipmunks scampering up and down tree trunks in search of food. The shiny object was an ordinary padlock that had replaced an older one lying on the porch by the door. It had been cut off and lay where it had fallen. Someone was not very tidy. My curiosity was intense. I wanted to see inside, but after circling the camp it was apparent that I would not be able to.

I sat down on a rock by the shore and tried to imagine a young Margaret playing in the summer sun. As I looked across the lake I saw an abundance of trees with only a smattering of man-made spaces and buildings. The location definitely offered privacy. It was pretty isolated for such a popular lake. I suppose it could actually be very lonely.

It suddenly occurred to me that the Murphys had probably sold off this land and the shiny new lock was from the new owners. All of a sudden I felt guilty, as if I was trespassing. I hadn't seen any uninviting signs, and as I looked over my shoulder at the cabin and its surroundings, I didn't see any indication that a family was using this great spot either. Then I heard a truck creaking up the road.

That old abandoned house episode washed over me, and I was consumed with a need to hide. I skittered up by the side of the cabin farthest from the road. As quietly as possible I tried to maneuver to the back, almost on my hands and knees because of all the brush. Just as I came to the corner, a truck pulled up and began to back into a clearing next to the cabin.

My heart was pounding, and my breathing sounded like thunder in my ears. I'd have to wait until the person went in the cabin and then scoot back to the road through the woods. What the ...? Drops of water started pelting me at the same time an "Oh, Fuck!" bellowed from the truck cab. It had started to rain one of those summer showers. This was going to be great! I'd be soaking wet by the time I got back to my truck, and I thought my windows were down. *Any time you want to run for the cabin so I can get out of here, I'd appreciate it.* I heard the truck door open and slam shut. I peeked around the corner to see if the person was headed for the cabin.

I quickly slapped my hand over my mouth as the gasp escaped my lips. The rain ceased to be of any concern when I saw who had gotten out of the truck. It was all I could do to stay quiet. Thank goodness the rain hitting the leaves made so much racket. I remembered my camera hanging on my neck. I wanted to get a shot of the truck and the license number, which I was already committing to memory. While I took the shots and crammed the camera into my backpack, I heard the hasp on the door swing open and the sound of footsteps on the cabin floor. The chanting of "curiosity killed the cat" rang in my head, replacing the pounding of my heart. What was going on here? Things weren't adding up. The shuttered windows hid me from sight but meant I couldn't see what was going on inside. *Margaret, get your butt out of here **now**!*

This time I listened to my little voice. I got soaked as I pawed my way along the underbrush at the side of the road. After a few turns in the road so I was out of sight of the cabin, I made my way onto the dirt ruts and started to jog back to my truck. The action of my muscles felt good and helped to counter the effects of the adrenalin that had been pumped into my bloodstream.

It was late and darker than usual because of the rain. I tore ass getting back to my place until I nearly ran into a deer that leapt out of a ditch. The last thing I wanted to do was make contact with a big furry. My truck had taken enough punishment. I eased off the gas and took some deep breaths. *Get a grip, Margaret, and take some drama out of the situation.*

Back at the apartment I stripped, took a quick shower, and put on my sweats. My mind was racing but I was trying to ignore it. Making some dinner helped. I ate out on the deck after I toweled off the chairs. The rain had stopped as suddenly as it had begun. The sky was clearing with raggedy gray clouds rent by currents that were only visible through the resultant moving clouds. The backdrop was tinged with yellow and turquoise.

I was settled down now. Food had worked its magic. It was too late to call Jeff, and besides Lizard Lids hadn't done anything wrong. It wasn't like he broke in. He had a key. Let's face it I just freaked out because he gave me the creeps. It was me that had been skulking around. I had almost forgotten why I was even out there in the first place. I could call Josie and let her know the blueberries were ripe and ready to go. I'd even offer to rake some for her.

As I contemplated all my possibilities for the future the phone rang.

"Margaret is that you?" Why did people insist on starting conversations that way? Who else would it be?

"Yes, of course it's me. Is that you Joanne? You sound terrible."

"Tina is in jail. She got busted shooting an Oxy eighty and I guess she was holding."

"Slow down Joanne. Are you using? And please be straight with me."

"I swear to God I'm clean."

"You don't need to swear to God, he knows. I'm not going to ask why she went back out. Were you guys going to meetings?"

"Well we started to but then she kept begging off when I'd call to see if she wanted to go. She was all nervous and kept saying they were going to take her kids. She was getting crazy and paranoid. I think the last meeting she went to was right after we talked to you but something spooked her."

"I tried calling you both but didn't get any answer."

"The people from drug court that showed up at the meeting last night told me what they know. I guess she was real wasted, and boy is she going to be sick. They came and got her kids."

"Wait a minute. Who are 'they' and what about her husband or her boyfriend?"

"Oh, Jim took off. He hasn't been around for a long time."

"So Tina is in jail waiting for arraignment?"

"Yeah, and I don't have any money to bail her out. I thought you should know. She sort of thought of you as her sponsor."

"Joanne, I can't bail her out. Besides she needs to be the one to call me if she needs help, and I'm not her sponsor. I'm not ready for that."

"But you have three years. That's the longest anyone I know has been sober." I wasn't going into that craziness with her. She was a newcomer, and old-timers like Winfield, Del and Kenny weren't female. "If you've been going to meetings you must have met some women with longer than that."

"Oh I did. I asked this old woman down at the Washington meeting to be my sponsor. She's a real kick ass kind of person. She's got ten years in. Can you believe it? She came in when she was forty, but she did drugs too."

"Well it sounds like you want to be sober and you haven't been threatened by your dealer or anything like that have you?"

"No. Why? I'm doing okay."

"I'm glad to hear it. Maybe we can start making some meetings together."

I heard a click on the line. "Margaret I've got to go. I've got another call and I'm meeting my sponsor. I'll call you if I hear anything more, and you can call me if you hear anything. Oh I got a job too, which is why I'm not home during the day. See ya."

"Talk to you later."

I still needed to call Josie, but it felt awfully good talking to Joanne. Even in the short time I had been in the program, people going to jail or back to jail was common. It was a statistic I didn't want to join. Catsy told me if I stayed in the middle of the program I'd have less chance of falling off the edge into a drug and alcohol grave. It was like being in the middle of a life boat so that even if things got rocky you wouldn't fall out. The only thing I seemed to be able to stay in the middle of was trouble, other people's trouble.

The call to Josie was short and sweet. She needed a couple of quarts to begin with, and I said I'd see what I could do but it would probably be on Monday afternoon and I'd pick up a rake. It was either that or hand pick them in a squatting position.

It was too late to get to a meeting so I sat down and continued to go through the top drawer of Dad's filing cabinet. Among the family pictures were notes that Dad had kept along with Mom's birth certificate and mine. I might need that at some point. I'd figured I'd have to send away for a copy from New York if it was ever absolutely necessary. He had kept mementos of his courtship of Mom. It's difficult to think of your parents as once having been boyfriend and girlfriend. My dad was truly a pack rat. The pile of papers and pictures needled me into thinking about organizing all this stuff. I don't think I really knew where to begin. My first job would be to sort out what I would take to Margaret's.

It felt luxurious sleeping in late the next day. The morning was gray and misty, so I fixed a big breakfast and padded around in my slippers. My belly full, I was tempted to go back to bed, but it dawned on me that I had forgotten to get a paper the day before so figured I'd get one this morning. It would be nice to read national and state news rather than the local hysterics. As far as teaching was concerned, I might have to expand my parameters to include something other than teaching just high school social studies.

I squeezed into a pair of jeans and a sweatshirt, eyeing the growing pile of dirty laundry accumulating in the bathroom. I had been putting off the inevitable but not for much longer. I stuck some money in my pocket and shook out my rain jacket. That didn't help. It was still full of wrinkles but, what the heck; I was just running down to the Quik Stop for a paper. Once outside, I took my time. The weather was keeping the town quiet.

At the Quik Stop the regular crowd was hanging out, plus one. Leaning up against the outside, one foot planted on the wall and out of uniform was Howard Jones. Seeing him slowed my stride. Shit! This guy kept turning up like a bad penny. I had to walk close by him to get into the store. I could always do an about face and go to the market, but it would be rather obvious and besides who was this guy to keep me from going where I wanted to go? Nobody was going to get in my way. I squared my shoulders, picked up the pace, and barged right past him, not giving him a chance to say a word.

There wasn't anyone I recognized inside, and there wasn't anything I needed except a paper, so I paid for it and headed right back out the door. Even though I had been fast, it was enough time to give Howie a chance to come up with something to say. "I'd watch my step if I were you." Well, duh. That must have taken a lot of brainwork.

Back at the apartment, I perused the classifieds but the pickings were slim. There was an opening in Tylerville for a combination English/social studies position in the junior high that might be promising. I could call Beth on that one. It was exciting thinking about teaching in Tylerville. It was hard not to be impatient about a job. Wanda would probably be back on her feet soon and want her job back. I didn't know what the scoop was about Wanda and when she'd want to come back to work, and I couldn't afford to live on a waitress's salary through the winter. Fear of financial insecurity was creeping in. Catsy would tell me to leave it in God's hands, but I still thought I should help him along.

I had time to print out a cover letter and resume and put the packet together for Monday's mail. Now what? Sorting through all the pictures I wanted to take to Margaret's brought back some bittersweet memories. It also reminded me that somewhere in my junk was a scrapbook that had been given to me as a farewell gift from the faculty at my last job. Scrap booking had become all the rage, although I had never gotten into it. Maybe I could find it and stuff all the pictures and notes in it, just to keep them flat. I scrounged through bags and boxes and finally came up with it just in time to leave.

Margaret was still dressed in her church clothes, and I felt like a slob. She led me into the living room this time. The room was cheery and inviting. Two loveseats upholstered in a floral design flanked a stone fireplace. A broad coffee table held a tea service at one end, complete with lemon, cream, cookies, and delicate china cups and saucers. Now I was really feeling out of place. The other end of the coffee table held old albums. You could tell they were old because the covers were black and so were the pages, nothing like the bright colors and designs of the modern scrapbooks. I set my own contribution down, thinking that it looked pretty conspicuous.

Margaret gestured for me to sit, and she sat beside me offering me tea. This was like going back in time and having tea with the queen. I was suddenly afraid I was going to break something because I felt like the proverbial bull in a China shop. I gazed at the rest of the room to take my mind off my awkwardness. The windows were hung with the same simple white broadcloth curtains as the kitchen, trimmed with ball fringe and tied back. It was cool in the room, in part because the sun wasn't beating in. There was a baby grand piano in the corner draped with a shawl and festooned with photos of Margaret and her husband. It was an elegant setting and Margaret and her husband looked like a happy couple.

"I really don't have these things in any kind of order. I just discovered them in a filing cabinet my dad had. I've only gotten into the top drawer. I'm thinking of framing some of these and creating a wall collage." I was babbling, which I tend to do when I'm very nervous.

"Dear, you don't have to have anything in order. The albums I have were things my mother and I put together when I was a young girl. They are a bit musty and faded, mostly black and white photographs. It was a mother-daughter activity in a household full of men. But I'm excited to see your pictures." I could sense her genuine enthusiasm even if I couldn't understand it, and that put me more at ease. Margaret was able to do that to me.

I opened up the scrapbook. There was my high school graduation picture with my Dad. My girl friend's mother had taken it. Mom had been gone for a couple of years by then. The sense of loss swept over me. Margaret held the pictures in her hand with a kind of reverence. We went through the goofy shots of me at my birthday parties, holidays, and family outings. There were Mom and Dad, smiles on their faces as they held one another. You could see that they were in love. I had brought a wedding picture that I had found. Mom was wearing a dress suit and Dad was wearing a suit, not a tux. Of course, it hadn't been formal with bridesmaids and pomp. Dad and Mom had been on their own with no family to speak of.

Margaret spent a long time gazing at the wedding picture. "Your mother was very beautiful and delicate."

"Yes. I wished I'd inherited some of those qualities from her but Dad endowed me with most of my features." Hal's comment about my heritage came drifting back to me. I had gotten testy with him, but here I was saying the same thing about myself to Margaret. We chatted about hair, freckles, and sunburns then Margaret asked if Dad had been my protector.

"Oh, he was my protector even when I was being an obnoxious brat. I hated the thought of needing protecting. He was there for my mom. She was strong in her own way, but when she got sick she depended on both of us. I really wasn't there for her as much as I should have been." I hadn't been. I had been out getting drunk and in trouble, which my father would get me out of and then smooth it over so as not to upset Mom. I could hear him now. "Your mother doesn't need to be troubled about this. It will be just between you and me." How selfish could I get?

Margaret heard the regret in my voice and seemed to understand the churning that was going on in my mind. She patted my hand. She was still holding the wedding picture as she looked into my eyes, her own eyes filled with tears. "We must not regret the past, Margaret. There is nothing we can do to change it. What's done is done."

Wow, she sounded just like my sponsor. Some of the program must have rubbed off on her from Kenny and Winfield. Hoping to lighten the mood, I showed her Dad's note to me. It still made me emotional reading it again, but it was good to share with someone. However, I was not prepared for the reaction it elicited from Margaret. She started sobbing. I was dumbfounded. He had been talking about leprechauns and our special sharing. I missed him especially because of those times, but why was Margaret so sensitive about it? Maybe it went against her religion or something.

She put down the wedding picture, squeezed my hand and said, "It's time I shared my photos with you." There were baby pictures of John Jr. and his mother and father. Margaret's mother's name was Mary too. She looked very shy, almost frightened, whereas John Sr. looked condescending. There wasn't the same love in these pictures but more like a dark undertone. Tommy had been a pudgy little thing when he was born, and I didn't say anything, but he and Margaret looked like pudgy little twins from her baby pictures. Boy had she changed. The photos were grainy black and whites as Margaret had said. There was the camp. Even after all the time that had passed since the picture was taken, I still recognized the view from the shore and the design of the camp. I didn't know if it would be appropriate to bring up the camp and the questions I had about it. I wasn't sure I wanted to be responsible for causing more irritation with a sore subject just to satisfy my curiosity, but that selfish need to know reared its ugly head. "Margaret, did your family sell the camp after the accident?"

"No. It's a strange thing, but Father actually had it set up in trust for Tommy. Why in God's name—oh pardon my swearing, but it seemed like a cruel thing to do with what happened. But then, I never understood my father; I just tried to stay out of his way. Tommy didn't know anything about it. He left before it all came out."

Now I was excited. "Margaret, would anyone else in the family be using the camp?"

"Not to my knowledge, unless Kenny's children went up there. After our mother died it was left to me to handle the estate. I put a padlock on it, and it's been left that way. It was Tommy's and is still held in trust for him and his family. Why all these questions about the camp?"

"I was up in that area checking on Josie's blueberries and I was just curious." I didn't want to alarm her with the fact that someone was using the camp for who knew what.

Margaret had picked up the last album and was caressing the cover. She hadn't opened it but gave me that strange look again. "Margaret, these are pictures that were taken in the last couple of years before Tommy left." She wasn't ready to relinquish them and it suddenly dawned on me that the most vivid and special memories she had of her brother were wrapped up in that album tightly clasped in her lap. Finally she handed me the album and picked up the wedding photo like a trade.

I opened the album to high school portraits and a senior picture. I just stared. My mind was paralyzed, as if I'd been shot with a TASer. There in black and white was a young version of my dad not much different from his wedding picture, although there was a distinct innocence in his senior picture that had been replaced in the wedding photo with more worldliness. I knew Margaret was watching me. My mind was on fire and I railed against the thoughts that came pouring in. It can't be. It just isn't possible. A sense of betrayal crowded my thoughts and I could barely breathe. I needed air. I jumped up. I couldn't look at Margaret. All I could do was gulp for air and try to stifle the cry that was in my throat.

I couldn't accept that my whole life was based on a lie and I could not accept that my father could have killed anyone accidentally or otherwise. He had always protected us. All this time I had wanted family, felt deprived because I had none, then this. This was insane. I should be happy, but I found myself pacing up and down the living room clenching my hands in an attempt to get a grip.

"Margaret, I don't know what to say or think." That was a crashing understatement. I owed her a better response than that but I had none.

"Come sit back down." She dabbed at tears with her lace hanky and I was suddenly aware that there were tears streaming down my own face. "When Winfield told me about you, I had great hope that I would see my Tommy again, and when I met you I knew. You are my brother's daughter. There were so many things you shared that brought back memories. I was your father's little Maggot. It was our secret little code name. There were so many things I wanted to ask and so many things I wanted to tell you but I didn't know how. I had to find a way for you to see for yourself. You have brought me so much happiness just by letting me know that Tommy found love and happiness in his life, that he had you and your mom to share it with. Words can't express what that means to me after all these years." A restful peace enveloped her. I was able to catch my breath and sit back down next to her.

"I've always wanted a family. I felt like there was this big hole in me that nothing filled up, and believe me, I tried. When Dad died I guess I just ran as far as I could, but now all I can think of are the nasty things that were said by Wayne, Howie and the ones who painted that nasty stuff on Josie's. Kenny said families come with their own set of problems. Does Kenny know?"

"No, but he has an inkling that something is up since you came to town. Winfield knows. He has always been able to read me like a book, plus he was the one who spotted the resemblance coupled with your name." I nodded. "I didn't want to get my hopes up, so I told myself it might all be a coincidence. There is so much of Tommy about you that it was like he was with me again."

"It's going to take me awhile to get adjusted to having a family. Right now I'm pretty scared. How will this change things with Kenny and everyone else I'm related to." I couldn't tell Margaret that I couldn't accept all the things that she had accepted about Dad and what happened to drive him away from his family. It was totally incomprehensible to me. I knew I wasn't being any too rational, but what else was new?

The afternoon had flown by. We laughed and cried together, sharing memories of the person we had both loved. Inside there still was that pocket of disbelief. I felt like I needed more proof, and the image of Doubting Thomas came to mind from a deep childhood memory. Did I need to stick my hands in the wounds to believe? Did I only want to know half of who my father was? It was definitely going to take time to get acclimated to all this.

When I left her home I was bursting to share the news with someone, and at the same time I wanted to cradle and protect the information from prying eyes.

Chapter Twenty One

There was so much to do this week. At the top of my list after work was calling Jeff about what I had discovered at the Murphy camp. Then there was the serious laundry issue, blueberry raking, and a meeting or two or three. My face gave me away when I walked into work. "Did you have a hot date this weekend that I wasn't privy to?"

"No, Josie, no secret liaisons. I spent a very lean job hunting Sunday morning and a very interesting afternoon with Margaret Doyle."

"You went job hunting on a Sunday morning? No wonder you didn't have any luck."

"No, silly, I went through the paper looking for openings, and there wasn't much of anything there."

"You know, you don't have to worry about leaving this job for awhile. Wanda won't be ready to come back right away, and I'm sure she'll want to spend as much time with her baby as she can."

"Thanks for easing the pressure. I guess I'm used to having a teaching job lined up for the fall. That might not happen this year. You've been positively great, but I don't want to impose on you or Wanda. I'm sure Shirley has never quite accepted me working here. I think she classifies me as an intruder."

"That's her problem; besides, she wouldn't be happy if she didn't have something to bitch about. You just take your time. I really don't want to lose you."

"Thanks, Josie. That means a lot to me. Either way, it won't be any earlier than the end of August. I don't know when they start school around here, but it can't be much different from the rest of the state." Josie was being sweet about everything and I felt guilty not confiding in her about my newfound family. It was hard to share when I didn't know how I felt about it, or maybe I hadn't accepted it as being for real yet. I was certain—especially in this town—that it would be difficult to keep the discovery under wraps. Who was I kidding? At least two other people—Wayne and Howie—seemed to have already made the connection.

When Hal came in, I was all butterflies. I didn't know how much I wanted to say to him either, but whatever we discussed would have to be done some place other than the diner. This place was a hotbed of gossip, and there was no sense in making a public broadcast.

"You're bright and cheery this morning. No more teasing about the mud run today, I hope. You really know how to reel a guy in and then dangle him."

"I promise, no more teasing. Actually I'm really excited about going, but I have a question to ask you."

"There's that 'but' and that's never a good sign." There was a 'here we go again' roll of his eyes and an 'okay, give it to me' expression on his face. I just didn't know when to quit, and Hal didn't take jokes well. He was far too serious, but that was an alluring quality for someone like me.

"Kenny Murphy is having a picnic before the mud run and I've been invited and so have you. I really want to go, so what do you say?" I put on my best pleading damsel look.

"Is that all?"

"Well, yes, I guess. I don't want to be too pushy or anything. I wasn't sure how you'd feel about going. If you don't want to…."

"No problem. I'm going to be on call. I was going to suggest we take our own vehicles. We can meet and go from here. When are we supposed to be at the picnic?"

"Around noon, I think. Josie and Dwight are going, and Josie is bringing her potato salad. I haven't decided what I'll bring yet."

"Whatever it is it will be great, I'm sure. Do I have to bring something? I could always bring some chips."

"You don't have to, but if you want that would be great too. I can't wait. Oh, I do have something else to tell you, but I'd rather share it with you in private." This last bit I said in a hushed tone as I bent toward him. He got a wicked grin on his face and said, "I'm ready and willing whenever you are." I was reminded of our first encounter and the devil with the deep brown eyes. A shiver went up my spine and I wanted to jump in the sack with him right then. I could feel the heat in my face, and I turned away only to run smack into Josie who was wearing her own wicked smirk.

After work I ran upstairs and called Jeff. I was glad he was the one who answered the phone. "Jeff, this is Maggie. You'll never guess whose hangout I found."

"Maggie what's this all about?"

"You know that Cleaves character, the one I call Lizard Lids? Well, he is camped out at the old Murphy place off the Bolton Lake Road. I have it on good authority that he hasn't been given permission by the owners to be there. He put a new padlock on the place and keeps it closed tight when he's not there. Oh, and I got his license plate number and a picture of his truck too."

"Slow down, Maggie. What were you doing out there?"

"I was checking out blueberries across the road for Josie, and I had permission to explore over there." This last was a lie and I held my fingers crossed as I said it.

"I told you there were no outstanding warrants on the guy. All we can do is keep an eye out for him."

"What about trespassing and breaking and entering?"

"Well, for one thing, we have no proof that it happened, and we have no complaints from the owners. Besides, where do you come up with breaking and entering?"

I told Jeff about the original padlock and the new one. I had to admit that in the telling it sounded a bit lame. There was no way they were going to be able to do anything about it. I really wanted to get this guy, but Jeff wasn't having any of it. This was the pits!

"Margaret, I'm just going to tell you again that you need to be careful. You don't know anything about this guy or why he's here. Why are you so intent on getting involved with him? Just let it go." I didn't want to hear this from Jeff, and I hated it when people asked me questions I had no answer for, not even a snappy comeback. My chat with Jeff was severely unfulfilling – more like frustrating – to say the least.

The day had cleared off, and Josie had given me a rake and bucket so I could get some berries for the diner. Recipes for blueberries danced through my head as did the thought of another beach walk if the tide was right. Who was I kidding? In the back of my mind was the idea of making another trip across the road and down to the cabin. It was an insane idea, but when did I ever claim to be sane?

It didn't take long at all to fill the bucket with berries, though I had to figure out how to rake them and what position was the most comfortable. It was a far cry from picking high bush blueberries.

Once I had accomplished the raking, I went over to the edge of the cliff to peer down at the beach that I had explored on my first visit to the blueberry barren. It was almost invisible as water lapped against the rocks, continuing to carve out nooks and crannies that I could check out at low tide. What I really wanted to do at that moment was go back to the main road and head over to the Murphy camp. This time I wouldn't feel like I was trespassing. I turned the truck around and headed out. No sooner had I gotten to where I could see the road when Hal's cruiser turned into the lane. He was still on duty. He hailed me down, and I got out of the truck as he opened his door.

"Josie told me you'd be up this way so I thought I'd see if I could catch you."

"What's up?"

"You tell me. You looked like you wanted to talk but not in the diner. This looks pretty damn private to me." Seeing him in his uniform in this secluded spot, I was beginning to get all gooey inside.

"I know where Jason Cleaves is hiding out." He gave a quizzical gaze and I wanted to back off, but I was excited about my other news of being part of the Murphy clan.

"Hiding out? What makes you think this guy is hiding out?"

"Well, it just so happens that he is staying in the Murphy cabin across the road, and I was just on my way to check it out. He could be the one responsible for Sheila and Bear's deaths. He was following me, you know."

"Don't take this wrong, Margaret, but you have an extremely overactive imagination. It's hard to keep up with the leaps you make. Of course it's kind of cute in a way." Ooh, I hate being patronized. *Kind of cute*, my ass! I could see he didn't feel any excitement over my news.

"Fine. Let's go check it out."

"I don't think that is such a good idea. If we need to get a hold of him, we'll know where to look. If you don't mind me asking, what makes you think he's at the old Murphy place?" I gave him the short version but included getting the license plate number and calling Jeff this afternoon.

"I know you think this guy might be following you, but you seem to be doing a little stalking of your own. You should let it go. What was Lt. Chandler's reaction to your information?" I could feel myself getting testy. "About the same as yours." Did I detect a hint of jealousy, or was that just wishful thinking on my part?

"Margaret, if you don't want to take my suggestion then maybe you'll take Lt. Chandler's advice. You don't need to be running into harm's way all the time." That was sweet coming from Hal, but my insecurities were still in control.

"Well, I'm not trying to…it's just that…Look, Howie has been threatening me every time I see him, and it makes me wonder. If it wasn't Lizard Lids, maybe Howie's being all broken up about his sister is an act, a cover-up for the fact that he had a hand in her death. It wouldn't be the first time siblings got into it with each other. Besides, it doesn't seem right that he has fixated on me as the one who caused her death. I think he has something to hide."

"Margaret, you need to let us do our job instead of accusing everyone you come in contact with. You say you don't want to be part of this case but it seems to me you're the one who keeps sticking yourself in the middle of it." Before I could open my mouth to answer, he became eerily calm. "I assure you, Margaret, Howie is not acting. He and his sister were very close, closer than Del and me. Perhaps it's something you can't understand because you have never had brothers or sisters. I've known Howie all my life, and you are way off base." I had been severely reprimanded. He was right. I couldn't know about the bond between siblings. I had always been a loner.

"Forget it. You're right, I'll let it go, but could you just tell Howie to lay off the nasty comments when he sees me, since he's such a friend of yours?"

"It's a deal. Was there anything else you wanted to tell me that couldn't be said in the diner?" I wasn't sure if I was ready to share the Murphy connection. I still had some foreboding; it felt too good to be true. There had to be a catch, and I didn't want to leave myself open to Hal's pointing it out to me.

Hal had to get to work, but not before wrapping me in his arms and giving me a nice tongue lashing. "You sure there isn't more you want to *discuss?* We could have a few minutes before I'm missed." Oh what I wouldn't give for a good *discussion,* but I had a lot more than a few minutes in mind. Reluctantly we parted company, and I was faced with the dreaded prospect of doing laundry. Yuk!

I could tell the only things that were going to get me through this week were meetings and more meetings. I had to stop planning all kinds of outcomes for this weekend, but I wanted to take my relationship with Hal to the bedroom and make mad passionate love. I'd had enough of this goody two shoes routine. Time was dragging.

The Tylerville meeting was good. There were a lot of people my age, but from what I gathered in conversations before and after the meeting, most of them had been sent by the court and didn't want to be here. They didn't say a word. I was hoping I might see Tina, but I didn't. She was probably still in jail. If only Joanne had been there, I could have gotten the scoop from her. I was like the drug court people; I just sat and listened. It was calming and took my mind off the future for a time. I tried to hang around after the meeting, drifting from one clatch of people to another, but for some reason I couldn't bring myself to open my mouth. All this time I had been looking for people my own age, and yet here I was with another wish fulfilled, and I wasn't happy. It reminded me to be careful what I wished for – sometimes it just didn't pan out.

I jumped in the truck and took off out of the church parking lot, berating myself for not introducing myself or getting phone numbers. Oh well, the opportunity was over for tonight, but I could look forward to tomorrow's meeting at the Grange. There I went again, off into the future. I just couldn't seem to stay in focus today. It was obvious I still had some serious walls to clamber over.

Shortly after I was on the road back to Mundy and feeling sorry for myself, I picked up a sheriff's cruiser. I made sure I was obeying the traffic laws and was even ready to use hand signals for turning when the cruiser's flashing lights went on and a chirp of the siren sounded. Now what? I heard the engine throttle up. The cruiser barreled past me doing seventy-five. The fear that had shot adrenalin through me eased off a bit as my heart tried to ratchet down to an even pounding. At this rate I was going to be a basket case and aging beyond my years. I had this built in feeling of guilt that rose up every time I saw police. It might be those years of driving drunk for which I never got caught. I knew it was irrational, but I couldn't help myself. Then there was Lizard Lids to dwell on. Where did I know him from? What did he want with me?

The next morning, down at the diner, I got right into baking with Josie. I was all fired up and started with lemon blueberry muffins. Just a hint of lemon and a pinch of cinnamon brought out the tang in the berries, and they were sweet muffins with two cups of sugar. I made a blueberry streusel coffee cake, and Josie made two kinds of blueberry pies for the afternoon. It was plain that we would need more blueberries as our creations flew off the shelves.

Back in the apartment, I got a call from the Mundy Consolidated School System. They wanted to set up an interview as soon as possible. We agreed on Thursday afternoon. It was the first follow up I had received, and my hopes started to rise. *Easy girl...no expectations, no disappointments.*

I hadn't done laundry yesterday, as I just couldn't bring myself to face the drudgery. Today I *had* to do it or I'd have to go to the mud run smelling like greasy fish and looking like a dumpster diver. The prospective interview also helped stimulate my need to do a wash. You'd think it would actually have been more important than the mud run, but my priorities did tend to be skewed.

The Wash Tub was busy with tourists and single guys doing their laundry. I decided I'd be claustrophobic if I stayed here the whole time. There were no prospects in the guy department either. They were either enormous around the middle, smelly, or missing teeth—sometimes all three. No wonder they were stuck doing their own laundry. I dumped my things in the only available machine – so much for sorting whites and colors, but I had no patience to wait for another one. Checking my watch so I could be back in time to put my things in the dryer, I loped down to the library. I loved the library! I could just sink into a comfy overstuffed chair in front of the empty fireplace and imagine being in a medieval castle. Sarah wasn't anywhere to be seen, so I went down to my little hide-away of local history and Mundy memorabilia. It felt different now that I had a connection. I was trying to break in this new family relationship like a new pair of jeans, and it was stiff and uncomfortable at the moment. I found myself eyeing everyone I met as a potential cousin, and I was going to check out those genealogy books that Sarah had told me about.

Twenty minutes fly when you're doing something you enjoy. I rushed back to the Wash Tub with fingers crossed that there might be two dryers available. Fat chance. Now there were all kinds of empty washers, but all the dryers were in use. There were several that had only five minutes left to go. I could wait that long, so I piled the clothes from the washer into two baskets sorted by color.

A very long hour later I was back at the apartment for dinner and ready for a meeting. It was difficult to sit still. How was I going to get through the meeting without looking like a newcomer with the jitters? *Just do it, that's all.*

When I arrived at the Grange Hall, Winfield and Kenny were already there, sitting on the steps having a smoke. I was glad to see them. How would they react to the news that I was part of the Murphy clan? Both had become very important to my sobriety.

I stumbled from the truck, dragging my backpack and feeling like a newborn colt struggling to get its balance. Winfield and Kenny stood up simultaneously and then sauntered toward me, grinning at each other. "Welcome to the family, Maggie. Looks like Charlie wasn't that far off after all." Kenny gave me a warm hug, and it felt so great. This little leprechaun had a strong grip, and I experienced a sense of security that had been long missing in my life. I started to cry—I couldn't help myself—huge sobs came pouring out. Winfield just nodded in a knowing old sage way while he sucked on his pipe.

I was safe and among family. My anxiety drained away, replaced by an excitement and willingness to soak up everything I could at the meeting. Kenny had been really good about the whole thing, but at the same time, he seemed to understand my hesitation about accepting all that goes with gaining a family.

The meeting and being around friends in the fellowship left me pumped up. Del offered to follow me home 'just in case,' and I took him up on his offer. I was tired of trying to prove how tough I was. It turned out to be very enjoyable. Del waved goodbye at the diner and I parked the truck and went to bed.

"It's just the two of us now, Maggot. We've got to stick together through thick and thin. Don't shut me out." That's what he said when Mom died but I shut him out all the same. I woke sobbing to the cadence of my alarm clock mixed with Dad's words. I had dreamed about him, and for some reason a feeling that I had deserted him came tumbling down on me. Was I shutting out the possibility that my dad had needed me because he wasn't perfect? I couldn't keep all this crammed inside. I had to share it.

It was way too early to call Catsy. The first thing she'd ask me would be, "Are you going to drink over it? If not call me later." Well I wasn't about to get drunk so I had best just get down to work.

At our break Josie and I sat down at our back table. It had been slow so far. The overcast weather with intermittent drizzle was putting a damper on tourist activity, but I liked it better than blazing sun because it fit my mood. Even the anticipation of the mud run wasn't enough to pull me out of the doldrums.

"You are bursting with something. You better let it loose or there'll be an explosion, and I don't think that will be a pretty sight."

"Oh, Josie, so much is going on in my head I can't get a handle on any of it. You're right; if I don't unload, I think I'll go insane." So I proceeded to tell Josie what had transpired in the last week, and it was easier than I'd thought, sharing with her about my fears and lack of acceptance about my father's other life. I was amazed at the weight that was lifted off my shoulders when I had finished.

"You know, Maggie, it's no big deal to anyone but you. All of us have family dirty laundry, like members backstabbing or not speaking to each other. It's stuff that's been going on since the beginning of time. I couldn't begin to tell you some of the family secrets around this place. I guess you are seeing the tip of the iceberg. You know I don't wish to speak ill of the dead, but the Coxes and Joneses— and the McCarthy's for that matter—don't have lily white family histories. That's probably why they have always been so quick to point the finger at others."

"You're right, Josie. I guess I was just feeling terminally unique. Thank you for bringing me back to earth."

"Speaking of earth, could you get some more blueberries for me this afternoon?"

We laughed together. "Sure, no problem. It will give me something to do to get my mind off me."

Driscoll swaggered in through the door and lifted a finger in the air, for service I presumed. He glanced at the goody case as he aimed for the table that Josie and I had just vacated. The more I saw of this guy, the more of a pompous ass he seemed, and I wanted to tell him to go back to New York. But that would be rather hypocritical since that's where I was from—well, from upstate New York, which was different…

"Josie, have you heard about a member of our constabulary?"

"John, why are you whispering, and evidently I haven't been privy to any goings on in the local constabulary." This was all Driscoll needed in order to be in his glory as the town crier. It suddenly occurred to me that I hadn't seen Hal yet this morning, and now I was concerned that something had happened to him.

"Miss Murphy, you might be interest in my little tidbit of news unless you already know and are showing tight-lipped restraint in not sharing it with Josie."

"I am sure I have no idea what in the world you are talking about." I feigned indifference, but my anxiety level was skyrocketing.

"It seems a friend of yours has been put on extended leave, or perhaps paid suspension. It isn't quite clear which, since the sheriff's office is playing it close to the vest."

"You mean Hal is in trouble?" Now the anxiety was quite evident in my voice. Driscoll gave me a quizzical smirk that I was certain was meant to torture me.

"No, as far as I know Deputy Grimes is in no difficulty."

"Has something happened to Jeff?" I regretted saying that the minute his name left my lips. I hadn't meant to even talk to this jerk, let alone blurt out something that he could twist, but it was too late to take it back.

Thankfully Josie intervened. "John, stop beating around the bush and upsetting Margaret. If you have something to say, spit it out and stop mincing words." *Bless you Josie.* I loved watching her put him in his place.

"First I want to know who this Jeff person is you referred to."

"John, that is neither here nor there. Who are you talking about, or can it wait until the paper comes out tomorrow?"

That brought him up short, and he filled us in on how apparently Howie had been acting a trifle strange since his sister's death, and the authorities figured it would be better for all concerned if he wasn't going around fully armed. Tell me about it. They put him on an extended leave of absence. The fact that his truck was part of a hit and run investigation didn't hurt their cause either. Hopefully he'll pull himself together. *I* certainly hoped so. Maybe Hal had said something to either him or his boss. The Sheriff's Department was worried about lawsuits and misconduct that might make the department look bad. Needless to say, this hadn't done much for Howie's disposition. I could see it coming. Somehow he would blame me for his predicament. It was obvious that Driscoll had drawn the same conclusion, but at least I wouldn't have to worry about Howie pulling me over in an official capacity.

It was at this point that John Driscoll turned his full attention to me. I anticipated another finger in the face, and sure enough, after imparting his revelation about Howie, he started in on me again. "So who is this Jeff person you are so concerned about? Will he have any bearing on your plans for the future? How is it going anyway?"

He was disgusting. He had slipped back into investigative reporter mode, and I had no intention of getting roped in.

"Pardon me. I have customers to take care of as part of my *job!*" I replied testily as I got up and left, frantic to wait on anyone. *Please, Josie, don't say anything to that creep about the Murphys.* The plea went over and over in my head as if I could transmit it telepathically. *Please, God, don't let Driscoll con her into saying anything.*

I couldn't wait for him to leave. It felt like he was going to stay here forever, and there weren't enough customers to keep me busy. Fleeing to the kitchen was my only other option. I chatted with Robby and Dwight. Robby was going to the mud run and that seemed to help bring him out of the funk he had gone into when Bear was killed. He was too innocent to be burdened with that kind of emotional junk. I wasn't quite sure what his actual relationship to Bear was, and frankly, finding out hadn't even rated an honorable mention on my priority list. I had just stayed clear of the subject altogether, but it was nice seeing his enthusiasm return. I told him that he could tell me all about what went on at the mud run because I had never been to one. He was astonished and relished teaching me all about it.

When I got ready to leave work, Hal hadn't come in, so I told Josie to let him know I'd be out raking blueberries for awhile. She said she'd take as many as I could rake and freeze what we didn't use immediately, and she offered me as many as I wanted for my own use as payment for the work. I said we had a deal.

Raking blueberries is back breaking work. It let me work up a sweat and concentrate on my body rather than getting lost in the muck of my mind. I played number games to keep from thinking about anything else. How much area held how many buckets of berries and how long did it take me to fill a bucket? It was pure nonsense-figuring to pass the time. I had backed my truck into some shade since the sun had decided to come out in full force, and I didn't want the berries baking just yet. I took my time walking back and forth to the truck in the heat. Josie had given me these green and yellow plastic bins that stacked nicely in the bed of my truck. She didn't expect me to fill them all but said I might as well take them all. Of course, that sounded like a challenge I couldn't refuse. As the bins filled and piled up I imagined that my truck and I could pass for part of a convoy of migrant workers. Funny but in a lot of ways there were similarities that went beyond my beat up old truck. I had been constantly on the move until my dad's illness had required that I stay put.

Nearing exhaustion, I took the last load to the truck, put away the rake, and pulled out my backpack and an old blanket I carried for impromptu picnics. I ambled over to a small copse of trees on the cliff edge and laid it out. My legs ached as well as my back and arms. It had been a workout, and I had probably overdone it. I would regret this tomorrow. I could see myself now, hobbling into the interview like an old lady. Oops, I'd better let go of that image.

Lying there listening to the buzz of insects and the breeze singing through the branches, I felt at peace. I must have fallen asleep because I was startled by a sound that didn't fit into the concerto of nature. I lifted myself up on my elbows to see what it was. Hal's truck had pulled up and he had gotten out and was looking all around. He didn't see me and started to call my name.

"Over here!" I was trying to get up, but stiffness had settled in and I was having a rough go of it. Hal saw me and rushed over.

"Are you all right?"

"My pride is giving me a pain. I think I raked a tad too many berries, and I'm stiff as a board."

"You're all right then. Don't get up. I'll sit down with you. I have something to tell you." Of course I had to say, "You mean about Howie?" Hal just got sort of a disgusted look on his face. "How the hell do you know everything that goes on?"

"Hal, don't get all bent out of shape. I work at Josie's, gossip central and that creep Driscoll showed up this morning just dying to tell us all about it. I thought something had happened to you at first, and I was worried, especially when you didn't come in. Driscoll's a real snake."

"What is it with you and reptiles?" He cracked a smile and we both laughed.

I smiled back at him. "Anyway, I'm glad you're not in trouble."

"Do you mean that, Margaret?"

"Yes, and I've got something to share with you too, but please promise me you won't get crazy on me. I'm really not all that comfortable with it yet." I had his undivided attention. "You go first. Driscoll wasn't very nice this morning, and I'd rather you told me."

After he told me about Howie and the excessive drinking and how concerned he was about Howie doing or saying something stupid, I told him about what I had discovered at Margaret's. I didn't know how to start but I wanted to let him know I could understand a little better some of what had been going on in town. I circumvented actually admitting that I was closely related to the Murphys but let Hal know that I had every right to be at the camp. He didn't argue with anything I said and sat attentively, taking in what I was trying to convey. When I had finally finished all that I was willing to share, I sat back and waited for his reaction. Hal measured his response but kept any judgment out of his words. We hashed over the ancient Murphy history. If the conversation hadn't been so intense, I would have been interested in doing more than talking. I got the impression that Hal might be thinking the same thing. It was getting late. He was being the perfect gentleman and wanted to get together the next day, but I had the interview and didn't want to say anything about it. I was afraid of jinxing it, so I just said I had a prior engagement. "You enjoy being cryptic, don't you?" he asked.

"Will you miss me?"

"What do you think?" We embraced with a certain amount of groping and considerable heavy breathing. We both knew we needed to leave but I didn't want to stop. Once again, Hal was the one to be my conscience and not take advantage of my obvious horny state of body and mind. Dammit! It made me want to try that much harder to break down his resolution. And maddeningly, it made him even more desirable.

Chapter Twenty Two

I was on edge all morning. I told Josie that I had to leave early, and I wasn't waiting around for Shirley to make an appearance. I wanted to have time to take a cleansing shower and time to check out the school before I had to actually be there for the interview.

It's amazing how I can sit in my apartment and the phone doesn't ring for days, but let me be on my way out the door and invariably that's when someone will call me. I was caught. Should I answer it or just pretend I'd already left? Like I could ignore it?

"Hello."

"Maggie, this is Margaret. I hope I'm not interrupting you."

"Actually I'm just on my way out."

"Well, I won't keep you, but do you remember seeing any single-entry bank ledgers among your father's things?"

"I can't say that I have, but there are still some things I haven't gone through. Is there something particular you wanted to know about?"

"Tommy kept a journal that he wrote in all the time, and he used the ledgers to camouflage what Father would have called a sissy's diary, totally unacceptable for a son of his. He left his old ones, but the one from his senior year is missing. I thought he might have taken it with him and continued to write in it."

"Okay Margaret, I'll look for it the first chance I get." I really wanted to get off the phone and be gone. It wasn't just about wanting to be on time for the interview. I was feeling very uncomfortable about what Margaret had said about Dad being responsible for his brother's death. Something inside my head was screaming, *not my father! He would never, not even accidentally, do something like that.* We couldn't be talking about the same person. It wasn't possible. I couldn't accept this whole situation.

"Maggie, dear, I don't want to hold you up, or put any pressure on you. I realize that this whole thing has been a shock. Just remember that I'm here if you ever need anything. Please don't hesitate to call me. Good luck today. If God wants you to have the job you'll get it. Trust him." I didn't want to put my trust in a God I had given up on years ago. That was fine for Margaret, but not me.

"Thank you, Margaret. I'll be in touch." How did she know I was going for a job interview? I hadn't told anyone. The woman was uncanny and it freaked me out, but it was kind of nice to have her there for me.

The school was tucked back in a wooded area that was hidden from the main road. No wonder I'd never seen it. The view from the rear of the building was of the river, hence the name Riverview High

School. I could imagine trying to keep the students on track when they could look out at the slowly undulating river. It was doing a number on me as I stood by the corner of the building.

I found it is always a good idea to know something about the school you are applying to so you don't look like a dummy at the interview. It never hurts to let them think their school is special to you. I had gotten some basic information from the school budget they had voted on. It was a public record and copies of the booklet were kept in the library. The school was tiny compared to Southern Maine standards with less than two hundred students in the high school, and the students weren't all from Mundy either. The school pulled in students from surrounding communities and townships.

It was difficult to grasp the layout of the school from the outside, but it was two stories high and had at least two wings with the main entrance at the place where they met. One wing showed classroom windows and the other side was a solid brick wall with the school's name on it. A parking lot separated the high school from a middle school or elementary school. It appeared to be one large campus. My schools in New York had been nestled together in a similar manner, but we didn't have the view or the landscaping.

When it was time for my interview, I was ushered into the principal's office where I had time to cool my heels while another applicant went through the gauntlet. Even being there for a job interview didn't change the old feelings that being in the principal's office brought to mind. I had spent more time than I cared to remember in an office like this – and not only as a student – but I tried to put that stuff out of my mind. I got the impression I was the last in a series of interviews for the day.

Schools in the summer are a jumble of desks, boxes of books, and equipment all piled up in the hallways as rooms are cleaned and painted. By the end of August or the beginning of September, everything would be shipshape.

When my turn came, I didn't want to appear too desperate. I sat at one end of a conference table, flanked by the superintendent, the department head, the principal, a parent representative, and the special education coordinator. I tried to take in the names and faces, but I was too nervous to remember most of them or even who held what positions. Roger Lowell, the principal, was the only one I could identify because he was the one who ran the meeting and did most of the talking. They took turns asking me questions, and I practiced the principles of honesty, patience, and tolerance for the same routine that goes on at all these interviews. It was all scripted. What they really want to know they don't dare ask because it would be politically incorrect, and you wouldn't get the job if you answered those questions honestly. The only part I actually enjoyed was describing some of the projects that my past students worked on. I was so proud of their accomplishments, and we'd had fun doing them.

It felt like a good interview. I liked the people, even though the parent seemed a bit overbearing, and the school looked well kept on the inside even in the middle of summer cleaning.

After the interview, Roger walked me through the building for the tour while giving me all the reasons why Riverview was such a great school to work in. The school had an elevator for the staff and the handicapped that brought back memories of a teaching job I had held with no classroom to call my own. I had shared a closet with two other teachers and carted my equipment and maps up and down in the elevator. I often looked like an albatross flying down the hall with these same maps flapping out behind me. I prided myself on my ability to adjust and give my all in any circumstances – something attainable, now that I was no longer drinking.

During this walk around, Roger talked about his family and that he and his wife and three girls lived in Tylerville. It was handy that I knew someone in Tylerville as well so that I didn't seem so much of an outsider. I told him about Jeff and Beth and, in this small world, found that Roger knew them too. Their kids were in the same classes.

Roger told me they were having a school board meeting the next night and that the superintendent would present the candidates to the board at that time. Once the vote had been taken, all the candidates would be notified of the outcome by phone or mail within the week. I said I appreciated that and that it was nice not to be left mentally floundering. Everything in this town moved at lightening speed compared to what I was used to, and at the same time it felt strangely like people were caught in a time warp that kept them in the past. It seemed eerily like the place that time forgot.

The blueberry raking had worn me out, and all the anxiety and anticipation about the interview had taken its toll on me. I felt like I'd climbed a mountain. Part of me wanted the security of a job, any job, and part of me kept asking, *do you honestly believe you can stay and work here?* This was my normal behavior pattern, and heaven forbid I should break it and make a commitment. I decided not to worry about it. As Margaret had said, it was in God's hands, wherever he might be, and the only decision I needed to make right now was whether to take a long hot shower or a long hot soaking bath when I got back to the apartment.

The bath won out, and I hit the sack early. No phone calls, no baking, no nothing. The bath had been just what the doctor ordered, but without candles and a bottle of wine, some of my former sleep aids. I slept sounder than if I had passed out, and in the morning I was much clearer without having to struggle through a wine-soaked haze.

At Josie's we collaborated on a multitude of blueberry delights. Considering the quantity that I had brought back, we had to. "So what do you think about some blueberry peach preserves that we could put on the tables for breakfast?" I suggested. Josie thought that was a grand idea, and I said I'd start work on the preserves after I put together my chocolate zucchini cake for the picnic. That would take up some time.

It was a big job that kept me busy. Thank goodness the market had canning jars, as they weren't exactly something I carried around as an essential item. All the while I was working on the preserves, Margaret's questions kept gnawing at me. My mind was waffling between happiness at being a part of a family with all kinds of relatives and denial that my father could have kept such a secret about his past from me and mom. Why? Why? Why?! Hal had been understanding, saying "It's not like you can pick your relatives," but that's what I wanted to do. Not only did I want to pick my relatives, but I wanted to control what part of their lives I chose to accept. Humility was *not* part of the equation here. I needed to talk to Catsy.

After sealing up the last jars and letting them cool on the counter, I gave Catsy a call. Catsy was in, and I entertained her with my domestic endeavors and all the anticipation of the mud run and my post-mud run plans with Hal. It was a delaying tactic. "You want to tell me why you really called?" Catsy knew when I was blowing smoke. It could be very unsettling.

I then told her what was going through my mind and what Margaret had asked.

"Have you looked for these ledgers in your father's things?"

"Well no, there hasn't been much time."

"Bullshit! You called me so you could have an excuse not to be doing it right now. You're stalling. You want proof one way or the other that Margaret's brother is your father. That requires an action on your part. Right now you're letting fear of the unknown rule your decisions. Mags, you can't keep running away. You can do this – just make a decision and carry through.

"But that's just it. I don't think I can accept that my dad could have done what Margaret said he did. What reason would Dad have to keep such a secret unless he really was responsible for his brother's death? It's all so jumbled up and complicated."

"From what you told me it sounds like you're making a lot of assumptions with no facts to speak of. I'd say that was contempt prior to investigation, wouldn't you?"

"I suppose you could be right."

"*Could* be right?! As your sponsor I *strongly suggest* you get off this phone and check out your father's things before you jump to any more conclusions."

I'm not a fast learner, and I don't follow directions well. All I could do was sit on my futon and scrutinize the filing cabinet as if I were planning to break into Fort Knox—the one with the gold, not the one in Maine. I'd have to sleep on it.

The next morning, I couldn't remember the night before. If I had dreamed at all, I had blocked it out, and that was just fine with me. The day was overcast again but with the promise of eventual clearing. I was glad that I'd be taking my own vehicle to the picnic and the mud run. It was my security blanket and it could hold everything I might possibly need to meet any contingency. The amorous kind came to mind. Both Josie and Hal had assured me that wet weather only added to the ambience – Josie's word – of the mud run. The more water the more mud, so that made sense. Of course, my wardrobe had to be revised because I hadn't taken weather into account. I wanted to look sexy for Hal, but no matter how tight the jeans, the baggy sweatshirt killed the effect. I had washed everything I owned so I'd have just the right thing. When would I learn that nothing ever worked out the way I thought it should?

My chocolate zucchini cake was rich and moist. Frosting it would seal in the flavors, and it gave me something to do this morning instead of watching the minutes go by until it was time to leave. Decisions were looming on the horizon, and I dreaded them. Even with the misgivings I had about family and Mundy, I didn't have the drive to pick up and move again.

The phone rang, and for the first time I didn't jump. "Hello."

"I'm calling for Margaret Murphy."

"This is Margaret speaking."

"Margaret, this is Roger Lowell principal at Riverview. I'm calling about the school board's decision." Oh hell. Be calm, you didn't want the job anyway, keep it light, but the anticipated letdown coursed through my body and all my insecurities came rushing back. I hated rejection and always took it so damned personally, but this was a first over the phone.

"I appreciate your calling." I was trying not to choke on my words. It was like pulling off a band-aid —do it quickly and the pain is over just as fast.

"Welcome to the Riverview Team." I was in shock. "We'll be having a staff breakfast in August plus orientation for the new teachers. I'll give you a call to set up a time for you to sign your contract. All the scheduling information will be mailed to you, and if you have any questions, you can reach me at the school. See you next month and have a great rest of the summer." I was at a loss for words. I babbled my thanks and that I looked forward to meeting everyone, stock answers because I couldn't get my mind around the fact that I had been hired. As I hung up the phone Hal tapped at the door.

"You ready to go? Josie and Dwight are on their way down the street. Can I help you with anything?"

"Yeah, you can take the cake down and put it in the front seat of my truck. I'll get my backpack." I was saying words but I was going through the motions. I was ecstatic and ready to explode, but I decided to pretend that the phone call hadn't happened and wait until I could take it all in. Right now, I'd focus on the mud run, savoring one glorious moment at a time.

"Did you shove a change of clothes in there, and rain gear?"

"How could you tell?"

"The thing is bulging. It looks like it will pop a rivet!"

"Oh, come on, it isn't that bad." He hefted it.

"What else have you got in here, rocks? It weighs a ton."

I suddenly remembered all the treasures from my excursion to the blueberry barren. "Now that you mention it, I could take some things out." I could feel my face heating up and knew that I was beginning to blush. I pulled out my balled-up clothes and rummaged in the bottom. Handfuls of rocks, shells, and driftwood came up out of the bowels of my bag. Tiny crab bodies skittered across the table.

I didn't dare look in Hal's direction. I hustled out the door to dump out the residue of sand over the side of the deck and then jammed my clothes, wallet, camera and other items back in. The flotsam and jetsam I left on the table. "I think I'm ready." Hal had this big smirk on his face as he shook his head and sighed. He carried the cake as we headed to my truck. Josie and Dwight had pulled up along side.

"All set? Just follow me. You can park your vehicles on the side of the long driveway up to the house if there is room and then just walk up. There's no telling how many people will be there and you'll want to be able to get out for the mud run. Oh boy, that cake looks delicious. What flavor is it?"

"Chocolate zucchini cake with cream cheese frosting."

"Chocolate, my favorite flavor. We've got room for it right here in my truck."

"Down boy! You have to wait." This came from Josie who had a huge bowl of potato salad in her lap. She winked at me. Hal put the cake down gingerly on my seat. I plunked my backpack on the floor in front of it and hollered, "Wagons Ho!"

Cars and trucks were parked all over the place. We had to hike up the driveway, Hal lugging my backpack and Josie and I lugging our contributions to the feast. Kenny was jerry-rigging tarps over the food tables as Josie and I set down our things. "Margaret, it's so good that another member of the clan could come." He said, throwing his arms around me.

When I finally left Kenny's grasp and snagged a tall cold glass of ice tea, I joined up with Hal who was with his brother Del. The two looked like night and day with very little family resemblance. I guess making comparisons came with the idea of belonging to a family. We found a place to sit down in the yard under one of the tarps Kenny had rigged.

Sarah Carter arrived with her family, and we talked about the library. I didn't tell her about my new found family or my new employment, but knowing news travels in a small town, I wasn't surprised when she mentioned my new teaching job. "Sarah, I'd rather not broadcast the teaching position. I just got the call this morning, and I'm not sure how I'm going to handle teaching in the same town I live in.

"Well, it will be in the *Tidewater Times,* and you could say it already had been broadcast. They televise the School Board meetings for anyone that cares to watch, and the school cafeteria was packed last night." I thanked her for the heads-up and suddenly felt like I was living in a fish bowl. There was quite a crowd – the most people I had seen in one place since I'd gotten to Mundy.

Occasional showers sent people scattering for cover under various tarps. These developed pockets of water which would then overflow, resulting in a gushing stream followed by squeals of laughter. The food was gobbled up in waves. Josie's potato salad disappeared and so did my cake. It always makes me feel warm and snuggly when people like my cooking. It's the way I hope they feel, too.

As I was helping clear the tables, there was a commotion by the drive. I looked over to see Terry Murphy saunter up with an entourage of guys. "Look whose here everybody, a brand new Murphy cousin from New York. Hey coz!" I went over to say hello. Kenny was on his way over too, moving faster than I'd ever seen him move before, and he didn't look happy. The minute I got close to her, I realized she was shit-faced and I was guessing her companions were, too. Her face spoke volumes contradicting her greeting to me. I couldn't understand what was wrong. We had gotten along great at the hardware store, and she'd seemed like a nice person, a little intense but nice. Maybe she saw me as an interloper. I wasn't quite sure how I felt about being a member of the family, so I couldn't blame Terry for having similar misgivings. It was beginning to look like we had a lot of similarities and not just in the looks department.

"Good to see you again, Terry." Now I wanted to make a hasty retreat. Kenny came up alongside her and took her hand, which she struggled to release. In an undertone meant for Terry's ears only, Kenny whispered hoarsely, "Why don't you and your friends go in and grab something to eat. I'm sure your mother has something you'd like." Good old Kenny, trying to feed a drunk. As Kenny shuttled her off to the kitchen, I made my getaway to find Hal. I was ready to leave. I still don't do well dealing with drunks. I don't know if it's because I don't want to go there again or if I'm afraid that I *might* want to go there again.

"You okay? You look strange."

"I'm fine. Is it time for the mud run?"

"It's already started, but it's no great loss if you aren't there for the whole thing. I'll get my truck turned around and you can follow me out to the field. You sure you're alright? I saw Terry and her gang. They're feeling no pain, but they're relatives, right? You'll want to say goodbye; I mean they *are* family." Hal's point about relatives was extremely uncomfortable, and I wasn't sure how to take it. It might have been less of a strain if we'd all stayed together, but I'd lost track of Del, and Hal couldn't understand where I was coming from as well as Del could.

I was finally able to get through to Hal that I wanted to leave, and we boogied out of Kenny's and over to the mud run after I made the appropriate goodbyes. Fortunately, there was no Terry in sight.

The trip to the mud run was short, and the road was choked with all kinds of vehicles. The fields on either side of the road had sprouted cars and trucks like weeds. I didn't know there were so many people in this part of the country. The rain had stopped for now, and the sun looked like it was trying to peek out from behind the clouds. It still wasn't nice enough to take off the sweatshirt, but there was a promise of that later in the afternoon. Despite the meeting with Terry, I was upbeat, on edge, in high gear, and I was going to enjoy myself come hell or high water.

Hal motioned me to pull over near the corner of a field already loaded with vehicles. I jockeyed the truck into position and got out to see where Hal had ended up. Slinging my backpack over one shoulder, I mingled with the crowd that seemed to be milling in a particular direction. It was a good thing I wasn't short or Hal and I would have had trouble spotting each other.

The field had the air of a stadium tailgate party, but on a smaller scale. The spectators appeared to be getting well lubricated so they could appreciate the muddy, grotesque vehicles that still reminded me of childhood monsters. I was craning my neck to take in everything as Hal and I linked up and headed for what passed for a fairway of small local vendors and a gathering spot for various groups. A PA system set up on a flatbed was making quite a din. It was hard to distinguish what was being said, but I did catch what passed for snatches of the English language among the monikers of pet trucks that would be competing.

I felt Hal's arm around my waist guiding me through the maze of goings-on. Just as I was beginning to relax and feel secure, a familiar voice, highly intoxicated, came from behind. "Yo, bitch! I fucking warned you but you couldn't take the hint. You've ruined my fucking life. I otta fucking kill you!" With that, I felt this enormously heavy paw come down on my shoulder. My shoulder was still sore from all the raking I had done and I don't react well to pain.

I slipped away from Hal, whipped off my backpack, and let it fly like a mace. It dropped Howie on his ass as a trickle of blood slithered from his nose. Ouch! That had to hurt. Howie reached for his nose, saw blood, and went into a tirade of even more profanity. I was aware that we had gathered a crowd, and the tittering from Howie's cronies only helped fuel the fire. But to me it seemed surreal and in slow motion. I was vaguely aware of Hal grabbing my arm in an effort to restrain me. Howie's fury was feeding my own and I wanted to beat the crap out of him as he struggled to get back on his feet.

Hal was shaking me and yelling my name. Gradually I focused on him. "Margaret, calm down. Get a hold of yourself. He's drunk. He doesn't know what he's saying."

I wrenched myself from Hal's grasp. "I'm out of here!" I wanted to run as fast and as far as I could.

"Margaret, listen to me. It's going to be alright. I'll take care of Howie. If you really don't want to stay here, why don't you go up to the barren and I'll meet you there."

His voice was quiet now that he had my attention, and there was a hint of seductive intimacy that wasn't lost on my raging mind. "We can have the place all to ourselves away from the crowd." Now he was whispering in my ear, and his hot breath set my flesh on fire.

I breathed in deeply, looked down at the ground and back up into his eyes. "I'm sorry, Hal. I guess I overreacted, but I do want to get out of here. Will you meet me at the barren?"

He slid his arm around my waist and turned me back in the direction of my truck. "I'll be right there. Just let me smooth over this little fracas and I'm gone. Are you going to be okay?' I nodded and strained to maintain an even gait back to the truck.

I had time to think about what had happened on the way to the blueberry field. It wasn't pretty. My old behaviors had come back in a heartbeat. I was restless, irritable and discontented. I had been with a lot of drunks and, let's face it, it was crazy-making. Catsy had warned me about thinking my ego could handle things. Well I'd handled that situation really well!

But as I drove into the barren and parked my truck, I was feeling much calmer than I had all day. This was more my style. I had been so caught up in the melee that I hadn't noticed that the sky was clearing—at the same time as my brain. I walked over to the edge of the clearing and peered down over the cliff. No beach was showing, so the tide was either almost in or just starting to go out, but frankly I didn't care which. I went back to the truck, pulled out the old blanket, and rummaged for a plastic trash bag to use as a ground cloth. Just because it was no longer raining didn't mean it was dry. But I was finally able to ditch the sweatshirt. This would work out after all.

I sat clutching my knees, looking out at the ocean, trying to clear my mind of resentment and still my emotions. I tried to think of all the positive things in my life. It had stopped raining. That was a start. I have a place to live, I've had good food, and I have a teaching job for the fall, so I should have no material wants. I concentrated on enjoying where I was at the moment, determined to wash away Howie's negativity. As I performed this mental yoga, I saw Hal walking up the lane.

He waved and I ran to meet him. I was so happy to see him that I threw my arms around his neck and planted an enthusiastic kiss on his lips. Something was wrong. There was no response. Instead Hal went rigid. "What's wrong? Where's your truck?" I was confused.

"I've got to hand it to you, Margaret, you make it so easy. They ought to know better than to send a woman to do a man's job."

"What are you talking about, Hal?" He was starting to scare me. He wouldn't look at me but instead stared at the ocean. I took his hand in mine, but he shook it loose and grabbed my wrist with a vise-like grip as he started for the edge.

"It was time to move on. I hate this Hicksville. Only the Feds would come up with that lame story about finding out you're related to the Murphys in this backwater. You executed the story line perfectly after you discovered Cleaves at the cabin, but my plan is still right on schedule."

This was definitely not going according to *my* plans and it was *not* going on the positive side of the day. Maybe I was crazy, but Hal had gone off the deep end. I had passed scared and moved on to terror. Now he was dragging me. I was digging my heels in but I was no match for his strength. I twisted to loosen his grip but it only got tighter and more painful.

Oh God, if you're there help me, please! In answer to my plea, the sound of a truck tearing down the lane and kicking up dust halted our progress. I was saved!

Howie, the last person I expected or wanted to see, stumbled out of the truck with a shotgun in his hands. Could this nightmare get any worse? "You're early."

I recognized the malevolent glare in Howie's bloodshot eyes. How was I going to get out of this? I was out-weighed, out-numbered, and out-gunned. I didn't even have my backpack. Maybe I could reason with them. "Howie, Deputy Jones, I want to apologize for my behavior. It was uncalled for. All I can say is that I was caught off guard." My voice wavered and cracked.

"Shut up, Bitch!"

"What's the gun for Howie? Think about it. It's not too smart." Hal was being conciliatory and condescending at the same time. I wouldn't be so smug with someone who was pointing a gun at me.

"I know. You always have a better plan. You're the smartass. You have everything figured out. But I don't feel like being the patsy any more."

"Don't fuck this up. We've got a good thing going here. All you have to do is keep your mouth shut and ride it out." I was clueless, like I was listening to a conversation in a foreign language.

"I should kill you both." This was reassuring.

"Don't be stupid. You'd never get away with it."

"And you *would*? Don't call me stupid! I suppose you're the only one who can get away with murder. Why'd you have to kill Sheila? She never did nothing to you. If it hadn't been for Sheila, you wouldn'ta knowed about *her."* Know what about me? What was this lunatic raving about? Howie was starting to sob. Things were starting to click into place, and I didn't like it one bit. Hal had his eyes locked on Howie and the shotgun. His smug expression was gone but there was no fear, just disdain. I was still breathing and that was a plus. If they got into a fight, I might have an opportunity to slide out of Hal's grip. The shotgun was disconcerting. You didn't have to be sober or a good shot to do damage with that thing.

"I'm not as dumb as you think. Now we're going to do it my way. Get on your knees!"

"What the hell is going through that soused sponge you call a brain?" Hal's voice was more commanding, but it wouldn't be my choice of something to say to a guy with a gun.

"I would have thought that would be obvious for such a smart guy as you. Do it!" Howie was starting to sober up. I still didn't have a clue what he was planning on doing, but there was clearly no good scenario for me.

"You obviously haven't thought this through, but then your family never did."

"You've got a lot of nerve saying something like that after what you done to my sister."

"I had it all under control until your goddamn lush of a sister fucked things up."

"Yeah, right, you did a real good job romancing the bitch. Meanwhile, she's alive and Sheila's dead and so are Bear and Wayne. Was that your fucking genius plan? And you framed me. Now you're going to get what you deserve."

This heated exchange was escalating way out of control. Howie's rage was definitely in charge and who knew what was coming next. I was suddenly intent on trying to understand what was being said and what it meant so I could figure a way out. For once I kept my mouth shut. Hal and I were uncomfortably close to the precipice. As I squirmed and tried to edge away, Hal held me locked in his grip. I was a hostage on two counts. If I got away from Hal, Howie would shoot me. This was a lose-lose situation.

Howie was running out of comebacks in the face of Hal's unflappable cool.

"It's almost over. I'll take care of her, and we can put this all behind us. The tide is just right. They'll never find her."

My mind was racing, calculating the odds. *Stay calm. Keep your wits about you and think!* I didn't want to believe what was coming from Hal's mouth. All my paranoia had been well founded but way off the mark. How could I have been sooo off base about Hal? Never had every fiber of my being been so in tuned to run, but I had no way of going anywhere.

"It's not going to go away or be over for me. I'm not taking the fall on this." Howie had the shot gun trained on Hal. Then I spoke. "Hal there has been a huge misunderstanding. I don't know who you think I am but…"

At that point he looked at me as if just realizing that I was there, and he had a cold dead look in his eyes. With panic to be clear of that look I pulled away at the same time Hal wrenched my arm. The next thing I knew, I was flying through the air and down into the waves. I don't know if I screamed or not, but I hit the water hard. There was an explosion in my head and then nothing but cold blackness until I realized that I was gasping for breath and thrashing in the water.

My head was pounding and I was scared shitless, but I was alive and out of Howie and Hal's reach. Being in the water wasn't great but I was in no hurry to rejoin the two of them. I recognized where I was and headed for the place I had come up on the day I had gone exploring. It was difficult trying to swim in my clothes and shoes but I was grateful to have them when I finally got a hand hold on an outcrop of rock that formed a ledge. The rock was slippery and I would gain and lose my grip as waves pushed and pulled me in and out. I'm a strong swimmer, something my dad had always insisted on since we spent so much time at the lake when I was growing up. At that moment the memory of learning how to swim gave me an extra boost. Once I was up out of the water I closed my eyes. I needed to rest and this seemed a safe enough place. I may have passed out, I don't know—everything was a blur —but something jolted me back into awareness. I heard my name being called out, but I didn't respond. Self-preservation had taken the helm.

"Margaret! Are you all right, Margaret?" Hands were helping me up. It was Jeff though I barely recognized him in his riot gear and in my state of mind I wasn't sure about anything. "Margaret, look at me. It's Jeff. Are you with me? Can you walk?" My teeth were chattering from cold or shock. Someone threw a blanket over me. My arms and legs didn't want to follow direction. They had suddenly turned to gelatin.

"Jeff?" I managed weakly.

"You're in shock, Margaret. I'll get you to my car."

I sat in Jeff's cruiser soaking wet for what seemed an eternity, trying to get a handle on reality. There were state troopers, sheriff's deputies, and an ambulance and trucks scattered on the tiny dirt road and onto the blueberry field. I had an inane thought that all these people were ruining the blueberry barren and that it was a good thing I had raked all those blueberries. There were lines of yellow tape tied to random shrubs outlining the scene. Where were Hal and Howie? I couldn't take in any of it. Jeff came back toward the car peeling off a bulletproof vest.

"How are you doing?"

"I'm here, and I think I'm alive, thanks to you. How did you know I was in trouble?"

"Besides the fact that trouble is your middle name, you're going to have to tell me. We got an anonymous call saying there was a hostage situation. The magic words drugs and guns were all that were needed to mobilize the whole kit and kaboodle. We got here as fast as we could but it was too late.

Anonymous caller? That made no sense. "What do you mean, too late? Who could possibly know we were out here and what was going on? Where are Howie and Hal?" I could have convinced myself that this was all a bad dream if I wasn't soaking wet with welts on my wrists where Hal had held me. "Jeff, tell me what happened. Where are they?"

Jeff got an enigmatic look on his face, "Howard Jones has been taken into custody for murder and attempted murder." Jeff gave me a moment to let that sink in, but it wasn't helping.

"No, that's all wrong. It can't be."

"Maggie, I know you liked Deputy Grimes, but he's dead. Jones shot him. All we can figure out right now is that Jones was out to get both of you to protect his drug business. I'm sorry we couldn't save Grimes. Howie isn't doing much talking, so you'll need to help fill in the blanks.

Stop the hamster cage I want to get off! I tried to fit the pieces of what Jeff was saying with what had transpired before I hit the water. It wasn't easy. I had a sneaking suspicion from the concerto that the sledge hammer in my head was playing that I might be suffering from a concussion. Somehow Howie had gotten the idea that I was responsible for his sister's death, but he knew that Hal killed her and

Bear and who knew about Wayne. Howie knew that Hal had tried to frame him by using his truck and for some reason both of them had some mixed-up idea about me. "Jeff you've got it wrong."

"Maggie, you don't understand. You sort of fell right in the middle of months and months of undercover work to take down a ring of dealers in Tyler County."

"They thought I was working undercover, that explains a lot."

"Who are 'they'?"

"Hal and Howie. Hal was the ring leader, Howie was strictly a follower. Did you know all about this undercover business?"

"Well, not all of it. I'm not on the task force and it was on a need to know basis. It's hard to penetrate the drug dealers in a small community. The fewer people who know what's going on, the better. I was filled in when the call came in. Apparently their inside man used the paranoia over you being the snitch to his advantage. If I had known, I would have done something to get you out of it." I had come uneasily close to being just like the dead sailor I had found years ago, a case of mistaken identity.

My mind was attempting to ferret out who the undercover person was. Jeff was still talking, but I wasn't paying attention. The guy I wanted to sleep with, maybe settle down with, was a cold blooded killer who had done his best to kill *me*. I was angry and he was dead. "Jeff, Jeff wait a second you have to listen to me. *Hal* was going to kill me. Howie was pissed because Hal had tried to frame him for Bear's death."

"Maggie, you're confused and in shock."

"No, I'm telling you the way it was. You have to believe me. Hal came here to kill me, and then Howie showed up and stopped him— well tried to, at least. Oh, I'm not sure what he was doing. Howie was drunk and no match for Hal's wits. Howie always took orders from Hal and Hal admitted to taking care of Sheila and was going to try and do me in the same way."

"All right, don't get all worked up. There will be time enough to sort things out; right now we need to get you checked out at the hospital."

"No way am I going anywhere in an ambulance! I just want to go home."

Jeff shook his head. "I know you when you're like this. If you won't go to the hospital, an officer will take you home, but they will want a statement from you. You know the procedure, but at least you'll be able to get it over with. Remember, if you don't know something, just say so, okay? I hate to leave you alone. Are you sure you'll be alright?'

Of course I wasn't going to be alright, but being here wasn't helping. "I need to go home." It had a nice sound to it...home.

Chapter Twenty Three

By the time the officer who followed me home had gotten everything I could tell him, it was late. I turned on my Tiffany lamp, took a couple of aspirin, and waited for them to kick in. Common sense, reason, and logic had fled hours ago. My fingers found their way to the filing cabinet. I drummed the top of it, and then caressed it. I didn't know what to believe anymore or who to trust. Was everything a lie? Could my connection to the Murphy clan be the misguided dreams of a grieving woman, as illusive as my supposed relationship with Hal? Now, looking at the filing cabinet, I understood that I was afraid that I wouldn't find any ledgers, and that would be the end of everything. Yesterday I had a date and a family to look forward to. Today the guy I thought was so great was dead after trying to kill me, and if I didn't find the ledgers I would be out a family and alone again.

Right now my life felt like it couldn't go any lower. Let's face it, it looked like shit. I was obviously deadly at picking friends and having relationships. I'd moved up to Mundy and brought death and destruction in my wake, so what's the point? Why not drink myself into oblivion. My mind was in an ocean of hopelessness and I was struggling to find a foothold of hope. There had to be a purpose to all this.

The phone rang and I flew out of the chair like a cat that had just had its tail stepped on. How dare someone intrude on my silent hell? "What?" Not exactly a welcoming way to answer the phone.

"Margaret, this is Catsy. I saw the news. You must be a wreck after hearing about Hal." I almost wanted to laugh. Catsy had no idea. The whole sordid mess started to spill out of me and as I told Catsy how lousy everything was and how I had thought about drinking and killing myself, my anger over the whole situation came into play.

"Are you through? You know, on your recanting of 'this is my life and I hate it', you left out a few details." Now it was her turn to do 'this is your life'. For every negative I had come up with, she had a positive that topped it.

Suddenly I was frantic. I didn't want Catsy to hang up. She was my only contact with some kind of sanity, and she was right – I was being totally selfish. All the people who had helped me out who didn't even really know me flew through my mind. I cried, laughed, cried some more. She let me run the gambit of emotions.

"My suggestion about a cat still stands."

"With my track record do you really want me inflicting myself on your furry favorites?" That broke the morbidity of the moment.

"You're not alone, Maggie. You have me and the fellowship."

I drifted through the week like a rudderless ship. The best I could manage was a detachment from most of the aftermath of Tyler's great drug bust and latest death. Driscoll had another body to add to his drug death tally. The only names that were publicized were those of the people picked up in the sweep that happened after Howie was arrested. It sounded like mostly small time users who sold drugs to support their own habits. There was an arrest in the Westbrook area with possible out of state ties in connection with the bust up here. A haul of money, drugs, and guns was touted as making it all worthwhile. Strangely and thankfully, my experience was left out of the news, probably to protect their undercover agent. I had my suspicions as to who it had to be and that might have accounted for why he seemed so familiar. Cleaves, a.k.a. Lizard Lids, must have been the agent and the one who made the anonymous call but Jeff would neither confirm nor deny if he even knew.

Howie had a lawyer and was going to plead not guilty to murder and attempted murder. If it went to trial I'd have to testify. I was still smarting over being used but it was one of the things I had to accept.

Driscoll was zealous in calling for a full investigation of the Sheriff's Department from the top down. He had a new crusade. Even though my name had been kept out of the press, Driscoll came sniffing around for some kind of exclusive victim/narc angle. I was sorely tempted to make him a victim of an accident, say scalding hot coffee in his lap, but I curbed my impulses.

There was still everyday life to deal with. Work lost some of its thrill. Charlie called about fixing the truck. I appreciated the fact that the subject of Hal and Howie wasn't brought up. I had no intentions of playing anymore real life bumper car games.

A bright spot was the call from Superintendent Lawrence Bernard. He wanted me to come in and sign my contract. I couldn't begin to express how happy I was that they still wanted me. When I got to his office, he explained that due to circumstances beyond his control it might be necessary for me to pick up a couple of classes at the middle school—more fallout from the drug bust. One of the teachers had been arrested. He assured me that it would be no problem with my professional certification. I kept my misgivings to myself with a fervent hope that teaching middle school classes and dealing with that age group wouldn't be necessary.

The hardest part was going back to meetings. I rehearsed all kinds of scenarios about facing Del, and the more I thought about it, the harder it was to go. I hadn't called anyone or seen anyone in the program but Kenny and Winfield, and I was squirrelly.

Catsy called to check in on me. I should have been the one to call, but she seemed to understand and cut me a little slack. "You haven't been through your father's things yet, have you? You know procrastination is *not* a virtue. Face your fears."

When I got off the phone, I sat on the floor in front of the filing cabinet and unlocked it. A cursory look through the remaining items in the top drawer satisfied me that there was nothing left to find out about my dad there. I pulled on the handle of the bottom drawer. It was stuck until I wrenched it open with a hard yank that sent me sprawling. To my amazement, the drawer was crammed full. A small locked cash box on its side was jammed up against a row of leather looking spines. Each one had a simple code and word embossed in gold – single entry ledger. Their black, dark green, maroon, and brown bindings were scuffed and faded. I don't think there was a speck of room left in the drawer for anything else. The last bastion of denial about my father came crashing down.

The cash box was locked. After I pulled it out of the drawer, I shook it and then turned it over. There taped to the underside was a key. Now there was a novel idea. I opened it up. There were a couple of pictures of Margaret as a youngster, my dad's birth certificate, and some childhood items that meant nothing to me but must have been very special to him and perhaps to Margaret. Nestled in a pile were all kinds of newspaper clippings of which Margaret was the focus.

Setting aside the cash box, I took out the first ledger and flipped it open. In his concise blockish writing were entries and dates, some very short, others longer but not written in every day. All entries had a special significance to my dad, things he wanted to keep track of. This ledger was the most recent and spanned three years. At the back, the writing had deteriorated as his health had declined and ended shortly before he had become bedridden. He had never said a word about what he'd been writing all those years.

Knowing Dad's methodical nature, I guessed that he had probably kept these journals in order, so I reached in the back for the very last journal in the drawer. Here were the writings of a teenaged boy, one who was shy and full of insecurities. I was embarrassed to read the words. It didn't seem right. Wasn't I supposed to be the child in this scenario? I flipped through this one a bit more briskly. Dad deserved some dignity. I thought I knew what I was looking for or at least the time frame. I skimmed just the dates. Each page I turned began to weigh more as I was torn between wanting to know what happened and being afraid to find out. What if he'd just left it out of his journal altogether? But he hadn't.

I was ashamed of what I had feared and felt like I had betrayed him. I had to share what I had found with Margaret. Someone needed to help set the record straight after all these years. All the things that Margaret had told me about the relationship between Dad and his father—I couldn't bring myself to call him my grandfather—made sense to me but had been totally misinterpreted by Margaret. I read on as this young man who was my father strove to keep from having the spark of life and happiness crushed out of him. I felt his pain and anguish as if it was my own and then I found what he had tucked away in the pages.

I arranged to see Margaret in the early afternoon. She asked if I minded Winfield being there and I couldn't refuse her that. In a way it would be good for both of us if he were there, as much a comforting presence to me as to Margaret. Again I was amazed how strange and kind of nice it was that someone actually cared about what happened to me. I had been so dense about so many things, but I was learning.

The ride up to Margaret's home had a different feel to it than the first time I had walked up High Head, almost a month ago. The crisp hot summer air was filled with the occasional chirping of crickets, replacing the buzz of pollinating insects, and there was a scratchy sound to the waves of tall grass that had risen from the fields where the wildflowers had once been dominant. They had gone to seed preparing for another season.

At Margaret's, I still marveled over the changing view from her porch. She met me at the door with Winfield at her side, and we went out to the sun porch. The windows were open, and there was a cooling sea breeze meandering through the room ruffled by the ceiling fans quietly whispering overhead. Winfield sat close to Margaret holding her hand. She looked much frailer, almost like she had aged years since our first meeting. I felt guilt start to creep in and pushed it aside. I had to keep myself out of this and think of her.

I set down my backpack and pulled out the cash box to puzzled looks from both of them and then pulled out the first ledger that Dad had taken with him when he had left. Margaret's eyes fell on it and she seemed to glow. "Margaret, you were right about Dad being Tommy but you need to know some things. It's time to set things right for all of us. He loved you very much and tried to protect you as best he could." I opened the ledger to where I had found the scrap of paper he had tucked away there and handed it to her. Her hand shook as she reached out and drew it toward her. Winfield would have given her privacy, but she insisted that they read it together. As I waited, tears came to my eyes once again, seeing in my mind what was written on those pages and what, in a slobbering scrawl so unlike my dad's writing, was written on that scrap of paper, the secret that Dad had literally taken to his grave.

I can't go on living there is nothing left
I killed you Johnny please forgive an old man
Tommy you won't speak to me I feel your accusing eyes
What have I done I let you take the blame You'll never forgive me
I just can't take the pain

This was John Murphy's suicide note. Look what one selfish act had done to so many people, including me.

Winfield's arm went around Margaret's shoulder as she softly sobbed. Time was of no consequence. When she lifted her eyes to me I saw the same feelings of shame that I'd felt at having doubted Dad.

"Margaret, he wanted it that way so that you could have and believe in a family and be protected from the consequences of the truth coming out. It would probably have destroyed what was left for your mother, Kenny, and you. Remember you said he was your protector. He accepted those duties with love. You were always with him." I opened the cash box to show her the mementos he had saved including her wedding announcement from the paper and her husband's obituary. I just knew he had watched over her, and from the look on her face came a dawning recognition of long forgotten mysteries, the wedding gift with no name attached, congratulations for noteworthy accomplishments in her life as well as condolences when her husband died. All this she shared with me and I saw another side to my dad. I think I'm finally ready to let him go.

Printed in the United States
By Bookmasters